THANK YOU, DEATH ROBOT

Printed in the United States of America

Published by Silverthought Press
www.silverthought.com

"Thank You, Death Robot" title used with kind permission from Victor Giannini

Cover art by Len Nicholas
Cover design by Mark R. Brand and Paul Hughes

ISBN: 978-0-9815191-9-7

THANK YOU, DEATH ROBOT

Edited by Mark R. Brand

[silverthought]

Philadelphia | New York

This book is dedicated to my son John, that he may know someday the bewildering adventures that fueled my own imagination when I first learned to love the worlds hidden within books. I love you, little buddy.

I would also like to extend my deepest thanks to Silverthought's executive editor, Paul Hughes, our cover designer, Len Nicholas, and the authors of the stories herein. Without their enthusiasm, hard work, and endless patience, this book would never have happened. And a very special thanks to Vic Giannini for letting us use what has to be one of the greatest short story titles of all time.

—M.B.

CONTENTS

DEATH ROBOT: MYTHOLOGY AND IMAGINATION
A Foreword by Mark R. Brand

Like many fans of science fiction, I was raised on a steady diet of aliens, space exploration, and robots. From the terrific old Tor paperbacks with fantasy covers by artists like Boris Vallejo and Frank Frazetta to the breakout '80s sensation that was *The Transformers*, everything from my leisure reading to my Saturday morning cartoons was full of robots. Some were benevolent *Jetsons*-esque friends, but many (and of course the ones who interested me the most) were, for lack of a mechanical equivalent, thrillingly evil.

When I reached my grade-school years, I began to pick up on these characters in movies. IG-88, the bounty hunter from *The Empire Strikes Back*, had no speaking part, only a good long look at his coldly-lethal, garbage-disposal-shaped body and his unnecessarily large rifle. Maximilian from Disney's *The Black Hole* was terrifyingly silent until the blades on the ends of his hands started whirring. In *The Terminator*, Arnold Schwarzenegger brought a lifeless, computerized voice to his time-traveling killing machine. And who can forget the juggernaut-like Hunter Killers from the same film, or the armies of grim-faced steel skeletons wiping out mankind? *Robocop*'s ED-209 spoke in a menacing, amplified version of the voice that tells you your car door is ajar, and then growled like an animal. Robots from films like *Logan's Run, 2001: A Space Odyssey*, *Runaway* with Tom Selleck, Ralph Bakshi's *Wizards*, and even the NORAD computer from *WarGames* provided us with a motley assortment of technological terrors doing their best to fill the archetypical roles of spurned counselor, malevolent guardian, street criminal, repentant assassin, and maniacal scientist bent on global destruction. Roy from *Blade Runner*, Ash from Ridley Scott's *Alien*, and Zygon from *Starchaser* all showed us a chilly human face hiding a blackened, mechanical heart. Among our heroes these machines walked, and sometimes they could even imitate humans, but there was little doubt to my popcorn and soda-consuming sci-fi brain that these tall, dark, and scary characters lacked a soul.

Or *did* they?

The Terminator redeemed himself at last, as did Necron 99. Sometimes these mechanical monsters turned on their makers, Frankenstein-style, and abandoned or killed them in ironic twists. Sometimes the robots possessed a keen sense of right and wrong, and seemed to know when they were stepping across the moral boundaries. Sometimes you could read the subtext of these films and witness the point at which the robot decided to make up its own mind about whether or not to let our protagonists' sense of morality guide them. Then again, sometimes not. And that's what made this sort of character so compelling to me as a teenager. What lay behind their eyes: a thinking, strategic, intellectually-evolved sentience, or a calculator with a crosshairs for aiming its huge guns?

Not since the '80s have there been so many of these in popular culture, though the archetype has never completely died out. We saw them again as the scary parasitical Sentinels in *The Matrix*, the deceitful and overwhelming victims of metal-racism in the magnificent Sci-Fi Channel remake of *Battlestar Galactica*, and clever sequels, prequels, remakes, and spin-offs of the above mentioned titles. Here and there, new steel-skinned faces popped up. The ABC Warriors from *Judge Dredd* ground to life like the gears of a piece of ancient, mothballed farm equipment. The hive-minded Borg from *Star Trek* painted an alarming picture of a culture subsumed by our dependence on technology, where everyone is connected and isolated at the same time. By and large, however, robots became relegated to lesser and less-conspicuous roles in film as our growing boredom with the Space Age set in.

The literary genealogy of the death robot is circuitous, but no less storied. It can be traced back from the earliest days of widespread machine use to the beginning of the industrial revolution when workers deliberately sabotaged machines that threatened to reduce their lives to relentless production. Even before that, however, you can find references of mankind trying to create or control something lifeless such as a Golem or "manufactured person" like the monster (whose actual name was "Adam" inasmuch as he had a name) from Mary Shelley's *Frankenstein*. *Frankenstein* was published in 1818, only a few decades before *Galerie der Sippurim* in 1847, a collection of short stories which recounted the tale of a 16th century Jewish rabbi named Maharal who created a powerful and violent clay Golem to defend the Jewish ghetto of Prague.

The spark that lit the way for the death robot as we know it today was ignited by another familiar name. L. Frank Baum, the author of *The Wonderful Wizard of Oz*, is generally credited with the invention of one of the first robotic fictional characters. Around the turn of the century, he wrote of a mechanical man named "Tik-Tok" in his book *Ozma of Oz*. This character needed to be wound like a wind-up toy in order to function. *Ozma of Oz* was published in 1907, long before the term "robot" was even coined, but it nevertheless left a lasting impression upon the imaginations of its readers. Speaking perhaps to the strength of the archetype, Tik-Tok became the inspiration for another similar mechanical servant named

"Grommetik" from Gregory Maguire's *Wicked: the Life and Times of the Wicked Witch of the West*, who perpetrates a murder, thus ironically qualifying him to stand shoulder to shoulder with some of the best evil baddies from any of the stories and films I've already mentioned.

Neither was literature or popular fiction left out of the death robot craze of the late 20th century when some of the legends of science fiction were publishing stories with robots as antagonistic, sometimes homicidal characters. Isaac Asimov introduced the Three Laws of Robotics as a way to ideally approach the moral ambiguity inherent in powerful, semi-sentient beings mingling with their human creators. Philip K. Dick's Replicants in *Do Androids Dream of Electric Sheep?* explored the edges of what could be called the robotic version of "human" rights, and in *Fahrenheit 451*, Ray Bradbury conjures an implacable mechanical Hound that stalks Montag in the place of human pursuers. Frank Herbert's *Dune* outlines a culture where the computer, or "thinking machine" is outlawed under penalty of death because of a distant historical event called the Butlerian Jihad where humanity was enslaved for 900 years by machines.

And of course virtually every other sci-fi medium including television shows, tabletop and video games, and toys from then till now have included a long parade of intimidating, enigmatic death robots to flesh out their respective universes. Towering colossus or microbial-sized nano-machine, robots bring to our imagination the thrill and sometimes the terror of what it is to give life to something you cannot control. In addition to providing us with an almost endless vehicle for antagonistic narrative creativity, they also provoke relevant hypotheses of the very human variety. What would pure emotionlessness look like? Is something alive if we've built it? If the laptops we drag to work each morning could talk with us, what would that conversation sound like? How can you outthink something that can calculate data thousands of times faster than you?

It is estimated with exponential returns on the advancement of technology that within my generation's lifetime a computer will be built that can exceed the raw computational power of the human mind. And, terrifyingly, rocketing toward what some have called the Technological Singularity, a computer will be built shortly thereafter that can "think" faster than the human *race*. These theories, of course, come with the same cinderblock-sized grains of salt that we took with the 20th century predictions of flying cars, meals in pill form, and colonization of planets that we were supposed to have somewhere roughly in the middle of Bill Clinton's second term in office. Instead, we got the Internet and Reality TV, which, depending on your preference, could either be considered progress or sure signs of impending dystopian apocalypse.

But some truth is there, to be sure. We have the International Space Station in place of condos on Mars. We have cars that can run on electricity now, even though most of us are too poor to afford them, and we have genetically-engineered corn to pop in our microwaves. The same scientists that predict the computer hardware will be available to theoretically outthink humans in the semi-near future also are quick to add the caveat that it is the *software*, not the hardware, which is the difficult feat for the machines to match. The pure adaptability of human thought still vastly exceeds that capable of even the most advanced machine. Then again, my cell phone is several orders of magnitude more complex than the computers that helped send the first men to the moon, and it cost less than a good dinner.

Some truth is always there.

THANK YOU, DEATH ROBOT

Bitty-Brigit is Lonely

By Gayla Chaney

"Read me a song, please."

"No. It's *sing* me a song. Read me a story."

"Sing me a song… Read me a story… Sing me, please."

"I fear your perfection has been grossly exaggerated," Jillian Webster stated with disgust as she stared at the thing on her sofa. The ad had promised "the perfect companion," but from the moment she had opened the shipping crate, Jillian had been disappointed.

Ordering any mechanical device from the classified section of a magazine was probably not a brilliant move. And not just any magazine. Not *Harper's* or *The New Yorker* or *Ladies' Home Journal* or even *Mother Earth News*. No. In a rash moment, Jillian had ordered this doll-being from the ad section of a small, start-up survivalist pamphlet titled, *Beyond Doomsday: How to Thrive When Everyone around You is Perishing.* She found the strange tract on a park bench where she had gone to contemplate her future. "How to Thrive" caught her eye. Jillian liked the idea of thriving. That would be a nice change of pace. If the subtitle had been *How to Survive When Everyone around You is Perishing*, she wouldn't have bothered to pick the thing up.

"Kiss me goodnight, please."

Jillian sighed a deep, heavy sigh of exasperation. "It's morning." She pointed to the large picture window in her living room before continuing, "Sunlight means it is daytime. We've been over this before. I think you must be defective. You certainly are not as programmable as your manufacturer claimed. In fact," she sighed once more, "I think you just might be a mechanical idiot."

"I am a dependable companion. I can help you ward off loneliness and depression while we wait together for a safer time. I will not deplete your food or water rations, but I will accompany you through thin and thick."

"Thick and thin! It's thick and thin. Got that?" Jillian hissed. "Oh, forget it. Now, that's probably something you can do." She watched as the automated, miniature manikin nodded its head in agreement. What was advertised as "an elf-sized companion for the hard times ahead" appeared to be nothing more than a glorified Chatty-Cathy doll that could hobble across the room of its own accord and blather poorly-constructed sentences from some implanted vocal device. It wasn't even pretty with its mopey hair, the color and style reminding Jillian of grackles' wings glued to a naked scalp. Its pistachio-colored eyes were aglow like some stray alley cat out prowling at night. Suddenly, the rage Jillian had been carrying inside her for months spewed out.

"You piece of junk. You stupid, worthless piece of plastic. Oh, God, I've been exploited again," she sobbed. Her rant continued for a full five minutes as she lambasted the world, all men, her husband Jeff in particular, concluding with more superlatives hurled at her recently purchased companion. When Jillian ran out of insults, she reached out and shook the little robotic creature. When nothing happened, she slapped its silly face, once, twice, and then again. "How do you like that, huh?" Jillian knew her question was ridiculous, but it felt good to vent, and this replicated being was an easy target. The only response given was a tilted head before the thing asked, "Mad, sad, or bad?"

"Bad. You were bad. Horrible, actually. And you are going to get worse. Okay?" Jillian dropped the mechanical puppet back on the sofa and picked up the programming manual. She held it at eye level so she wouldn't have to see the peculiar face peering at her, waiting for a command. "Companion is a stupid name. Let's change that, shall we?" Jillian proposed. She mulled over possible names, hoping to select something that sounded totally innocuous, something appropriate for a child's toy, something her nemesis, the pregnant Suzanne, might find cute.

Cute. That had been how Jeff had first described his new receptionist. She hadn't picked up on the hidden attraction. Jillian and Jeff had been married nearly eleven years. Both were professionals. Well-suited, well-educated, and so comfortable in their lives, their careers, their marriage. She had never felt threatened. Not until Suzanne the Cute arrived.

Jillian couldn't conceive, and she had considered that a blessing. She didn't enjoyed being around other people's children. Why on earth would she want one of her own? She cringed whenever she spied toddlers whining and clinging to their mothers in the mall. At restaurants, she always requested to be seated away from anything in a high chair. Food flung from trays by squalling infants could ruin a good meal. Jeff agreed, citing some article from one of his medical journals about the detrimental effects of annoying noise on blood pressure.

19

What a liar he was, Jillian thought. He couldn't leave her fast enough once that slut Suzanne revealed her little secret. Jillian's eyes blazed as she recalled Jeff's confession. He cried as he admitted his infidelity. Jillian, however, remained stone faced as she listened. Afterwards, he hung his head as Jillian began her argument. She told him his behavior was adolescent. *Prurient.* Surely he could see what was happening. Did the phrase "midlife crisis" mean anything to him? Throwing away a life together because some bimbo conceived was not only stupid, it was pathetic. "Wake up, Jeff," Jillian sneered, and when he didn't respond, she repeated herself, her voice rising in a crescendo. "Wake up, you fool!"

Jeff apologized profusely. He swore it had nothing to do with his age. He had simply fallen in love. Maybe for the first time in his life, he added. A thoughtless remark. Jillian reached out and grabbed a nearby tulip-filled vase and threw it at him. "You fucking bastard. How dare you!" The vase had shattered on their Persian rug, the water and tulips spreading across Jeff's feet. "Go on. Get out. Go to your whore." Jeff bent to pick up the jagged porcelain pieces of the vase, but Jillian screamed again, threatening to throw a lamp if he didn't leave *now*. She probably hurled some other insults at him. She wasn't sure at all what she was saying but the rage kept her tears at bay until the door closed behind her retreating husband. And then, when she was all alone, when her husband was on his way back to his mistress, Jillian collapsed on the sofa and wept.

She cried sporadically for weeks, breaking down each time she realized Jeff was really gone. She was stunned repeatedly by the realization that he was *happy* with a woman who had barely completed high school, who chewed gum when she answered the phone for his clients and laughed like a donkey braying. He must have lost his mind was the only explanation Jillian could come up with. Now, Suzanne was pregnant, Jeff was thrilled, and Jillian was... lonely. That just wasn't fair.

She had determined not to make it easy for them. If she couldn't keep them apart, she could at least mar their bliss a bit. Despite his pleas, Jillian refused to give Jeff a quick divorce. The child would be born a bastard, if born at all. Jillian would keep their affairs tied up in the courts until Jeff came to his senses or until hell froze over. Jillian felt the tears welling up in her eyes at the thought of her predicament. "He was my husband," she mumbled. "That woman had no right to take what was mine." With a vengeful surge, Jillian grabbed the instruction manual and began to read again.

"Betsy? Bonnie? Bunny?" Jillian spoke aloud, pausing as though the thing might respond. "I want the 'B' sound, like in baby. I think that might appeal to a mommy-to-be." Yet, the more Jillian pondered new names, the less inclined she was to humanize it. What if Suzanne or Jeff knew someone by that name, someone they didn't care for? After what Jillian had paid for this little robotron, she couldn't risk it being shunned due to its name. She thought about it for a moment. Maybe some made up word that sounded babyish, but not an actual human moniker, would do the trick. Jillian stared at the child-like face with its bright, glowing eyes before blurting out, "Bitty-Bright! That's it. It is perfect for you."

Following the instructions outlined in the owner's manual, Jillian lifted the left arm and felt with her fingers until she located the pea-shaped nodule that allowed for commands to be inputted. "Hello. My name is Bitty-Bright," Jillian purred. "I'm lonely. Will you be my friend?" She smiled as the doll repeated her words.

21

Jillian would send the doll to Suzanne's baby shower and attach a card offering congratulations from the staff at Methodist Hospital. She pictured Jeff and Suzanne opening the gift at their shower as their guests looked on. Bitty-Bright would parrot all the phrases that Jillian downloaded and a few that came with the program, hopefully saying them correctly, charming the expecting parents and their friends with its sing-song voice as it hobbled across the room. If Bitty-Bright messed up a bit, who would really care? They might even find it... *cute*. She glanced over at Bitty-Bright, who sat upright on the sofa, head still in the tilted position waiting for Jillian's next directive. "Smile," Jillian commanded, and the lips curled upward. The head returned to its original angle. "That's pretty good," Jillian conceded before she went back to reading the owner's manual.

The manual explained that the companion was not a toy. It was not intended for children's entertainment; it was for something much more serious. "Indeed," Jillian whispered. Should disaster occur, and a person was in total isolation, a talking robot could lessen the anxiety of any exile, possibly alleviating some of the debilitating effects of depression. Jillian doubted that as she glanced over at the newly christened Bitty-Bright.

This type of technology hadn't come cheap. It would, however, be worth the money if it functioned as advertised. But as Jillian had already observed, it didn't have all the bugs worked out, either. Frustrating, Jillian thought as she searched for the section titled: "Self-Destruct Mode." The brochure explained that the companion could be used as a weapon, activated to destruct by word commands or it could be set to discharge on a pre-determined date. Jillian purchased it for that purpose alone. Its less than stellar conversational skills could be overlooked if it performed as promised. Jillian planned to use the date method for Bitty-Bright's self-destruct mode. She would make it in the morning after Jeff was out of the house, but early enough that Suzanne would still be home. Jeff did hospital rounds before he went into the office. That allowed for two hours, maybe more when Suzanne would still be sleeping or showering, preparing for the day. That's when Bitty-Bright could discharge and blow up their lovely little bungalow.

Jeff, of course, would be devastated, but he was overdue for a little emotional pain. After which, Jillian could be waiting in the wings, ready to offer consolation. She would be patient, forgiving, a virtual vessel of kindness. Grief would reveal to Jeff what real love looked like: It was a familiar, inviting hearth. It was a wife waiting patiently for her wayward husband to return. It was Jillian.

Bitty-Bright would surely be the most incredible gift at the baby shower. Everyone would ooh and ah. And if Bitty-Bright could be programmed with more endearing phrases guaranteed to please the expectant parents, all the better.

Jillian pulled Bitty-Bright's left eye out of its socket and located the tiny device described in the instruction manual. This gadget, when properly set, held the power to make all her dreams come true. The manual suggested using needle-nosed pliers, but Jillian thought she could do it with her fingernail. She slipped her index finger through the hole and gently turned the small wheels. She had to watch carefully to make sure the gears landed on the proper day and year. She would be so upset if the thing somehow detonated ten years down the road instead of next week. Jillian scrupulously coded in the detonation date: March fifteenth at eight a.m.

"Beware the ides of March, Suzie-Q," Jillian chimed as she pulled her finger away from the miniature dials inside Bitty-Bright's head. There was a lever that had to be switched and it took more effort than Jillian would have thought. She supposed that was for security purposes, but using her finger instead of pliers hurt. As she went to remove her finger from the eye socket, something pricked her finger.

"Ouch!" Jillian quickly withdrew her hand and brought the bleeding finger to her mouth. Instinctively, she sucked off the blood while staring at the baby-faced bomb in front of her. She wanted to slap that pudgy face again, but she hesitated. It was a weapon now, and she didn't want to blow up her own beautiful home all over a pinprick. Instead, she childishly stuck out her tongue at the creature, who mimicked her back. "Oh, aren't we clever?" Jillian quipped.

"We clever," Bitty-Bright chimed and began blinking its newly restored eye repeatedly until Jillian had to look away.

Others would think what she was doing was terrible, Jillian knew. They would call her a monster. Suzanne the Bimbo, the husband-thief, would get their pity, and Jillian the Jilted would be locked away. The world thought upside down when it came to true justice. Well, she didn't care what the world thought. She wanted her husband back and if killing Suzanne was the only way to accomplish that, then so be it.

"Sing me a story, please."

Jillian ignored the request. She didn't bother to correct the little robot. The baby shower was just three days off. Jillian would have the doll delivered, beautifully wrapped, irresistibly cute, and then she would wait for Suzanne to experience a doomsday first hand, compliments of some crazy survivalist-inventor and Jillian, of course.

Although Jillian went to bed happy, she awoke startled in the middle of the night. Frightened by something, she sat up to find Bitty-Bright standing at the foot of her bed. "What do you want?" Jillian asked, irritated by the thing's presence and suddenly aware of a dull, pulsating pain emanating from the pinprick on her finger.

"Bitty-Bright is lonely," the doll replied.

"No, you're not. You can't be. Now, get out of my room." Jillian watched as the doll shuffled back to the living room. The sight of it unnerved her. She wanted the thing out of her house. She would have it delivered early. Tomorrow, in fact. "Creepy piece of crap," she muttered as she closed her eyes. Jillian's whole arm felt feverish. She thought she needed an aspirin, but she could still hear those small, padded feet hobbling down the hall and she decided against getting up. She rolled over toward the wall and attempted to drift off to sleep again. Just as she managed to relax, she heard that shuffling sound again. Turning back over, Jillian found herself staring into the glazed, glowing eyes of Bitty-Bright standing— hesitantly—at her door.

"Bitty-Bright is—" it began in a childish tone.

"Shut up!" Jillian cried. She leapt from her bed, unnerved and flushed as she furiously slammed shut the bedroom door. "Bitty-Bright isn't anything. Do you hear me? You are nothing but a sitting time bomb, so go sit!" She listened and thought she heard the thing pitter-pattering away. "Stay on that sofa, and don't get up again," Jillian ordered through the closed door. Bitty-Bright did not reply. Relieved, Jillian took the silence as a sign of submission.

The ear-piercing sound that rang out from Jillian Webster's house before dawn awakened her neighbors. To the man next door, Allen Hines, it sounded too shrill to be a tornado siren, but too loud not to be something urgent. Looking out the window, he saw nothing. He dialed 911 and let the operator hear the sound. She assured him a police officer would be dispatched. Hines dressed quickly and waited for the police to arrive.

The police had to kick in the door when no one inside responded, yet when they called out, "Police!" and stepped into Jillian's house, the siren ceased. Allen Hines stood on the porch as the police located Jillian Webster dead in her bed. Hines overheard the call for an ambulance and he slipped inside, his morbid curiosity prompting him for a closer look. The police, upon seeing the curious Hines, ordered him out of the house, but not before he saw the doll with its pudgy cheeks and childlike face lying on the floor. Who would have ever guessed that the shrewd, childless Jillian Webster, a disciplined woman who appeared obsessively dedicated to her own career, would keep an imitation child in her bedroom for companionship? *The things people don't know about their neighbors*, Hines thought.

Jeff Webster was still her husband and therefore was notified immediately as next of kin. He arrived within the hour of being called, bringing his very pregnant mistress with him. Hines thought that was distasteful, but then again, Jillian was gone now, so what did it matter?

"I can't believe this," Jeff was saying as the police officers detailed what they had discovered. He noted the robotic doll that Jillian had acquired since he left. It resembled a child and that disturbed Jeff. He wondered what it meant. "She never showed the slightest inclination toward motherhood," he said as the ambulance from the morgue took away Jillian's body. There had been a red line running up Jillian's arm from a swollen finger. It looked like some kind of blood poisoning. Normally, Jillian would have sought medical attention immediately for the slightest scratch, but this infected finger appeared neglected. How long had she ignored the signs of blood poisoning? And why would she? And the doll. Oh, God, the doll! Shocked and saddened, Jeff bent down and stared at the creature.

"Bitty-Bright is lonely." It whimpered the words.

"Did you hear that?" Jeff asked, startled.

"How sad!" Suzanne said as she bent down, placing her arm on Jeff's shoulder for support as she stared at the sad, pudgy face of Jillian's inhuman companion. "We can't leave it here," she whispered. "It seems almost... like a child."

Jeff helped the pregnant Suzanne up and shook his head. "That is really not like Jillian at all," he muttered as he stared at Bitty-Bright.

"Oh, Jeff, please, let's take it home," Suzanne whispered. "It's lonely. You heard it say that, didn't you?"

Jeff looked into Suzanne's eyes, guileless in a way that Jillian's had never been, and he realized why he had fallen so hopelessly in love. He smiled. "Okay, but I'm not sure how the police will feel about us taking it."

"Maybe they won't notice me slip out with it if you keep them busy elsewhere." Suzanne spoke softly, giving Jeff a private wink, which Bitty-Bright mimicked as the expectant mother gathered the little robot in her arms. There was an almost inaudible chirp emitted by the doll, accompanied by a quick flicker in the iris, a glitch, perhaps, shooting out a tiny glint of light into the room. It was just a fleeting gleam, which went completely unnoticed by the couple, as did the twitching of Bitty-Bright's left eye, a motion that repeated itself all through the day and into the night, continuing with the regularity of a timer clicking off seconds, minutes, and hours, marking the days.

THANK YOU, DEATH ROBOT

By Victor Giannini

Archer sat down on an overturned garbage can, staring out over the tangled mass of debris that had once been Main Street. The theater where he saw his first movie, something about some sort of space odyssey, had collapsed in on itself. The marquee lay twisted on the cracked pavement below. Archer saw the small bleached bones littering the slides and jungle gym of the playground across the street.

Archer wasn't expecting a parade for his return, but he wasn't expecting a graveyard either. Up and down Main Street, abandoned vehicles baked under the sun like husks of giant insects. Charred flesh clung to the bones that choked the streets. Down the street, just past the shattered middle school, was one lone figure. It stood motionless and glittering by the bike rack where Archer had once left his ten-speed before class.

As he crept through the rubble, Archer recognized what was standing by the bike rack. A third-generation extermination model, a death robot, now in hibernation. Each piece of stone crunching under Archer's boot made his heart rate sky-rocket. He slowed his breathing and prayed his decisive actions would stop its self-reactivation.

Archer clasped his battle weary arms around the transparent dome containing its brain-like tangle of wiring. A flicker of lights began to dance amongst the wires. It sensed his presence. He wrenched it over to the side, kicked the control panel open on its lower back, and savagely tore at everything vital to its neural processing capabilities. A small display of sparks shot out, followed by a plume of smoke.

The death robot lay lifeless and inert, blanketed in the same coat of dust that choked what was left of the landscape. Archer sat back and took a deep breath, which shook his powerful chest. He looked out upon rows and rows of derelict homes and storefronts. Friends and relatives had once lived in this small town. They had all turned out for the big parade when he and his fellow soldiers left to fight the war.

Archer looked down at the death robot. He didn't delude himself; he knew there was no point in searching the whole town. The death robot had been dormant because its mission was completed.

"Everything I fought for," he said. "That whole goddamn war... all for nothing, because of you."

He spat on it. The delicate pattern of circuitry encased in a humanoid form did not respond. His face tightened, and he brought his boot down on it. A sharp clang echoed through the lifeless streets.

He was lucky the robot had gone into hibernation. It had probably been a couple months since it had run out of targets.

"What was it then, huh?" Archer said, grating his teeth. "What was most efficient? Disease? Gas? Bullets?"

Archer sighed and stood up. Military intelligence had briefed him about these machines before. The enemy deployed their death robots into civilian areas, under the programmed function of exterminating all bipedal life forms.

Somehow, he had clung to the hope that his town was spared. The same wellspring of fear and desperation that kept him alive through all his battles had also kept logic at bay.

The devastation of Main Street was all Archer needed to see. Bodies. Glass. Ash. Everything was cracked and crumbling from disuse. The only thing left was the death robot, a machine perfect in its design. Extremely talented scientists granted it the ability to learn, and then use that knowledge to kill. Just like a soldier.

"I guess we're not all that different," Archer said as he mopped the dirt and sweat off his coarse face. He walked over to the robot. *If any of them had my training*, he thought, *if any of them were prepared, they could have stopped you.*

Archer knew that was almost impossible. He had been lucky to find it dormant. The robot had probably killed everyone within a few hours. Far more expensive than the average soldier, but far more efficient as well.

Archer stared down at the mass of wiring, gears, circuit boards, and energy conductors. The maze of artificial organs that allowed the metal creature to learn and act did not intimidate him. Part of his military training had been taking advantage of the enemy's many mechanized weapons. The capture and manipulation of the enemy's Titan Hawks and Devastator Tanks had been instrumental in their victory. Archer knelt down and began to pluck at the wiring.

He decided the best he could do with the machine would be to cancel out its killing prerogative, but to leave its learning one intact. One of its two perfectly honed functions could possibly aid him.

The robot's tank-like treads made it difficult to turn over. Once he finally got it, Archer tried to pry the front panel open. Failing at that, he grabbed a rock and began beating the panel.

It dented enough to create a small opening at the seam. Again, Archer slipped his finger inside and began tearing.

The robot opened. Inside were many spring-loaded canisters. He made sure to disconnect the conductor to the hatch, so none of the vials could accidentally discharge. Some contained lethal chemicals like mustard gas; others contained neural viruses engineered to kill in minutes with automated needles retracted in them. Some were even worse, like reubanoid, which caused the victim's white blood cells to turn on the red ones. Archer tore them all out, dug a crude pit in the dirt, and buried them. He then found the hatch containing the various blades and small automatic rifles it used, as well as the gas canister for the flamethrower. He tore them all out and threw them to the street.

As the sun dipped below the nearby hills, Archer was still tinkering with the death robot's circuitry.

Archer sat on a hillcrest with the death robot, gazing out over the desolate ruins of his hometown. Here the grass was still growing a bit, though yellowed. The road was a few meters away, and degenerating into cracked and useless rubble. The shade of a tall oak tree kept them cool while Archer prepared one of his military rations.

The robot extended a gripper and lifted a clump of mashed potatoes from Archer's rations. It pressed the soggy potatoes against its sleek face, trying in vain to push them into a mouth that could not open. Archer laughed at it.

"I like that you're trying to be human," Archer said. "But there are some things you just can't do. You don't need to eat anyway. I have to eat," He looked down at the cracked egg that once was his hometown. "They told us not to expect much when we got back," Archer said while he stirred. "I mean, we won the war. Sort of. We heard about what was happening back home. The air raids, the chemical attacks, the robots..."

The robot beeped and swiveled its head towards Archer.

"Yeah, the robots," Archer said. "But they were programmed to do what they did. There was no choice involved."

The robot's generic, vaguely humanoid face plate stared back.

"Yeah, choice," Archer said. He sighed and looked away. "We didn't have much of a choice. Fight or die. No one was trying to kill you though, right?"

The robot beeped in acknowledgment, then turned its optic sensors towards the setting sun.

"No hero's welcome for us. Even the transports we landed in were falling apart and low on fuel," Archer continued. "They gave us the option of staying with the military, trying to rebuild what's left of the major cities and piece our country back together. Many stayed, but... I just had to come home. How could I not? I mean, the whole reason I fought that damn war was to protect my home. Last time I was here, I flew out on a huge ship, a parade of family and friends cheering and waving and fireworks going off. It was pathetic, really. Did you know that I walked here? Walked!"

Archer looked back at the robot. It hadn't moved.

"I had a feeling though, long before I got back. You can just feel it when someone you love goes away. Still, I fought for them. For this..."

The robot beeped, taking in all the data Archer was feeding it and assimilating it into its neuro-processor network. Archer resumed eating his ration. They sat there as the sun went down, blanketing them under a soft purple night.

"So yeah, I had to come home, even if all I was coming home to was…" He motioned dismissively toward the wreckage below them. "What else did I go to war for anyway? World peace, of course… but it was mostly for them. For my friends, my family. For Cynthia."

The robot beeped. Its clear eyes glazed over with a pale light. It rolled closer to Archer. He stood up and walked a few feet away, turning to face the hill at the edge of town.

"Cynthia was my girl," Archer said. "We've been together since… I mean we were together since high school."

Archer sat down again, facing the hill, his back to the robot. He silently cradled his head between his knees. He thought about how the robot sitting next to him had killed Cynthia. He wasn't positive, but it was most likely. Most logical. It was logical for the robot to kill her. That was all it knew. Like a baby feeding. It had no choice. She was just another target. Surely, it hadn't made a decision to kill her specifically…

"But now I can help you have a choice," Archer mumbled. He lifted his head from his hands. "You're just like a tank, right? But you can learn. You have a brain. They just forced you to use it the wrong way. I can help you be something more than a killing machine."

Archer stood up and approached the robot. He stared at its smooth, metallic surface, at his own face reflecting over it in the moonlight.

"You can't help what other people make you do, right?"

It did not respond.

Archer smacked it. Again, nothing. He smacked it harder. It beeped, but made no movement to defend itself, did not register any sign of pain or damage or even vague concern. Archer sat down again, directly in front of it.

"Everyone's gone now. I knew I might never see them again, but I thought it would be because I was dead... not them. I fought so hard to stop that. And now... now everyone's gone. Everyone except me, and you."

The death robot beeped.

"Yeah, that wood is perfect," Archer said as he watched the death robot tear apart a storefront. The wooden paneling read *Pop's* before splintering under the robot's grippers.

"That's dry enough to burn real well," Archer explained. "We're going to try to avoid using the trees, because they absorb carbon dioxide and release oxygen, which I need to live."

The robot beeped and added the wood to their growing pile. It looked at Archer expectantly.

"Yeah, it's not terribly cold, but we should get in the habit of making fires before it becomes vital. Let's go inside somewhere and I'll show you how to start one."

Archer walked down the street, wood under his arms, with the robot rolling beside him. The wheels within its treads squeaked incessantly as they rolled. Archer looked down at the robot's treads just in time to see them roll over a ribcage. Archer stopped dead in his tracks as the bone splintered beneath the metal creature.

"Don't do that," Archer said.

The robot swiveled its head towards Archer. It made a long, drawn out beep.

"It's disrespectful to violate the dead," Archer said.

The robot continued staring at Archer.

"Do you have to roll?" Archer asked, looking at the shattered bone. "I figured you'd be designed to be more mobile."

The robot's eyes lost their glow, and for a moment Archer became slightly alarmed. A deep rumble emanated from within its frame, and then the treads methodically collapsed and disappeared within it. The robot then shot up on two multi-segmented rods. It bent its new legs, and then began marching in place.

"Well... I guess that's a lot more convenient for both of us. Now normally we'd have to bury them all, us being the only two survivors," Archer said. "But that can wait, they're not going anywhere. For now, I should get warm and eat."

Archer saw the grocery store where he used to run with his friends to buy ice cream since there was no truck that would deliver it. Most of the time he would spend the money his mother gave him on Cynthia, getting her extra ice cream and having none for himself. The robot backed away from the skeleton and followed Archer.

The inside of the store was devastated. The aisles were split apart, shelves lying on each other, canned goods scattered everywhere and rotted produce littering the floor. And there were bodies. Streaks of dark brown trailed away from them across the tiled floor. Archer looked down at the robot, standing expectantly beside him.

"How about you clear out a space in the middle of the floor, away from anything that would catch fire easily, mostly wood and plastic," Archer said. "I'll start setting it up."

Archer began arranging the pieces in a manner so that they balanced on each other, creating a wooden tent over the pile. He watched the death robot sweep the cereal boxes and soup cans away. He was pleased to see the robot gently lift up one of the small skeletons that were nearby and place it in the back of the store.

"Until I can get the electricity working in these buildings, I have to stay warm the old fashioned way," Archer said when the robot returned. "Now the way to get a fire started is to create friction, and then hopefully a spark that would create a little flame that you would fan. However, in the military they taught us…"

Archer stopped when a hatch in the robot's chest opened up, revealing a small laser. It shot the glowing blue beam straight into the woodpile, igniting it instantly. The laser retracted and the hatch closed, leaving no trace of the deadly weapon.

"…I guess I forgot to disable that," Archer said, standing up slowly.

The robot beeped and stared at him. The flames reflected off its frame, casting a light on it that made its immobile face seem to smile. It beeped at him again, a short, direct sound, like a cat mewling for attention.

Beep.

Beep.

Archer ran both his hands through his hair, nearly pulling the thinning strands from his skull. His left eyelid twitched each time the robot beeped, the same lifeless sound, as if it were waiting for Archer to say anything. He ground his teeth, feeling the muscles across his face start to dance unnaturally, his very flesh responding to the incessant desire for communication. *It wants something. It wants me to take away the laser. Of course. It can't do it itself; it'd be like me tearing off my own thumb. Of course. Right.*

Beep.

"Good job on the fire, but I'd like to disable that laser," Archer said slowly as he approached the robot. "It's all right, come here. You're my friend now, not a killing machine. I can't be friends with someone who has the ability to kill."

The robot made an odd clanging sound. It was decidedly different than the short, high pitched beeps it made when listening to him.

"I know, but I'm a soldier, and that's different."

Archer reached forward. The robot clanged again.

"We have to kill. It's our orders, a soldier's duty. I never killed when I didn't have to."

The robot beeped. Archer sat in silence for a minute. The last rays of the day's sunlight filtered in through the broken windows. The robot beeped again and swiveled its head.

Beep.

"Yeah, you know I never thought about it that way. It was your duty too. And we even had a choice to accept that responsibility. You really didn't though, did you? You were just manufactured that way," Archer said. His stomach began to feel a slight burn as he realized he was befriending something crafted in the hands of the enemy. He reminded himself that wasn't true anymore. That was just the body, and Archer had broken that. Now he was creating his own friend instead. "You really are learning, aren't you?"

The robot beeped and moved closer to Archer. It opened its hatch, extending its laser.

"Thank you," Archer said. "It really is better if all your weapons are disabled."

He began tracing the wiring from the weapon to the robot's core, disconnecting them in the correct sequence to avoid an accidental firing.

"It's funny, robot," Archer said. "Here we are, friends and all, and I never really told you about my old friends." *The friends you killed,* Archer thought. *No, not you. The old machine that shared your body. Not you. You are my friend.*

The robot let out another slow beep.

"Yeah, let me tell you about Jeff, and Steve, and Matt," Archer said. Then he started laughing a little while he worked. "And Amy, and Amanda. Oh man, were they a pair. That time they got arrested for sneaking into the... But no, wait... I think... Yeah, I think I'll tell you about Cynthia."

The robot beeped again.

"Cynthia was my girl before I left for the war," Archer said. His grin began sagging, and then lifted again, as his thoughts danced around her. "Yes, let me tell you about Cynthia."

"Look at this," Archer said. He reached into his pocket and pulled out a compact digital image map. He pressed the corners down and it flickered to life. "This is her in our junior year of high school."

The hologram showed a girl with short, black, hair, full lips, a delicately sloping nose, soft set eyes, and slight creases at the corners of her mouth. She was wearing a black, short-sleeve t-shirt and paint-covered jeans.

"Me and Cynthia grew up in this town together," Archer said. "We were just friends at first, being so young and all. We hung out all the time, and we just kind of grew together. She used to wear this faint perfume that you could only notice if you were right near her. She wouldn't wear it when she was mad at me, for me having to go to soccer practice and other silly stuff instead of hanging out with her. She always wanted me to spend all my time with her. To tell you the truth, I loved to. And she had this awesome little skirt she wore on days she was feeling really flirty."

Archer pressed the corners of the digital image map and it began to morph. It finally settled into a hologram of a young woman, refined and matured with a few more years of age, but retaining her youthful glow.

"That's her right before I left. We dated straight through high school. I can still remember our first kiss. We went out to get pizza together, and we were just really enjoying each other's company. I guess I had been thinking about her... you know... as more than a friend. When we walked out to the car I remember holding her hand and feeling pretty nervous. I mean, I'd taken my parents' car without a driver's license or anything, but you know..."

Archer laughed. His eye twitched.

The robot beeped and assimilated the data.

"It was the first time since we started talking that I felt that way about her. We both kind of felt it, you know? We got in the car and there was a tension between us. We just sat there in the dark; I didn't even turn the car on. I think we were talking but I really don't remember anything we said, or if we were even paying attention. And then we both just leaned in at the same time."

Archer trailed off and stared at the moon, which was now peering in through the front of the grocery store. It hung peacefully over the hill where Archer and the robot had eaten before, rising up just over the tip of the town.

"God, I miss her," Archer said. "Just to feel her again, pressed against me. That was always the best. My hand fit perfectly on the small of her back, and I would just hold her against me with my other hand behind my head and stare up at the moon."

The robot beeped and pointed its claw toward the hill where they had sat earlier.

"Yup, you're right," Archer said. "That very hill is where we spent most of our time together, after class and all. We'd hang out there almost every night, watching the stars. I loved watching the moon hanging over us. One time, when it was full and bright, I told her that I thought that face in the moon was looking down on this world and screaming. And then she told me she thought it wasn't screaming, but that it was shocked, at how beautiful life is down here. I thought about that when I left for the war, to protect this beautiful world. Many nights I would just stare up at it when there was a break in the fighting. I'd be content just knowing that was the same moon up above that Cynthia and I lay beneath on that hill. In fact, it was on that hill where we…"

Archer stared at the ceiling in silence until the robot beeped.

"Well, where we 'became mature' together, I guess," Archer said. He began chuckling as he leaned back and placed his hand behind his head, with his other one resting on his stomach. "Why am I embarrassed in front of you, robot?" He laughed some more, and his eyes moistened. "Robot. Death robot. Why should I be embarrassed in front of the death robot that killed my Cynthia?"

Archer's breathing had quickened and small beads of sweat formed on his forehead. The robot beeped and whistled at Archer.

"Yeah, death robot. We fucked," Archer said through increasingly volatile breaths. "That's where we fucked, the first time, we fucked, up there on the hill where I took you to make you into a person that can make choices, robot. I'm giving you the gift of free will and you fucking took away the first person I fucked!"

The robot was silent.

"...fucked. Loved. I loved her. Oh God, I loved her so much," Archer whimpered. He rolled onto his side and tucked his knees up to his chest. Tears began to drip down his face. "I loved Cynthia so much. She... she told me... we would have a baby, together, when I got home. That I'd come home from the war and be a hero and a daddy."

The robot was silent. It looked through the window, up at the hill, and then back at Archer.

"Thank you. Thank you, death robot," Archer choked out. "No, I won't call you that. Even though you took away my future. You did what no bombs or lasers or gases in that fucking war could. But look what I did! I changed you! You stupid piece of shit killing machine! I'm going to make you better!"

Archer's erratically waving arms and heavy sweating caused the robot to back away from him. This caused Archer great alarm. He sprung up, arms outstretched as he pleaded to the robot.

"No, no, no, I love you," Archer gasped as he struggled to get a hold of himself. "You're my friend now. I don't blame you. We're both machines, you and I. Only I chose to kill. You didn't. Don't worry, death robot... I love you. It's just you and me out here now."

The robot remained motionless, watching Archer with the dark blue glowing holes in its face. Archer put his arm around the robot, hanging his head.

"I miss Cynthia so much, robot," Archer said. "I could last forever on her memory alone, if only I could reach out and feel her again. To feel how her skin was so warm and just a little fuzzy. To feel the blood pulsing under her skin, quickening as I kissed her neck... But she's gone now. That's life, love, war... You either go out with the climax or fade away in the aftermath, right? You and me together, robot, fading away in this garbage. Until I die, I will remember her. But I will never feel her love again."

The robot beeped, and then looked out at the hill again.

They had returned to the hill after the fire died down. The night was not as cold as Archer thought it would be, so he had decided to rest under the big oak tree. There, Archer reminisced further for his lost companions as he drifted into sleep, and the robot sat by his side, contemplating the pain that Archer felt. When talking of his other friends and close family, Archer had expressed similar emotions as he did earlier, but no story had made such an impression on the robot's central processing unit as that of his lost love.

Archer's chest rose and fell rhythmically. The death robot processed the assortment of fresh data. While listening to Archer it had accumulated information on human thoughts, emotions, and interactions. The intricate machinations that formed its brain began using this information to form its own conclusions. The very system that had previously allowed it to be the ultimate weapon of murder was now helping it make its first choice as a human being.

The robot began to understand that it was the source of the pain and loss that tore at Archer. It was its own actions, programmed or not, that had stolen Archer's most precious love. In return, Archer had loved it instead of destroying it, and rebuilt it to learn choice. The robot hung its head, as it saw Archer do when he was upset.

It accessed its data encryption files, recalling the older of the two digital image maps of Cynthia. It then began a rapid filtered search through all of its video files that were on backup. Archer had cleverly erased all the programming relating to the elimination of life forms, but he did not know that the robot kept an intensively detailed backup system of all its experiences. Finally, it came across a memory bank that showed a young girl who matched the image exactly.

The robot forced itself to watch the actions of its previous alter ego. It made a note of the exact sound of the scream that came from Cynthia as the bullets tore through her flesh. It then broke it down into smaller wavelengths and reconfigured them based on advanced algorithms. It took a few minutes of processing, but it finally had what it needed. It let out a quiet crackle to test out its long disused speakers. When it revealed its limited capacity for speech, the moment would be perfect.

It then watched the video clip again, watching Archer's lover fall to the ground and leak red. The robot then watched other files, seeing its own work that it could not actively remember with its current perception system. It decided that if its programming could change past events, it would have abstained from ending all of those lives. It realized that it used to be a thief. It had stolen life.

It had stolen love.

Archer had lapsed into a long account of how he and Cynthia had expressed their love under the very oak tree where it now stood. The robot had to make some highly educated inferences, but it finally found a logical path. A series of red and orange lights flickered across its head as the robot made a choice.

"It's me," Cynthia said. "I've come back to you on our hill. Isn't this place so special for us?"

Archer's weary eyes instantly burst open. Adrenaline flooded his senses.

"It's me, Cynthia," Cynthia said. "You can feel me again. Touch me again."

She was on all fours, shoulders close to the grass, boxy hips high. Even in the faint moonlight, Archer could see that she was wrong. No soft curves, only rough edges, sharp angles.

"I'm sorry I had to leave. I know you remember me," she said. "Let me hold you. Let me give you love."

Archer lurched back, feeling his stomach churn and his limbs shake. He shuffled back on his elbows as the robot drew closer. He felt the rough smack of the oak tree against his back. The robot reached out. It cupped its clumsy hand behind Archer's neck and drew him closer. Archer struggled against the steel limbs as the robot embraced him. A tremendous weight pinned him to the grass and strained his breathing. Cold metal dragged across his cheek.

"Love me," the robot said with her voice.

"No... no... You don't understand," Archer gasped as the robot began to gyrate slowly on top of him. The force of its dense metal body was too much for his softer form. He could barely turn his head as the hard face descended towards his.

The robot had a calculated and detailed schematic of how humans chose to show their love. It began to increase its gyrations as it ground its waist against Archer. Archer's head snapped forward and back as the intensity increased. He gurgled as his skull struck the ground with increasing force.

"I'm giving you love," the robot made Cynthia say. "I love you. I know you love both of us."

Archer felt his stomach churn as his ribs buckled and cracked under the pressure. Something warm burst inside. The robot wrapped its battle-designed arms around Archer's sagging form, pulling it close to its chest and simulating a heavy mechanical breathing in the young soldier's ear.

His eyes rolled skyward, focusing not on the frozen face that constantly ground itself upon him, but towards the moon. As darkness enveloped the edges of his vision, he concentrated on the fading glow, listening to Cynthia's voice as he sank within himself.

COMMISSION REPORT ON THE VIRGINIAN CONFESSOR PROGRAM

By Scott Lyerly

COMMISSION STAFF:

Linda B. Atwell:	Deputy Secretary of the State for the Commonwealth of Virginia
Francis A. Nifrog:	Chairman of Correctional Services for the Commonwealth of Virginia
Paul S. Sobrourski:	Virginia State Senator representing the 3rd District (Mr. Goodall's district)

WITNESSES:

Alan Embroy:	Warden, Clearwater Creek Correctional Facility, Warsaw, VA
Epatha Lee:	Mother of Beverly Lee
Brenda Magehey:	Sister of J.W. Goodall
Cal Taylor:	Systems Administrator, Clearwater Creek Correctional Facility, Warsaw, VA

OTHER NAMES:

James W. Goodall:	Prisoner (deceased)

Beverly Lee: Victim (deceased)
"The Bastard":   Media nickname for J.W. Goodall

PREFACE:

This report and its recommendations is presented to the Governor of the Commonwealth of Virginia and the citizens of the Commonwealth for their consideration.

CAPITAL PUNISHMENT IN VIRGINIA—A HISTORY:

It is no surprise that capital punishment has been a consistent form of sentencing in the Commonwealth of Virginia almost since its inception of a member state of the United States of America. Originally the most predominant form of capital punishment was hanging. This form remained the primary method of execution until 1909.

This is not to suggest that hanging was the only method of execution, as other forms were occasionally used. Individuals convicted of piracy were commonly gibbeted, while others were hanged in chains. A female slave convicted of trying to flee her white owner was burned in 1737.

Beginning in 1909 and lasting until approximately 1994, the electric chair was almost the exclusive form of execution in the Commonwealth. Indeed, during this time, all but one prisoner sentenced to capital punishment was executed via electrocution.

In 1994, legislation was enacted allowing inmates to choose their method of execution: lethal injection or the electric chair. Should no method be chosen, the default practice was then lethal injection. A handful of inmates have chosen the electric chair since this legislation. One petitioned successfully to be executed by hanging.

Executions were carried out at Greensville Correctional Center in Jarratt, VA until the opening of the Clearwater Creek Correctional Facility in Warsaw. Death row, previously located at the Sussex I State Prison near Waverly, VA, was relocated to the new Clearwater facility, thereby eliminating certain budgetary wastes in transportation and personnel costs. In addition, the legal process of execution is now carried out in a more expedient manner, since both death row and the execution chamber are located in the same facility.

State law specifies that at least six citizens that are not employees of the Department of Corrections must be present to serve as witnesses to the execution. In 1994, Governor George Allen signed an executive order granting relatives of the homicide victim(s) in the case the right to witness the execution. Relatives of the condemned inmate are barred from being present.

In the early part of the twenty-first century, legislation was enacted by the Commonwealth to allow the fledgling field of sentient robots to perform executions. At that time, the robots were restricted to lethal injection only. Shortly after the adoption of the robot executioner laws, their province was expanded to include the electric chair.

CONFESSOR PROGRAM HISTORY:

Without going into too much depth about the origin and social history of self-aware and sentient robots in today's society, it can be stated rather succinctly that the concept of robotic administrators of capital punishment came into early consideration during the overall development robots themselves.

Among the early models of these types of robots, the antecedents of the Confessor robot series, were a number of attempts at developing a robot that could simply administer the chemical combination for lethal injection without requiring human intervention.

Yet as this concept was matured and the earliest models put into field tests, it became apparent that robots designed simply to "push the plungers" were drawing criticism as well as showing an unsatisfactory level of performance. Part of the cause seemed to align directly with the fledgling robotics industry. As more and more companies attempted to enter the field of sentient artificial constructs, these robots were hastily coded, poorly built, and subject to malfunction and breakdowns.

It was at that time that the industry began to solidify. Robotics development and construction was eventually divided into two separate companies. One of these, Reval Industries, developed the progenitor of the current Confessor robot series. By folding into these robots the role typically assigned to clergymen and women, namely the listening to a last confession, as well as the physical act of legislated homicide, the Confessor series was born and became a decisive success. It should be noted here that while the Confessor robot program does listen to a final confession from the convicted, it is primarily for the use in closing old cases. The administering of last rites and absolution of sin rests still in the hands of the clergy.

"THE BASTARD"—A CASE HISTORY

The case in question that has ultimately led to this Commission is that of one James W. Goodall. What follows is a brief account of Goodall's life up to and including the crime for which he was convicted and eventually executed.

James Wayne Goodall was born in Warsaw, VA, a rural community situated close to the edge of the Potomac River. His father, John Goodall, Jr., was a large man and a millworker by trade. His mother, Betty Goodall, née Harking, was a slight woman whose primary occupation was homemaker, though when times were tight she would waitress at a local restaurant called The Shanty.

John Goodall, Jr. was a heavy drinker who eventually died from cirrhosis of the liver. During his life, he had been arrested no fewer than seven times for domestic assault of his wife. This cycle of violence would eventually extend to his son, James.

As an example of the type of violence James W. Goodall grew up experiencing, he had his left arm cast on three separate occasions due to spiral fractures, which indicate that the arm had been twisted until it broke.

As a result of this troubling family life, James himself encountered other problems throughout his school years. Before his seventeenth birthday, he had been in legal trouble for public drunkenness and underage drinking, selling marijuana, and extreme injury to local pets. From an early age he gained a reputation for being a ruthless and cruel killer of small animals. His "friends," such as they were, nicknamed him "Pet Killer." On one occasion, he was arrested for a game he described as "cat mowing." The practice involved burying a stray cat in the ground up to its neck and then, with a lawn mower, running it down.

When he was seventeen, he was implicated—though never charged—with the Warsaw High School Fire, a deliberately set fire that destroyed the high school, its surrounding support buildings, and cost the lives of three support services personnel who had been working inside. The fire was clearly defined as arson by the local fire investigator, and James W. Goodall was the prime suspect. Due to a lack of sufficient prosecutorial evidence, he was never charged.

It is unclear when Goodall became a murderer. While the fire (if he did in fact set it) killed three people, homicide did not appear to be the primary motive. However, when he was arrested for the death of Beverly Lee, murder—and cold-blooded murder at that—was in fact the primary motive.

Goodall seemed to enjoy inflicting pain. The state psychiatrist attributes this to an inability to emotionally understand or cope with the pain inflicted upon him by his father. Additionally, when Goodall was twenty-two, his mother disappeared. While her fate remains unknown, the few times Goodall has mentioned her has led detectives to believe that he may have had something to do with her disappearance. Again, this is not surprising to the state psychiatrist, who feels that Goodall may have blamed his mother for her inability to keep him safe as a child from his alcoholic, abusive father. That blame might very well have transformed into a rage, and, given his tendencies, that rage might have translated into some type of terrible action. At this time, Betty Goodall's disappearance remains unsolved.

Given Goodall's history and his violent nature, it is possible to state that it was only a matter of time before he murdered someone in cold blood. That victim ended up being Beverly Lee, a seven-year-old girl who he happened to come across alone one warm summer day.

In August of that year, following a short investigation, James W. Goodall was convicted of raping and murdering Beverly Lee.

"I THINK HE'S AWAKE"—AN INCIDENT SUMMARY

Following his conviction for the murder of Beverly Lee, James W. Goodall was sentenced to die by lethal injection at the Clearwater facility. He was convicted in August and transported to Clearwater that September to sit on death row. Goodall remained incarcerated and on death row for the next twenty-two months while his lawyers attempted to lessen his sentence on appeal. Once the final appeal attempt failed, his execution was immediately scheduled for the following month.

On the night before his execution, Goodall was visited by the Clearwater facility's Confessor robot. Specifications of the Confessor robot as well as the transcript of this visit are detailed in other sections of this report, and so will not be repeated here.

Once the visit by the Confessor had concluded, Goodall was left alone. His last meal was served approximately thirty minutes prior to his execution. It consisted of pizza and a bottle of Coke.

Goodall was led from his cell and into the "death chamber," where lethal injection is administered. The Confessor was already present. In the observation gallery, the required witnesses were present and seated. Goodall lay down on the gurney and the restraints were strapped across his wrists, ankles, and chest. One of the facility's five medical technicians then set out the instruments required for completing the end-of-life process.

The technician exited the chamber, leaving Goodall alone with the Confessor robot. The Confessor went through the normal process of inserting the IV into Goodall's arm[1] and coupling it to the three-chemical administration device that is used in lethal injection housed within the robot itself.[2]

---

[1] The ability to administer an IV is a recent development in the Confessor program. The XMT series is the first series of Confessor to have been developed with enough fine motor skills to perform a task so delicate.

[2] This is another recent development within the XMT series. Once the Confessor robots were able to set up an IV, an executive order was signed to require the robot to house the chemicals in a secured storage compartment on the left side of its chest cavity.

With the setup complete, the Confessor awaited the final command from the main facility administrator. Until this command is given, the Confessor can take no action. When the appointed time came, the administrator spoke into a microphone from with the observation gallery. He is reported to have said: "You may begin." At that time, the process of lethal injection began.

James W. Goodall had closed his eyes prior to the start of the procedure. As each phase was completed, the Confessor would issue a verbal statement saying as much.

Everything was assumed to be going according to routine until one witness leaned forward in her chair. Something had caught her eye and she leaned forward to get a better view. After what appeared to the administrator to be deep scrutiny on her part, she put a hand to her mouth. She is then reported to have said the following:

"Is that a tear rolling down the side of his head?"

This caused all of the witnesses to look first at her and then lean in closer to see if they could discern what she was seeing. The administrator counts himself among those who leaned in for a closer look. He claims to have seen nothing at first, and then, after looking a moment longer, he claims to have seen in the overhead fluorescent light a glint of the trail of water coming from Goodall's eyes. It was at that moment another of the witnesses, a man, is reported to have said:

"My god. I think he's awake."

After James W. Goodall was pronounced dead, an audit of the process was performed. The syringe of sodium thiopental was found to be still full. The implications of this were discussed by Warden Alan Embroy in the subsequent committee hearings and are presented at the end of this document. It was, however, determined that a malfunction occurred during this execution and the subsequent formation of this Commission was convened.

COMMITTEE HEARINGS:

Upon the discovery of the malfunction of the Confessor for the Clearwater Correctional Facility, all scheduled capital punishments were suspended and an inquiry undertaken. The inquiry was designed to gain as much knowledge of the incident as possible. To that end, a special task force was organized under the offices of Francis A. Nifrog, Chairman of Correctional Services for the Commonwealth of Virginia. This task force was charged with the interview of personnel in the Clearwater Correctional Facility, the gathering of physical evidence, compiling an exhaustive history of the Confessor program (presented in this narrative as simply a summary of the program), an exhaustive investigation of the case file of James W. Goodall, and many other more trivial administrative tasks.

In addition to this task force, a set of hearings was commissioned where Mr. Nifrog, as well as two additional individuals selected by the Governor of Virginia, would sit as the committee panel and oversee the testimony given by a select number of witnesses.

While these hearings went largely as expected, it was revealed as the opinion of one of those individuals closest to the program that the end result of the "incident" was unexpected, disturbing in its potential scope, yet completely within the robot's parameters. To quote in brief, the robot "worked as designed."

For the transcripts of the committee hearings, see Appendix A.

CONCLUSIONS:

Regarding the Confessor program currently practiced in correctional facilities in the Commonwealth of Virginia: the Confessor for the Clearwater Correctional Facility appears to have worked as designed. This indicates a flaw in the basic programming design of the Confessor robots, XMT series. Said flaw resulted in the breach of protocol for the administration of lethal injection for prisoners convicted of capital offense(s).

RECOMMENDATIONS:

The Confessor robots, XMT series, should be updated with programming code patches to alleviate this issue and prevent it from occurring in other executions. This patch should be added to the base programming of the next generation of Confessor models, the XMZ series. The XMZ models are currently under construction. Requirements and Design documentation will require updating, and the scope for time and cost recalculated.

In regards to the Confessor program itself, there is no reason to expect that it will continue to be flawed in the future. It is the opinion of this panel that the Confessor program remain active and be expanded to include other regional correctional facilities.

APPENDIX A: TRANSCRIPT FROM THE SENATORIAL COMMITTEE HEARING ON THE CONFESSOR PROGRAM (truncated where required):

F. Nifrog   Are we ready? (indistinct voice) Is the recording machine on? (indistinct voice) Okay, good. Today is May 12th and this is the closed-door session to determine what went wrong on the night of April 7th in the death of inmate James Wayne Goodall, also known as Jimmy Wayne Goodall, Jimmy Goodall, or, as he is sometimes referred to in the local press, "The Bastard." Paneling this hearing will be myself, Francis A. Nifrog, Chairman of Correctional Services for the Commonwealth of Virginia; Linda B. Atwell, Deputy Secretary of the State for the Commonwealth of Virginia; and Virginia State Senator Paul S. Sobrourski, representing the district Mr. Goodall was from. Okay, are we ready to begin? Okay, let's begin this, folks. Can we have the first witness brought in please? Mr. Embroy, thank you for coming. Can you please state your name and position for the record, sir?

A. Embroy: Alan Embroy, Warden for the Clearwater Creek Correctional Facility in Warsaw, Virginia.

F. Nifrog: Thank you. Can you please begin by relaying the facts of the matter at hand?

A. Embroy: On the night of April 7 of this year, Jimmy Wayne Goodall was in his cell for his final night in Clearwater. He was due to be executed the next day.

L. Atwell: Can you please state the nature of his crime, Mr. Embroy?

A. Embroy: He was convicted of one count of rape of a minor and one count of murder in the first degree. He was convicted in August, two years previous.

L. Atwell: Thank you. Please continue.

A. Embroy: On the night of April 7, as per standard death row practice in Clearwater, a Confessor was sent to Mr. Goodall's cell.

F. Nifrog: And a Confessor is?

A. Embroy: A Confessor is a robot specially designed for the administration of death sentence convictions.

F. Nifrog: Which model Confessor was this?

A. Embroy: I believe it was the XMT model, which would make it the next-to-newest model produced.

F. Nifrog: How did this model come to your facility?

A. Embroy: It was purchased with funding specifically budgeted for the administration of correctional facilities.

SEN. Sobr: So the state purchased this model for you?

A. Embroy: That is correct.

SEN. Sobr: At whose request were the funds secured and this purchase made?

A. Embroy: At my request, Senator.

SEN. Sobr: Thank you.

F. Nifrog: Please continue, Mr. Embroy.

A. Embroy: At approximately 9:30, 9:45 PM, the Confessor arrived at the cell. At this time it engaged Mr. Goodall.

L. Atwell: I'm sorry. I'm not familiar with the Confessor program. I understand that the Confessor actually administers the injection, but why was it in Mr. Goodall's cell the prior evening? Can you please explain how the Confessor robot relates to death row inmates beyond its intended function? While you're at it, can you explain why it administers the injection in the first place?

A. Embroy: Certainly. The Confessor serves a dual purpose. Its primary directive is to be the administrator for the end procedure for such categorized inmates in the correctional facility.

L. Atwell: So the robot kills the death row prisoners.

A. Embroy: That's correct.

L. Atwell: And why is that?

A. Embroy: Well, a number of years ago it was determined that the administration of a euthanasia protocol had a negative effect on the individuals charged with the actual act of termination. In addition, there were concerns regarding the quality of training of such administrators and the comfort of those being terminated.

L. Atwell: So to paraphrase: we were worried about the people we hired to kill condemned prisoners, and whether they were trained enough to do it without botching it and causing the inmate to suffer. Is that about right?

A. Embroy: Uh, yes, ma'am.

L. Atwell: And the other purpose?

A. Embroy: It seems that inmates facing their last night before being put to death had a desire and tendency to speak at length about all topics ranging from the weather to their last meal to their crimes. Psychological studies indicate that this may be a coping mechanism against the stress that knowing your last day is tomorrow can cause. They refer to it as Persistent Cognitive Reconnection.

L. Atwell: Which means?

A. Embroy: Which means they are trying to maintain some type of mental or emotional connection to the real world in order to keep calm in the face of literally certain death.

L. Atwell: And how does this relate to the Confessor?

A. Embroy: One of the things death row inmates tended to discuss was their crimes. It turns out they seem to be much more willing to discuss their crimes with a robot rather than a human. In an effort to clear some cold cases in police precincts, a law was established to allow Confessors to sit with inmates, discuss their crimes, record these crimes on audiotape, and for the recordings to be subsequently handed over to law enforcement in an effort to clear out dead ends and close cases.

L. Atwell: Are these audiotapes viable evidence for law enforcement?

A. Embroy: Yes, they are. They are admissible as evidence as they are considered deathbed confessions. Which is how the Confessor robots became known and even referred to as "Confessors."

L. Atwell: Does this program replace the role of clergy members as they relate to death row inmates?

A. Embroy: At times, although that was not the original intention. And clergy are still required for specific end-of-life rituals. Things like last rites, final confessions, things like that.

L. Atwell: But you just said the Confessors take final confessions.

A. Embroy: Yes, that's true, but that's only if the inmate wished to discuss his crimes or anything else before being put to death. A Confessor can't administer religious rites, so an inmate wishing to make a last confession and be absolved of his sins, depending on your religion, would require someone such as a priest or rabbi or similar person.

L. Atwell: So we give the inmates robots with which to converse before their death, but we give them clergy to cleanse their conscience?

A. Embroy: I guess, in a manner of speaking, that's correct, ma'am.

F. Nifrog: Thank you, Mr. Embroy. I appreciate you providing us with the background information regarding the Confessor program. However, without panel objection, I'd like to get back on the topic of Mr. Goodall. Objections?

Stenographer's Note: No objections raised.

F. Nifrog: Okay. Mr. Embroy, if you could proceed, please.

A. Embroy: At approximately 9:40 PM the Confessor arrived at Mr. Goodall's cell. It was allowed entrance and sat with Mr. Goodall until the next morning, when Mr. Goodall was schedule to die. At the appointed time, officers entered the cell and shackled Mr. Goodall.

L. Atwell: Is it standard procedure to shackle a prisoner as they make their way to the death chamber?

A. Embroy: Yes, it is. Mr. Goodall was shackled. He was then led down the cell block and into the center building where the administration offices are.

This is where the death chamber is located. He was led into the death chamber and his shackles were removed. He was assisted onto the gurney and strapped to it.

F. Nifrog: Strapped how?

A. Embroy: There are leather restraints attached to the gurney. They restrain the inmate's wrists, ankles, and one restraint across the chest.

L. Atwell: Why the restraint across the chest?

A. Embroy: To minimize the chance of the inmate bucking during a procedure. Sometimes an inmate has an emotional reaction just prior to the procedure and begins to panic. If they panic they begin to buck against the restraints. The restraint across the chest aids in minimizing any movement that would otherwise interrupt the procedure. Once appropriately restrained, the Confessor then administered the lethal injection.

L. Atwell: Could you explain that injection please?

F. Nifrog: As Chairman of Correctional Services, let me explain this one. Lethal injection is a three-part process. There are three drugs that are administered in order to terminate an inmate's life. The first is sodium thiopental. This drug is used to induce a state of unconsciousness, which is supposed to last while the other two injections take effect. This is to keep the inmate from feeling pain during the rest of the procedure. The second drug can be either pancuronium or tubocurarine. We use tubocurarine in the Commonwealth. This drug stops all muscle movement except for the heart. It causes complete muscle paralysis. If the third drug were not administered, the prisoner would eventually die by asphyxiation due to paralysis of the diaphragm. The third and final drug is potassium chloride. This drug stops the heart. This is obviously a cardiac arrest and leads to subsequent death. This has been the standard practice for decades and it seems it will continue to be the standard practice, at least until the law changes. Does anyone have any questions?

Approximately fifteen seconds of silence.

F. Nifrog: No? Okay, Mr. Embroy, you can proceed again.

A. Embroy: Thank you. After the Confessor administered the lethal injection, we performed the routine audit that we perform after every execution. We examine the room, the instruments, the body, and the robot. It was during the examination of the instruments that we discovered...

SEN. Sobr: Yes, Mr. Embroy? What did you find?

A. Embroy: Um, well... Well. It was in the examination of the instruments that we discovered that the full dose of sodium thiopental was not administered.

SEN. Sobr: Meaning that Mr. Goodall may have very well been awake during the procedure?

A. Embroy: Correct.

F. Nifrog: Order. Order, please. Mr. Embroy, are you telling this panel that you believe Mr. Goodall was conscious during his own execution?

A. Embroy: Yes sir. Under normal conditions, the inmate is rendered unconscious, as the rest of the procedure would be very painful to experience.

F. Nifrog: So by being awake during his execution—

A. Embroy: He would have been in pain.

F. Nifrog: How much pain?

A. Embroy: A great deal of pain.

CHANGE OF WITNESS.

F. Nifrog: Thank you for coming. Can you please state your name for the record, ma'am?

E. Lee: Epatha Lee.

F. Nifrog: Thank you, Ms. Lee. You are here today for what purpose?

E. Lee: I'm here to testify about Jimmy Goodall.

F. Nifrog: Can you give us some clarification of the relationship between you and the late Mr. Goodall?

E. Lee: We don't have a relationship. Jimmy Goodall killed my girl.

F. Nifrog: Order. Order please. Okay folks, the excitement's over. Let's have everybody take your seats and continue or I'll ask the room be cleared.

F. Nifrog: I'm sorry Ms. Lee for the outburst. Would you continue please?

E. Lee: This is Beverly Lee. This is my daughter. My girl. She's gone now. Not a day goes by I don't think about her. Not a day goes by I don't look at this picture and wonder why. Not a day goes by I don't talk to her about what a good girl she was and how much I miss her. Not a day goes by I don't cry like a baby when I wake up in the morning and when I go to bed at night. Not one single day.

F. Nifrog: Tell us your story, if you would please, Ms. Lee. As long or short as you wish.

TRANSCRIPT TRUNCATED: This part of the hearing is currently unavailable due to a pending civil action against the Commonwealth of Virginia in which Mrs. Lee is a potential witness.

CHANGE OF WITNESS.

F. Nifrog: Thank you for coming. Can you please state your name for the record, ma'am?

B. Magehey: Brenda Magehey.

F. Nifrog: Thank you, Mrs. Magehey. You are here today for what purpose?

B. Magehey: I'm here about Jimmy Goodall.

F. Nifrog: And your relationship to Mr. Goodall?

B. Magehey: He was my brother.

F. Nifrog: Thank you, ma'am. Do you have something you want to say before we begin?

B. Magehey: Yes. I know my brother was guilty. None of us doubt that. He knew they had him dead to rights. That's why he didn't appeal. He knew he'd lose. And yes, maybe he deserved to die. Maybe he didn't just kill that little girl like everyone said. Maybe he did do worse. But even if he did deserve to die, he didn't deserve to die like that. His life was already being taken. He didn't need to be tortured as well.

F. Nifrog: Mrs. Magehey, your brother was not tortured purposefully.

B. Magehey: Really? How do you know? Were you there? Cause I wasn't. I wasn't allowed in the gallery when they brought him in. Bullshit state laws. I was the only one who should have been there, the only one who gave a damn about my brother. I know he was a killer, a lowlife piece of shit, but he still deserved to have some family around him. Instead, I had to watch the video feed in another room. I got to sit in a nice comfy chair in front of a closed-circuit TV while I watched them strap him down and then that godforsaken thing rolled in on its big, ugly-ass wheels and took over at the plunger station. I watched my brother, Mr. Nifrog. I watched him close his eyes and not open them. But I saw it. I saw the tears, the tears as they leaked out of the corners of his eyes... Do you know how long it took him to die?

F. Nifrog: Mrs. Magehey, this isn't the time or place for this. We have asked you here for some specific questions—

B. Magehey: Do you know how long it took him to die? Eighteen minutes from the moment the second plunger went down. You know how long it should have taken? About five. My brother lay there, bound to that goddamned gurney, suffocating while that goddamned robot stood by and didn't do nothing.

L. Atwell: Mrs. Magehey, we understand you're upset but we must ask you to refrain from such outbursts.

We hate to dredge up bad memories here, but we need to understand exactly what happened so we can avoid it in the future. And, just so you know, there are some on this panel who agree with your views. Now, we do have some questions we must ask and we'd ask for your cooperation and respect. We'll try to get through this quickly so that you can get back to moving past this incident.

B. Magehey: Yeah, right. Move past this incident. You know something? I got no issue with the death penalty. I got no problem with putting down those that kill in cold blood. I know that means my brother, and that's that. But we need to find a way to do it without torturing them. They're already going to die. Why put such a hurt on them before they go?

TRANSCRIPT TRUNCATED: This part of the hearing is currently unavailable due to a pending civil action against the Commonwealth of Virginia in which Miss Magehey is a plaintiff.

CHANGE OF WITNESS.

F. Nifrog: Can you please state your name and position for the record?

C. Taylor: Cal Taylor, Systems Administrator for Clearwater prison in Warsaw. I oversee the Confessor program there.

F. Nifrog: Thank you, Mr. Taylor. If you could, please, give us your account of what happened on the

	night of April 7 as it specifically relates to the execution of James Wayne Goodall.
C. Taylor:	The Bastard? Don't know much about him except what I read in the papers. And that he was executed. I will say that it sure sounded like he got what was coming to him.
L. Atwell:	Actually, Mr. Taylor, we're interested in what happened as it pertains to the Confessor robot on that night, during said execution.
C. Taylor:	Oh, that. Well, that's tougher.
L. Atwell:	Tougher?
C. Taylor:	Yeah. Tougher.
L. Atwell:	How so?
C. Taylor:	Well, mainly because what happened is so technical. I'll try to explain it in English.
L. Atwell:	Please do.
C. Taylor:	Well, okay. Here's the thing. The robot didn't really malfunction.
SEN. Sobr:	What do you mean?
C. Taylor:	What I mean is that it worked as designed.
SEN. Sobr:	Continue, please.
C. Taylor:	See, the robot did what it was supposed to do. It listened to the confessions and last statements of the Bastard—oh, excuse me, of Mr. Goodall—and then in the morning it executed him. Plain and simple.
SEN. Sobr:	Plain and simple?
C. Taylor:	Yep. Plain and simple.
SEN. Sobr:	Mr. Taylor, plain and simple doesn't really work for me here.
SEN. Sobr:	Are you familiar with the particulars of this situation?

C. Taylor: You mean the ones where the robot used two plungers instead of three?

SEN. Sobr: Yes.

C. Taylor: Yeah, I'm familiar with it. I was the one that tore apart the code, looking for a break. There wasn't one.

L. Atwell: What did you find when you dug into the code, Mr. Taylor?

C. Taylor: Well, I found a lot of instances where the base code was different from what it should have been.

L. Atwell: Can you please explain that a little clearer? First of all, what is base code?

C. Taylor: Oh, uh... sure. Base code is the code that runs the robot. Well, I guess all the code runs the robot, really, but the base code is just that. It's the minimal stuff you need for the robot to function. It controls movement and inputs and outputs—

L. Atwell: Inputs and outputs?

C. Taylor: Yes. Things like mechanical eyes and ears so it can see and hear. Those are inputs because they take information in, like we do with seeing and hearing. Outputs would be vocalizations, kind of like talking.

L. Atwell: Thank you.

C. Taylor: Sure. So base code controls all that stuff, as well as the primary functions of the robot. Obviously this is going to differ robot type to robot type. A stenographer robot is programmed to transcribe court records, a sanitation robot is programmed to pick up people's trash, and a

Confessor robot is programmed to give people the needle. All of these things are wrapped into the base code.

L. Atwell: And so, what you found were changes in the base code?

C. Taylor: Yeah. I saw that the robot had been reprogrammed to give people the needle, but to do it wrong. Instead of three plungers, it only gave a little of the first and then the full dose of plungers two and three. And the time elapsed between plunger two and three was longer than it should have been. By a lot.

F. Nifrog: So what did you look at next?

C. Taylor: Well, so then I looked at the custom code.

L. Atwell: And the custom code does what?

C. Taylor: The custom code controls the finer points of robotic behavior. How does it interact with humans, how well does it obey commands, how fine are its motor skills... that sort of thing. For a Confessor there's an awful lot of custom code. The custom code library also houses the self-diagnostics.

SEN. Sobr: And what are those?

C. Taylor: Those are designed to evaluate the robot to see if it's functioning correctly. If it is, great, but if it isn't, this part of the programming takes action.

SEN. Sobr: What sort of action?

C. Taylor: Well, that can be anything from slight mechanical repairs to a full-fledged shutdown.

SEN. Sobr: It can shut itself down?

C. Taylor:	Sure. If it detects that it has been infected by a virus or something, let's say during a routine data dump, then it can shut itself down to avoid further contamination. Kind of like a medically-induced coma in humans.
SEN. Sobr:	Do you think these self-diagnostics had anything to do with what happened?
C. Taylor:	I think they have everything to do with what happened.
F. Nifrog:	How so?
C. Taylor:	Well, in review the robot's actions, what I found is that it ran some self-diagnostics and then began to reprogram itself.
L. Atwell:	Can it do that?
C. Taylor:	Oh sure. Can and did.
L. Atwell:	Why?
C. Taylor:	Well, I can't say one hundred percent. If I were to take a guess, I'd say it did it so that it could change the way it administers the lethal injection.
L. Atwell:	So what you're saying is that the robot reprogrammed itself to alter its base functionality?
C. Taylor:	More or less. What I'm saying is that the robot reprogrammed itself to inject a small part of the first plunger, just enough to knock the Bastard out for a moment or two. Then when he woke up, the robot injected the second plunger, then, after waiting too long, it injected the third plunger.
L. Atwell:	Why?
C. Taylor:	I think it did it based on its conversations with Mr. Goodall.

71

L. Atwell:	You believe it reprogrammed itself after it sat with Mr. Goodall all night?
C. Taylor:	Yes, or sometime during the night. Reprogramming is actually a pretty fast process. It can be done in the background while the robot does other stuff.
L. Atwell:	But why would it reprogram itself to intentionally inflict pain?
C. Taylor:	Have you listened to the audiotape of the Confessor's conversation with Goodall?
F. Nifrog:	We were saving that for the last portion of the hearing.
C. Taylor:	You should listen to it now.
F. Nifrog:	Why?
C. Taylor:	I think my opinion will make more sense after you listen to it.
F. Nifrog:	Can we get the tape set up? (indistinct voice) Five? Okay, everyone, we'll adjourn from this hearing for five minutes, after which time we'll come back and listen to the tape.

AUDIO PLAYBACK[3]

---

[3]The following is audio playback from the confessor's conversation with prisoner Goodall, with a few brief interjections from the Correctional Officer on duty at the time:

J. Goodall:	What the hell is this thing?
C. Officer:	This is your Confessor.
J. Goodall:	My what?
CO:	Your Confessor. You got one night left on earth, Bastard. This robot is gonna put you down tomorrow morning. Before he does, you get the chance to know him. And if you wanna tell him anything else, got any other crimes to confess to, he'll listen to those. Stand away from the door.

J. Goodall:	I gotta have this thing in my cell? Shit, man, I don't want this hunk of metal sitting in here with me. It spooks me out. Hey! You listenin'?
C. Officer:	You got ten hours, Bastard. Use 'em wisely.

Approximately thirty seconds of silence.

J. Goodall:	So what are you supposed to do, anyways?
Confessor:	I am here to get to know you.
J. Goodall:	Get to know me?
Confessor:	Yes.
J. Goodall:	That's about the stupidest thing I ever heard.
Confessor:	Why?
J. Goodall:	Why? Why're you here to get to know me when in ten hours you're gonna kill me?
Confessor:	No doubt this seems to be an awkward situation, but it has been found that inmates enjoy discussing things with robots prior to their final appointment rather than with humans. It seems that robots are non-judgmental and are therefore willing and able listeners. It also gives the inmate the chance to air any last issues, concerns, and sometimes confessions.
J. Goodall:	Oh, I get it. You're here to try and get me talking about myself and maybe anything else I done to see if you can close some cases. Well you can forget about it. I got nothing to confess.
Confessor:	We certainly do not need to talk about anything in your past. We can discuss your views on politics, or even something as mundane as the weather.
J. Goodall:	My views on politics? Shit. Okay, how about this one: I think capital punishment is wrong and should be abolished. How's that? Think you can push that one through for me? Sometime in the next ten hours, maybe?

Approximately thirty seconds of silence.

J. Goodall:	I tell you what though, I guess I got it coming.
Confessor:	How so?
J. Goodall:	You read the case file?
Confessor:	It was uploaded to me digitally.
J. Goodall:	That a yes?
Confessor:	Yes.
J. Goodall:	Then you know all about my conviction.
Confessor:	Yes.
J. Goodall:	Well, I don't mind saying that, yes, I did indeed do it.
Confessor:	So it would seem from your conviction.
J. Goodall:	Yeah, but what the case file don't tell you is how much I enjoyed it.

73

F. Nifrog: Okay, we've heard it. So what are you trying to tell me about it?

Confessor: Enjoyed?
J. Goodall: Oh yeah. I enjoyed it terribly much.
Confessor: How so?
J. Goodall: You wouldn't understand. You're just a robot.
Confessor: Yes I am.
J. Goodall: So you wouldn't get it. It's a life and death thing, man. The power of life over death. Power of death in your hands. I strangled that little girl and I got my rocks off doin' it.
Confessor: Rocks off?
J. Goodall: Ain't familiar with that term?
Confessor: No, but I do not have a full spectrum of colloquialisms programmed into my base vocabulary.
J. Goodall: Huh?
Confessor: I am not familiar with the phrase 'rocks off.'
J. Goodall: Well, that just means that I got my jollies killin' her.
Confessor: Jollies?
J. Goodall: Jesus Christ, boy, don't you got any vocabulary in there?
Confessor: Are you stating that you became sexually aroused when you killed her?
J. Goodall: There you go! I knew you'd get it eventually.
Confessor: Is that in fact what you are saying?
J. Goodall: Sure is. I had even more fun after I choked the life outta her.
Confessor: Again, I do not understand.
J. Goodall: Well, then, let me explain it to you, son. You see, when a man gets a certain amount of control over a woman, it gives him a kick. Not all men, mind you, but some. And what I found in my life is that I get my kicks by hurtin 'em. And the more I hurt 'em, the more harder I get. You following me?
Confessor: I am.
J. Goodall: So, there I was, mindin' my own business, when I saw her. That little black girl. She was so sweet looking, so young. And I had the perfect chance to have her. So I took her.
Confessor: This is when you kidnapped her?
J. Goodall: You betcha. And I had some fun with her. But then she was all crying and sobbing. So I hit her. And that's when I really started to get my rocks off.
Confessor: So for you, pain equals pleasure.
J. Goodall: Long as it's someone else's pain, it sure does.
Confessor: Which is why you strangled her.
J. Goodall: Yep. Strangled and humped at the same time. Her pain, my pleasure.
Confessor: I see.

C. Taylor: What I'm saying is that, based on all the things Mr. Goodall told the Confessor, the robot rewrote its own programming to inflict as much pain as it could on the Bastard.

SEN. Sobr: Are you telling me that you believe the robot reprogrammed itself to kill Mr. Goodall slowly on purpose? Based on their conversation?

C. Taylor: I know it did. Digital audit trails in the robot's programming told me that. I found that out in about thirty minutes. What I'm talking about is why. Why did it do that? Why did it reprogram itself?

SEN. Sobr: And the answer is?

C. Taylor: Well, I'm not quite sure. But I have a theory.

SEN. Sobr: Which is?

C. Taylor: I think maybe the robot was trying to understand what Goodall was talking about. I think it tried to get its own rocks off.

CROWD NOISE GROWS INTOLERABLE. ROOM CLEARED.

A BETTER MOUSETRAP

By Norm Vigeant

Smithy hated people, that fact could not be denied. In the Old Days, the feeling had been mutual, as most found him self-serving, acidic and rude. Before the Purge, he'd been a damned good computer programmer. So good, in fact, that before he realized it, he related to machines better than people. He could make systems and servers dance on his fingertips, but had trouble communicating with flesh and blood. He tried to improve his feeble social life, but his own ineptitude only opened him to mockery and shame. He retreated from society, wishing more than once for everyone to simply leave him alone.

Then the Purge came. Six years ago, for some chemical, environmental, or theological reason, a chromosome in the human strain had shifted, causing a mutation in red blood cells; a fast moving, mass-leukemia outbreak. In Smithy's pro-grammer-speak, a virus had been introduced to the system. Within three years of the first diagnosis, a full ninety percent of the planetary human population became ill and died, leaving a slew of diseased, decaying bodies behind. Furthermore, the infection decimated females more than the males, so *Homo sa-*

piens had less of a chance to re-populate the planet. Eventually, humanity would cease to exist.

Unlike the other survivors, who were burdened with the demise of family and friends, Smithy wasn't affected with a great sense of loss. He had no friends, and his family passed away before the Purge. He had no idea why he, along with the other survivors, had been spared, concluding that a special mutation allowed his immune system to remain intact. Call it built-in antivirus protection. A practical realist in his previous life, he turned his focus to survival. He was happy to finally have peace and quiet in his life. He moved from his apartment in suburban Philadelphia to an old, rambling farmhouse on the fringes of Amish country. Why? He knew an Amish farm could be fully self-sufficient by producing its own food, electricity, and running water, and he would enjoy the sense of space the farm provided. The relative remoteness of the area meant less chance that he would be discovered and removed by another survivor. After coolly dumping the previous tenants into a family grave in an anonymous cornfield, he set up shop.

Farming proved difficult, but certainly not impossible. Much of the first six months at his new home were spent making horse and carriage trips into the nearby towns. He disliked the forays immensely, what with all of the rotting corpses about, but he needed supplies and, more importantly, books from the local libraries. He read everything he could get his hands on about making a small farm self-sufficient. In no time, he had the windmill and waterwheel back up and running, providing enough power for electricity and clean water. He fed and tended the remainder of the chickens and livestock, and upgraded the barn, fences and pens to better protect them from predators. He took a gun and ammunition from a sporting goods store and learned to shoot. One couldn't be too care-

77

ful. He prepared the fields for the following spring's planting, knowing the canned and dry goods he looted from local stores would spoil eventually. Preparation would be the key to his long-term welfare. The foresight paid off, and within a season he had himself a productive, working farm.

In many ways, he'd been too busy to miss contact with the rest of humanity. At least part of him wanted to admit that. He had little use for people at this stage of the game, figuring they would just get in his way. Recently though, he reluctantly admitted to loneliness. Sometimes, as he lay in bed at night, he longed for the touch of a female. Unfortunately, companionship had been dreadfully difficult to come by in the new era. He hadn't seen a woman in over a year, and frankly, none of the females he'd seen since the Purge appealed to him all that much. His chances at finding a breathing, attractive woman were slim at best.

Then, from the back of his mind during his fall harvest, the idea of building one surfaced. Could it be done? The raw materials were around. He could use robotics and silicone for flesh, bone, and joints; processors, hardware and software for brains. Smithy could reprogram old computer chips to make a female robot do whatever he wanted. The idea intrigued him.

The more the idea burned, the more he liked it. Smithy the programmer had not exactly been a ladies man. No, he'd probably done more to repulse the opposite sex than anything else. He wasn't very attractive, didn't have a lot of money, and lacked anything resembling a magnetic personality. Now, assuming he could work out the obvious anatomical pitfalls, he had the chance to make the most attractive woman ever, whose sole purpose would be to serve his every whim. He immediately brought up the image of a girl who worked at his company in the Old Days, before she became a rotting, stinking corpse. He'd been smitten with other women before her, but this one took his breath away. She had long flowing hair, a radiant smile, eyes full of mystery and a face that could only be classified as incomparable. She even seemed friendly, chatting with him on occasion. After six months of obvious puppy dog infatuation, he worked up the courage to ask her on a date. She turned him away with vicious, mocking laugher. Losing her had stung much worse than the others. Now, Smithy stroked his chin and sneered. Yes, it could work. And it would be more than worth the effort.

Back into the surrounding towns he went, to scavenge for materials. Much to his surprise, he found the components and hardware to complete his project rather easily. The final item, the silicone he'd need to reproduce a person's flesh, proved to be somewhat more difficult. In the pre-Purge era, the best places to find the stuff were called 'adult' shops. Smithy wanted no part of that. He thought a large medical center with a burn and trauma center might have used the material for skin grafting. The closest hospital, Lancaster County, was a half-day's ride away.

So, in the early fall, he hitched the horse up to the carriage, and set off to the Lancaster County Hospital. He skulked through the center, ignoring the molding piles of six-year-old corpses he encountered upon entering, and found what he needed. He attempted to exit quickly before another living creature could discover him, but to no avail; a raggedy looking woman sat on a bench near the exit, regarding him curiously.

"What you got there, Mister?" she asked.

Smithy recoiled in surprise. She might have been a decent looking creature before the Purge, but now she resembled little more than a crude, living scarecrow.

"Come on, don't be shy," she said with a smile, showing all of her five broken teeth. "I haven't seen anyone in a long time."

Smithy quickly looked left and right, then swallowed nervously and stared at his feet, unable to utter a sound. The horse and carriage were perhaps twenty paces away.

"Where'd you come from, and why you carryin' around all that skin an' stuff?"

Smithy opened his mouth to say something, anything. As usual, the words would not be found, and he angrily scurried away, leaving the woman to stare at his back.

By the next planting season, Smithy's 'woman' was nearly complete. It was a good thing, too, as the mere thought of being with her drove him mad. All through the winter, as he worked her over, he could think only of the many ways he would be with her. The more he thought of her, the more difficult it became to put aside the carnal thoughts and concentrate. On one of the darkest and coldest nights of the year, just after solstice, he panted and perspired heavily as he stretched her soft, beautiful new skin across her midsection. He nearly gave in to his desires, but the fleeting image of him atop an incomplete torso stopped him. No, he couldn't defile his creation before she was finished. He would force himself to wait. To relieve the tension, Smithy mopped the sweat from his brow, bit his lower lip, and dreamed of the nights ahead.

He decided to call her Ani, after the woman whose features he lifted. And oh how amazing she looked. Smithy congratulated himself as he leered hungrily at his creation. Her deep auburn hair had a marvelous sheen that resembled embers afire, her eyes a glistening emerald green, her body the shape

of an hourglass. Each and every detail was perfect to his specifications. He couldn't help himself one of those final nights,
and kissed her ruby lips, relishing in the sweetness of her. Her
movements were as graceful as a gymnast's. The construction
of her joints and tendons had been time consuming, but it had
paid off. Her range of motion was incredibly fluid, nearly human. How could he have ever been interested in women, when
he could have this immaculate creature? Clearly, he had not
simply built a robot, but crafted a work of art.

The real genius of the construction was the programming.
He constructed Ani with a built in filter to weed out certain
functions and vocabulary that he thought she would find con-
fusing. For instance, she could dress herself, but had no concept of reading or writing. In short, she could perform her services for him when asked and leave him alone the rest of the
time. In his opinion, she'd make the perfect wife, or at least a
good way to exact revenge on all the pretty girls who maligned
him through the years.

Ani ran on very little power. She had a small switch and a
node hidden discreetly under her flowing hair. The switch set
her in motion. It sent a small pulse through her systems with
enough juice to keep her running for up to eight hours. When
the eight hours were up, Smithy would use the node to hook
her up to her own renewal station. A quick jolt of electricity,
and she'd be good to go again.

Finally, after a week of minor testing and tweaking to ensure proper results, Ani had been completed to Smithy's satisfaction. He would not be forced to wait for her any longer.
Tonight would be the special event. He turned her on, then
ordered her to dress for the evening in whatever woman's

clothes he could find, and positioned her appropriately for his arrival. His idea of 'setting the mood' consisted of cleaning himself after dinner.

Unfortunately, the evening did not go as planned. Smithy became so excited with the thought of being with Ani, albeit the replica of her, that he quickly removed her clothing and stuffed himself inside of her with unparalleled abandon. Everything about her was as exquisite as he imagined. That, coupled with the fact he hadn't been with a woman in a painfully long time, brought things to a quick and decisive conclusion.

Smithy collapsed backward in his bed when he had finished and wiped himself off with the sheet. It hadn't been good, but he still felt satisfied. Perhaps a few minor tweaks would help. No matter; there would be time for fun and games later. Hell, he built one over the course of the winter; perhaps he could build more. Imagine an entire harem ready and willing to do his bidding. He chuckled aloud.

"Smithy," Ani said in that silky sweet voice of hers from the other side of the bed.

"What?" he replied, remembering that she was still in the room.

"Bad," she answered.

So, she wanted him again, eh? Nice, but she would just have to wait. "Not now, woman. I need some time to myself. I'll get around to you later."

Ani shook her head emphatically. "No again. Never again. I don't like."

Wait a minute, did she just put me down? he wondered. "What do you mean, Ani?" he asked, getting angrier. He hadn't programmed anything like this. Or had he?

Ani paused for a moment. If she had been human, one would have believed she had been searching for the right words. "I don't like that!" she finally spat.

Yes, he decided, she was putting him down, just like all the others did. Bitch. Smithy's anger sparked and flared. "You ungrateful whore!" he shouted. "I gave you a life!"

"Don't care! Don't like that!" she yelled back.

Smithy had enough. He shot up, reared back and smacked her, open-handed, across the cheek. "I'll tear you limb from limb and toss your components out to rust in the rain, goddamn it!" he shouted. "And then I'll build another one, just like you without the attitude!"

Ani didn't seem to initially react to the verbal and physical abuse, being a robot and all, but Smithy swore he saw a flicker of expression cross her face.

"Sorry, Smithy," she said at last, moving closer to him. "I kiss you now."

"That's more like it," he replied, closing his eyes in anticipation.

Ani put her hands on his cheeks, then wrenched his head so suddenly and so violently that Smithy didn't have time to be surprised before his neck snapped.

"Don't like that," Ani replied softly as she kicked Smithy's lifeless body off the bed. Then she dressed slowly and walked deliberately to her station.

DEADLINES

By Andy Laughton and Paul Hughes

There will be rest, and sure stars shining
Over the roof-tops crowned with snow
A reign of rest, serene forgetting,
The music of stillness, holy and low.

I will make this world of my devising
Out of a dream in my lonely mind,
I shall find the crystal of peace; and above me
Stars I shall find.

—Sara Teasdale

The music has fallen silent above me, leaving all that precious little left beneath the shell a hollow echo of everything we could have been, now struck beyond extinct with the brutal grace of the deception.

I breathe out to ten beats staggered through my throat.

The boy is choking below me.

What's left of him isn't much. I survey the wound but there's more wound to him now than not. How he's singing with such a concave head and half of him garroted off, it's more than a little disconcerting. My hands can't cradle that tenderly enough through the copper torrent. I lay his head to rest and wipe what I can to clear his mouth.

"I have no doubt," he says, "we'll reach to strike the stars from the sky."

Something in that cores me. I don't know if it's a direct translation. The growing dead in his eyes is a slow approximation of others I've seen.

My claws retreat to the guts of the thing. Calliope writhes.

"We'll know the dead lines in their collapse."

My fingertips stumble over three studded papules. Three. Six, seven, nine. Fourteen.

"The song will find you."

That stops me.

I tear the mask from my face and breathe deeply.

By the time I realize she's stopped talking, Clare is dead.

Bill is singing something I don't recognize, something brisk and atonal as the duck shudders on the line. Cal's staccato responses ring through the pit and the undertones churn something black and restless in my stomach. I don't need to speak their language to understand that something is wrong; the speed of sound paints their panic thickly through the chamber.

I'd turned away from the panel in anger, and now I rock back to see the image of my wife slumping in her seat, face slack, all tension removed from what had been an unpleasant exchange. Gravity drags. Her chin comes to rest on her chest, furrowing the flesh a way her affected vanity would hate. Her head pivots gently to the left, a thin line of wetness spilling from her open mouth, the slack tongue lolling silent nonsenses.

Her eyes are a kind of empty that constructs a foundation of new horror within me. Matte. Then blood. On edge for the duration of our quarrel, she now tilts out of the seat, leaving the panel to display nothing but the chair and the wall, the seat spinning exactly one orbit and back into place, the wall catching only its shadow and then resuming its function as staid backdrop. I watch Clare's eyes as she falls, like that locked gaze can hold her in place and buffer her from striking the cold limit of the floor.

The sound Cal is making, it isn't music.

"Clare?" I say into the link, knowing nothing more appropriate, hoping she'll climb back up into the chair, wishing my last words to her had been something a little more not what they were, quickly realizing that the great falling feeling in my chest isn't going away and is in fact taking hold with a branding edge I already suspect will last the duration of this lost life.

The usual chiming resonance of the embassy has been replaced with silence—no, there is something. The sound of impacts. Things hitting the floor. Bouncing, rolling, some of them. Most sounding like what I hope aren't bodies, the meat slap of flesh on steel.

And still all I can see is a chair, a wall. No Clare.

Scrambling footsteps near me—Billy jogging from panel to panel, Cal chuffing along behind him, the hum and whistle of his jets barely audible beneath the frightening stream of notes.

"Billy?" I say, calling up the diagnostics. "Something's wrong with the line. I think Clare—"

"Nothing's wrong with the line." He runs to my side, waves away a test window. "All the connections, the embassies, even the outposts, they've muted."

The view of Clare's chair is pushed off to the side as Billy adjusts to display every available link.

A quick survey of the hundred-plus connections reveals a lot of empty chairs.

And a lot of bodies.

There is a clanking crash that brings the incessant hum of the heaters to silence, and the background drone warming the embassy becomes nothing.

And something in me breaks.

There's a new definition of helplessness that forty light years and counting hammers home. We are trapped in a fowl bauble traversing the sky in the wrong direction. Earth and everything we know slip silently away from us, highlighting the uncertainty of what we've witnessed.

Billy taps out a rhythm that isn't anything on the tabletop in our galley. He pushes a glass to me, fills it with something that I know will burn from our rapidly dwindling supply of firewater.

I watch him scrutinize my trembling hand as I raise a half-hearted toast. Intact hearts are for men with certifiably alive wives. I've now been wondering for six hours, and still all I see is a chair and a wall. Clare hasn't gotten up.

None of them have.

Cal tinkles something cheery. Or it sounds cheery. It could be a weather report or a drive status check or a wad of math meant for Bill to translate for me.

"Shut him up." I sip. It burns.

"Don't be like—"

"You shut that fucking duck up."

His nod is slow and borders resentful, but he does his little humming whistling thing to Cal, whose song stops abruptly. The duck's featureless face reveals nothing. He floats out of the galley without protest, tugging with him the undertones that color his presence.

"It's not like it's his fault. We don't know—"

I throw my glass across the room, knowing the janitor fields will prevent any satisfaction I would have derived from the jagged fireworks burst of glass and alcohol. They do.

"We need to go back."

Still with the fingertip tapping on the table. Bill shrugs. "You know we can't do that."

"They can tie fucking solar systems together but they can't shift into reverse? Find a way."

"Even if we find someone heading in that direction, we don't know if it's safe to go back. We don't know what happened."

"Yet."

"Yet."

I reach over for the bottle, drink from it directly, although the thrumming janitors have already sealed my glass back into shape.

"When will we know?"

He keeps tapping.

Over the standard days after the attack, I spend most of my time calling out to different links, always going back to Clare's, always hoping for a change in that view. A shift of a micrometer in the position of her chair will save me. A shadow, a sound, an anything. I beg with every inhalation, plead with every exhalation. Please let her be okay. Please let her sit up. Please let her get back into the chair. Please let her whisper to me. Please let it be a connection problem. I can fix that.

That's what I'm here to do. I can fix that, even if I couldn't fix us.

I pray that there won't be frost.

And as we pull farther away, I realize in the marrow of me the reality of losing her. Of losing them.

It is greed, needing her to be alive, discounting the four billion others of us and the however many of them. If only Clare is okay, then it all will be okay.

And still the chair is empty.

Cal eventually gets brave enough to sing again, as does Bill. I plug my ears with teeth, listening only to the whisper of dead space that is the Seattle embassy. Gone are the hourly chimes, the public announcements, the bleed through of other conversations. Gone are the dignitaries, the homefront representatives, the sounders and the roadies, the families who drop in from the cold for a quick chat with loved ones on the outward haul.

I search for hope in my survey of the links, but they offer nothing beyond a sterile stillness. I squint to see my people breathing, lean forward to witness any evidence that the ducks are venting their silver garlic lifeblood. The glass of the link coolly confirms absolutely nothing. Pressing the teeth deeper into my ears, I pray for the barest waver in the flat line of silence. My eyes throb, scraping across the spectrum to catch a duck rolling that steel floor or a human hand grasping for help. I beg the void. Something, anything, please. And still the bodies—the people—lie motionless.

Soon I will myself back to Clare's link, abandoning the others to focus hope solely on that wall, that chair. Station 05-617-2, direct line to outbound duck Calliope. All line tests indicate nothing amiss.

Bill leaves me alone for the most part, just coming in to deliver a meal or two a day. He is smart enough to know not to talk. But reflected in his quick nods and stares at the screen, the stolen glances toward the link as he sets a sandwich or a cup of soup down in front of me, I see his concern, appreciate his friendship even if all I can give him is blinked back despair and choked off fear.

And the last time, as he walks away, I turn to him, full of questions, wanting just, I don't know. Wanting reassurance. Human contact. Wanting to tell him thanks. Wanting to tell him of the boy in the rehearsal room. But I let him walk back to the pit to be with Cal. I know they'll soon be lost together in a conversation never crescendoing past pianissimo in deference to the fugue into which they are losing me. I turn back to the screen, the teeth in my ears splitting something soft and vital as I listen for Clare.

Then one day I wake at my post to see an intricate scroll of ice obscuring the screen. I watch the veil of frost build until I can no longer see the chair, the wall.

I sob because now I know the heat has died.

I think that scares Bill because I haven't cried yet.

There is much more drinking after that. I drink until there is one bottle of firewater left, then I sober up and get angry and pull the teeth from my ears and start talking out loud again, even if all I can do is yell.

Since the arrival of the ducks, I've abandoned everything I've ever believed about extraterrestrial life. We all had to, since first contact came in the form of beautiful songs from the sky performed by a chorus of duck-shaped metal bags of gaseous arsenic, not a "Take me to your leader" delivered by an egg-headed gray.

Just seven years after the ducks arrived with their incessant song and their solution to our ice age, I shouldn't have been surprised at all that while I was off with Bill on a trip to one of their arsine extractors that a machine intelligence would initiate a targeted detonation of Barnard's Star and effectively result in the statistical extinction of humanity. Sure, we have a few hundred translation crews out on the lines in transit to and from the ducks' bases sprinkled throughout our sliver of the Way galaxy, but with the Sol and Centauri systems baked out, it is going to be difficult to find a new home.

Me, I'm a roadie. Bill is the sounder. Our teamwork guarantees successful communication between us monkeys and the gasbags. I have to admit, the tech side of it all wasn't too terribly hard, and the pay was good. Clare and I would finally be able to own, not rent. No more student loans. We'd get the credit cards off of our backs. Har-de-har-har. And free heat for life. Those concerns might sound ridiculous when considering I'd be paying off our debt with government money I earned on a forty-light-year superstring roadtrip with my amnesiac friend and a shiny aluminum foil swan sculpture of poison, but still, we all have our obligations. And if I could achieve financial solvency by running wires and checking levels and troubleshooting wireless signals and maintaining our connection to home, good enough. Was it touring with Journey? Not quite, but beggars can't be choosers when a gig comes along during tough times. And honestly, I preferred Bill's music.

He was one of those child genius types who taps out the classics on their parents' piano before they've learned how to successfully shit on the potty. Way before puberty even considered taking its first swipe at him, he was an accomplished concert pianist with half a dozen albums and a room full of plaques in his parents' condo. If he'd kept at it, well, he'd be dead with the rest of them, gamma-rayed by Barney. Instead, he decided to rebel and matriculate. He wanted to be a composer, because as far as I can tell, he didn't want to live a cover band life. He wanted people to hear the inside of his head, not just the echoes of someone else banged out through his fingers. It was a lofty goal for a five-year-old perfect pitch savant who'd never even spent a night away from home and who still couldn't correctly pronounce "spaghetti."

I introduced myself to him late one night while I was cutting through one of the many rehearsal spaces at our university. He introduced himself to me in the form of six notes, repeating in various arrangements, tapped out into the midnight quiet during trimester study break. McCreary Hall offered brief respite from the growing cold, and I treasured the opportunity to melt a little snow from my parka as I traversed the hundred feet of heat the hallway offered on my nightly journey home.

And the cold, it was getting worse all over.

I was a wires and levels guy, and I didn't know much about music beyond what I liked and what I could make sound better. But those notes... I paused in my shortcut just long enough for something of those notes to work their way into me, and after walking a few hallways flanked on both sides by rooms each containing real pianos donated by alumni a century or two ago, I found the kid with the song stuck in his brain.

"Hey," I said.

He turned around. "Hey."

"Sounds good," I said.

He frowned.

Kids shouldn't have frowns like that.

I hadn't expected a little boy to be the source of that music. His hands were paused over the keys, maybe in expectation, maybe frustration, maybe just confusion over being interrupted when he thought he was alone in the practice building. Most nights on my shortcut through that space I was assaulted with two dozen personal depictions of hopeful brilliance, mostly undergrad shit ripped off from Music 101 classes where the kids heard compositions new to them, but that night the usual performance and comp students were back in their rooms cramming for the end-of-terms.

But this kid—but those six notes.

He didn't need to cram.

He released his face from frown and played the first three-note chord again. The second. First, second. He looked at me and transitioned into a third chord that was so striking in its dissonance I paused mid-inhalation and I don't think I ever really breathed again after that.

"What do we know?"

"Cal confirms that Barnard's Star is the probable source of the gamma ray burst."

"English, please."

"It went boom."

"Right. And the radiation?"

A trill from the duck.

"He doesn't know. We're trying to piece together the outbound and inbound traffic logs."

"A lot'll be dead, right?"

"We're guessing anyone within ten lys of Barney."

"How many were in transit?"

"We don't know. You aren't the least bit concerned about how a star—"

"Was anyone else on our line?"

"Signal integrity check says no. Which you would know if you'd been doing your job."

I ignore the boy's jab. "So we have a straight shot home. No roadkill to go around."

Cal hums.

Bill shrugs. "You know there's no reverse."

"Has he been able to contact any of the other ducks?"

"We're working on it."

"Work harder. If we can find an inbound transport close enough, we should be able to point-to-point over."

Bill nods but the set of his eyes and the crumple of his mouth indicates frustration.

"What?"

"It's just that we're getting into language we've never covered before. Cal has to dig deep to learn the words."

"How deep?"

"I can't remember high school anymore."

"You never went to high school."

"That's a relief. And, I guess, kind of not."

"If he starts going after important parts of your brain, be sure to let me know."

"Yeah. Will do."

They found the first line three months after it sheared the wing from a commercial liftliner with improbable precision. Whatever Israel has for an FAA retrieved the wing from the Mediterranean floor two months after they'd recovered various portions of seven hundred passenger bodies and somewhat some of the rest of the plane from the slushy mess of the sea.

When someone cuts your wing off, you fall.

They thought laser weaponry.

They thought that until an oil tanker was split in half in the same exact spot, but what are the chances of that happening?

Pretty good, with all those icebergs. But still, it was a clean cut.

What are the chances a hurricane would develop there, its eye an unblinking reminder of two big metal things being cleaved open right fucking there?

Even better.

So they looked around.

And looked around some more.

And drove right into the thing. Drove their little boat right into the line struck through the world.

So they looked up.

The science guys looked up.

And then the singing started.

Three notes, six, seven, nine. Fourteen. The kid never stopped playing.

He couldn't vote yet, couldn't buy smokes, certainly couldn't walk into a bar and order himself a drink. He was still too short to meet the height requirement for some roller coasters. We were both juniors.

We developed a hesitant friendship over the years, with me visiting him on my walks home. We bonded over the one thing in life we shared at a base level, our love for music, although he was performance and composition and I was just a wire runner and engineer. We talked big about cutting an album, but we never got around to it. I think the kid was lonely. I know he was lonely. Clare thought it was sweet that I spent time with him when I could have been jogging home to wrestle with her, but as months drew out into years and as the reality of our poverty in the face of a new ice age set in, truth is we wrestled less and fought more. Stopping to see the kid became less about warming up and more about avoidance.

He was in the practice room as usual when I shortcutted my way through McCreary. It was a particularly cold autumn night, carrying with it the dread of the impending winter, forcing particular attention to the thin, inadequate protection my parka offered. I figured a visit to the kid would both warm me up and maybe make his day a little less lonely. When you're age eight in college, you don't have a social life.

I knocked once on the door and opened it after seeing him, back to the slit window, in there. I had no idea how long he'd been practicing, and since there wasn't a panel in the room and I'd never seen him with any form of berry, I thought I'd tell him about the big news of the evening. How many times do you get to announce first contact?

"Hey, man."

Three notes. This was typical.

"You hear about the UFOs?"

Three notes. Six. He didn't turn around.

"Bill?"

Six, seven, nine.

"Hey…"

Ten fingers mashed against fourteen keys.

"Billy?"

Mash and mash, hands balling to fists. He struck the keyboard with such savage intent I expected at each impact to hear bones surrender.

I shook his shoulder and that contact made him jump. He swung his arm around and scrambled from the piano bench, his knobby knees pistoning him into the corner, shielding his face with the delicate palms of a genius. His eyes were wet and two tears dropped from his jawline to his t-shirt: one two.

His face was a grimace, a smile, a dance of muscle under that flawless brown. He tore at a breath, scudded it back out as he worked tears away from his eyes with fists.

"The singing…" he sobbed.

His eyes, all I could see was white.

I picked him up and ran.

Cal pipes a jaunty tune and for a second I'm certain we're infested with nightingales.

"We found someone."

I swim over to Bill's panel, upon which the display indicates another duck not too far away, relatively speaking. At point-seven light years, they're our next-door neighbors.

"Anyone we know?"

"Manifest says they're a sounder team heading home from a tour at the mines."

"And they're the closest?"

"The closest we've found so far. The only lined duck in range for point-to-point."

"What's our window?"

"We think they noticed us—they've slowed to a crawl. If we cut our velocity to ambient, we should be able to maintain contact long enough."

"What do you say, Cal? Want to hitch a ride?" I look up to the metal bubble, waiting for Bill to translate.

The sound he makes, it's like a whale playing a saxophone.

"He says it'll be safer to just continue on to the base."

"Who's in charge here?"

"He is."

"Wrong."

"This is his ship. This is *him*. We're guests of the—"

"Fuck that. Call the other transport and arrange for point-to-point. Cal can come along if he wants, but he can't keep me here."

The saxophone squawks.

"He says he'll go."

We lived off campus in a shitty studio apartment. I had two of the three deadbolts unlocked by the time Clare realized I was home and unstrung the chain and popped the last bolt and threw open the door and almost knocked me down into the hallway beyond with her hug and her, "Where have you been? Did you hear about the—Den? What's wrong?"

What struck me first when I looked past her into the apartment was that the president was on the television standing next to a big metal rubber duckie kind of thing that was floating four or five feet off the ground. On any other day I would have been concerned about this. I'd seen footage of the UFOs but this little one was new to me.

"Denny?"

"I took the kid down to the health services building. I think he was having some kind of seizure. They sent him to the hospital."

"Oh, baby." She cupped my face in her hands in that way she did when concern overrode personal space, as if feeling fingers on my cheeks would wick the stress away. "Is he okay?"

"I don't know. Not a relative, so they wouldn't tell me anything." She helped me unbuckle the maze that held my parka securely around me. I kicked off my moon boots, leaving them to thaw puddles of salt and black snow at the doorway. I took her hand and dragged her into a slow collapse, a tangle of limbs, into our Salvation Army couch. That pile of us was where we were at our best.

Her eyes were locked to the television as my lips warmed themselves against her neck. "So I take it you heard about this?"

"No one on campus'll shut up about it. I went to tell Billy, but—"

Snap. The press conference audio dropped out and was replaced by a barrage of static hiss for a moment, loud enough for Clare to down volume on the remote. "It's been doing that all day. First the sound cuts out, then SHHHHHHHH, now, wait for it—"

Tones. Flat, simple notes issued from the speakers.

"Turn it up." I dropped my attention from the warm velvet of her and sat up.

"It's just the same notes. They'll play over and over again for a—"

"Turn it up!" Noting her inaction I grabbed for the remote and held the volume button down until the bars filled the bottom of the panel left to right.

Three notes. Six. Six, seven, nine.

Fourteen.

"We're at ambient resonance."

"And them?"

"Them too."

"Okay, I'll bring the hook online and see if we can reach their line."

Cal sputters something low behind me.

"What?" I turn to Bill.

"Working on it." His right hand reaches up to massage his temple, as if kneading flesh can force the translation through the filter of his soft wet gray faster.

"Well?"

He shakes his head. "I don't know these words. Give me a minute."

"The hook is searching for a cross-string."

Cal drifts in an awkward figure eight as he lets loose another tuba sounding something.

"All I'm getting is that he wants us to be quiet. Keeps saying 'quiet.'"

I frown at Cal.

Bill nods. "Yeah, quiet. Be quiet, or speak quietly, or—whisper? Why should we whisper, Cal?"

The trumpeting exhaust of the gasbag is familiar enough to Bill that he doesn't need to translate.

"Okay, wrong. No whispering, no speaking quietly... Be quiet. You want us to be quiet. Why do you—"

"Shut up." Something has caught my eye on the main screen, something that shoots out from the periphery of my vision and streaks across everything. The harsh cautery of its passing gives me fear the screen has shattered.

Cal pipes almost inaudibly, shying away from the display.

Whatever is streaking across our main screen is big, bright, and fast, burning a line across my vision that stays. Our computer chugs along, attempting to present it in real-time on our little map of local space.

"Is that..."

Bill shakes his head, in disagreement or seeking clarity, I don't know. Cal blows two successions of notes.

"Is that an *anchor*?" I look back at Bill and Cal, knowing already in the meat of me the destination of this thing.

Bill clears his throat. "Cal keeps repeating two words."

This thing is traveling almost parallel to our superstring, which will, of course, take it to the Sol system.

"What words?"

"Dead…"

"That's one."

"Lines."

Billy walked up to me in the staging area. He watched me eat whatever canned meat the meal of the day was. With the crops dead, I was thankful for the tin of something. Continents were starving to death.

"Hi. I'm Billy, your sounder."

The hand he extended was still baby ass innocent and I wondered over that texture, knowing the brilliance that once flowed from the tapping of those fingers over ivory.

He was three times the age then than when I first met him but he still couldn't vote or buy cigarettes. And I doubt the last seven years had offered him many opportunities to ride roller coasters.

"I'm Denny."

There was no sign of recognition, but then again, all I ever had been to him was a guy trying to get warm by walking through a building. That was back when I thought I knew what cold was.

"Nice to meet you, Denny."

"Likewise."

"Have you been in the program long?"
"Yeah."
"Yeah?"
"Seven years."
"Me too."

What the ducks offered—when they revealed themselves—
was a gentle nudge.

They couldn't really talk then, but we got the idea. This
was after they raided the music schools for savants like Billy,
kids who couldn't get the song out of their heads, but before
they realized they'd need roadies to handle the tech end of
things. We had hands.

We called them ducks because they looked vaguely like big
fat rubber ducks and they floated in the air, which seemed kind
of cool because they were metal. They showed up in bigger
versions of themselves that I'm guessing weren't alive but I
don't speak quack. And by bigger I mean fucking bigger. By
fucking bigger I mean big enough to block out the moon.

They apologized for the airplane and the oil tanker and the
scientist boat. They felt bad about those incidents. They
hadn't intended to even reveal themselves, but once the science
guys noticed, they felt the need to say hi and sorry. And to accomplish saying those things, first they needed band geeks and
then they needed audio engineers.

Somewhere something with a sense of humor figured it
would be cool to reunite Billy and me. The catch was that his
brain was now half arsenic and he had no idea who I was. I
was okay with that because I was never much to know in the
first place.

"Why did you volunteer?"

I let the question hang there but since it was the only sound beyond muffled footsteps at our gate, I felt obligated to answer the kid.

"Wives are expensive."

There was a pause and I wasn't sure if he was waiting for the ducks to give him an explanation or if he was using some limited allotment of embassy etiquette to put it together for himself.

"That was a joke…?"

I said nothing. I caught a whisper of music in the bright air, decided maybe there was something left of him in that shell.

But still, I felt my opinion of this imposter tilting toward dislike. This wasn't the boy I'd known once from his relentless nighttime piano practice and his strict succession of notes.

Then again, was I the same? What skin I exposed broadcast the frostbitten duration of my tenure on our tow. No parka, no helmet could cast all that cold away. On our dying world, something happened to you, away from the white sterility of the embassy's warmth. Every time you came back inside, more of your blood was ice. That explained my attitude some. There was an ice in me that had been building up, and it was the kind of ice that stops hearts dead.

So I ignored his words in favor of dragging eyes across the place his ears should have been. The whole of the staging area transformed the muffs into reflected sparks. Maybe they didn't want us to scrutinize the hardware. Maybe I was supposed to see myself in the metal of him where ears would distract.

Three notes and who knows how many others. His posture became something else and for two, maybe three seconds his attention forgot me. He was lost in a rigid nowhere, less boy then than just another tool.

"They're ready for us. Maybe you should—"

So I crushed the lunch can as I stood, let it fall and bounce to the white floor, where it barely made a sound. I pulled my top on and locked it in place over the thermal vest, the reactor already spinning up in spurts of strange particles. With two scooping fingers I signaled him to follow me to the launch line.

The transition from our gate to the duck vessel was seamless. As we got in, there were more edges to my hearing, so I knew he was having a chat with something. His humming only reinforced that suspicion.

There was a hollow sound in my head that proved I was normal.

What the ducks had needed to be able to communicate with our species was a bunch of musical brains. Only a certain set of the folds would spark that magical tête-à-tête between corked up poison gas and little old us. People like me helped engineer interfaces like the one Billy had drilled into his head, but I'd never felt the tidal pull of the ducks' song inside of me, only heard the public version falling from the sky in those first days and pieces of melody from sounders ever since.

The chairs in the duck's pit were comfortable. I experienced the internal conflict that questioned whether I should be grateful for this. I wanted to hate them. I wanted to wonder what alien coercions were used to elicit such success in ergonomics, how many corpses were autopsied to end result in such plush furnishings. I had my doubts about the number of interior designers who had collaborated with our potential saviors.

Billy raised his index finger. My attention focused inadvertently on him. I knew he was now doing his job.

"Cal says we'll depart in three minutes. He's waiting for confirmation of a free string. The verification should be quick. After launch, he'll hand over line integrity checks to you."

Those minutes spindled out in sugary silence to me. The kid nodded four times, the humming punctuated by the occasional throat thing. Kind of a grunt, a clearing, some substantial clicking that meant nothing to me because I have ears. I knew somewhere in this vessel the operator lurked, calling its singsong out across the stars, grasping for purchase on the fundamental underpinnings of our universe.

When the sub-vocal conversation came to a suspected end, I drummed up enough curiosity to ask: "Cal?"

"Our duck chose the name Cal. Short for Calliope."

"Cute."

The kid smiled blankly. He'd forgotten sarcasm. And I thought he probably didn't know much about extinct musical instruments.

"Cal, what was that?" I test the first word with a whisper and gradually brave louder words in succession.

The duck still dances his figure-eight, venting jets of something in his shifting wakes that I hope won't kill me with my next breath.

Billy doesn't wait for an answer; he's already throwing new panels around the pit. "Definitely a string, but I don't recognize the vessel that was on it. Wasn't a duck. Cal?"

Silence from the gasbag.

"It looked like a goddamned anchor." I sit next to Billy, splitting his display and rolling back one half of the screen to replay the mystery ship.

Cal offers a quick chirp. At least he's not catatonic.

"What did he say?"

Billy squints as something jagged gropes his brain. He doesn't chirp, but the little throat sound he makes is just about as disconcerting.

A chime from the panel startles me. I see we have an incoming point-to-point request from our neighbors. They've done the tough work for us; a perpendicular string is highlighted on the map, one that passes through our probability halos. Our ducks are still drifting away from each other at the ambience of the strings, but we're well within range for merging.

With the sounder and the duck not singing, it's probably a good time for me to do my job.

Trips out on the lines aren't short things.

The duck base Billy and I were going to was almost a quarter of a quadrillion miles away from Earth. That might sound like a lot but we'd be there and back in four months. Nothing compared to the 93 billion light years it would take to truly traverse this everything.

As a roadie I knew a little of how the whole process of being yanked around the universe on the lines worked, but I didn't really care and I didn't want the level of brain intrusion required to truly grasp how the ducks did it. That was for sounders. All I wanted was the paycheck. And a four-month break from Clare.

I guess she was right most of the time but I was too much of a dick to let her know I knew that.

Cities were freezing. We looked back on that last unexpectedly cool summer as our twilight. Everyone had been so fucking concerned about warming for so long that this came as a punch to our collective gut. We were lazily drifting away from the sun, and there was nothing we could do about it except put on another pair of socks and pray.

Then the ducks showed up, all cute and apologetic.

What they'd been doing for longer than forever was zipping around the Milky Way on the connective tissue of existence, jumping from string to string like commuters changing trains. Some lines went one way. Others went the other. But one thing was clear—there were lines everywhere; you just needed to hammer the right one to hitch a ride to the right place.

Sometimes a line would detach from its foundation while the ducks were riding along. That's what happened to the one driven through the Arabian Plate, emerging out the Juan de Fuca. The ducks never intended to come to Earth, but one innocent jump and they'd snagged a planet and killed a few hundred people, shifting us just enough out of place to begin to freeze a few billion more.

Upon investigating the anomaly in the line, they realized that this was one sick world. So they came down with their song and their sweetness and told us they'd help tow us back into place. Accidents happen.

On my first trip with Billy, our species had been working together for seven years. Those first few shy ducks called in thousands more. They were kind benefactors, evacuating those they could to their bases throughout the Way while everyone else shivered at home until renovations were complete.

Megascale engineering is a tenuous process. Our planet had taken eons to seriously fuck up, but that didn't mean we weren't impatient over the thirty or forty years it would take to gently nudge us back into a safe orbit.

Billy and I would serve a two-month tour at a duck base translating for the workers. We'd provide the human touch to a few hundred people canned up in a birthing mine. The more miners we had releasing arsine gas from the metal trash rocks of the galaxy, the more ducks we'd have to help us.

The pay was good. More importantly, Clare would be warm at home, tucked away in the Seattle duck embassy. She'd even be able to contact me through the line they'd tethered there. We'd be able to continue our ongoing verbal assault daily. We were a lucky couple.

Billy clears his throat behind me. "Den?"

The panel is chewing through the math necessary to connect to the line that will provide our perpendicular leap to our neighbors. It's calculating probabilities for things I can't begin to wrap my brain around.

"How are you feeling, kid?"

"Headache."

"Yeah, both of you were out of it."

"Sorry."

"Is Cal okay?"

There's a soft murmur of tone from the duck, so I assume he's reading me through Billy.

"He's afraid."

This is an alien who is made of arsenic. He could kill us both instantly with a big enough belch. His species travels the galaxy by strumming the superstring foundation of reality. They push planets around. They have ships that block out the stars. And he's afraid of something. That makes me want to open the last bottle of firewater.

"Of?"

"He says they found us."

"They."

"They."

"The anchor thing is a they."

"The anchor thing is an anchor."

Fantastic.

It was the kind of fight we shouldn't have been having from seventeen light years apart.

The trip so far had been okay. It took me a while to get used to the fact that the kid I'd known for three years was no longer entirely inside of his brain and he preferred the company of the gasbag to that of the only other member of his species for who knows how many parsecs in any direction. The thing about the size of outer space is that it turns lonely into your everything, a taste on the edge of every breath, an underlying hum that won't go away. We were cats in a box and I already felt dead.

Being able to talk to Clare daily didn't help that.

She hadn't wanted me to go but she certainly didn't complain about her upgraded accommodations at the embassy or the food or the walls that held out the howling of the winds. She cried a little when she told me she tried to get my parents a pass but they were already among the frozen. I felt something at that but mostly just wanted her to shut up.

She didn't understand why I needed to be out there helping the aliens with the kid I'd known from college. Maybe I didn't understand that either but a part of me knew that at least it would be quieter on the lines.

When she told me she'd be in her second trimester by the time I got home, I threw a little static into the mix of our conversation and turned away from the screen.

Then Barnard's Star went boom.

We are everywhere all at once so it doesn't take much to jump ship.

Billy and Cal and me, we point over to our neighbor, the duck going in the direction of home. Cal is still tooting to himself and Billy is still translating and a streak of fire still paints the way home.

When we emerge from the slit in the other duck we're met by its sounder and its roadie and a gasbag a little smaller than Cal.

I go to the human who has ears and shake her hand. "Den."

"Dix."

"And them?"

"Lonnie and Gertie."

"Let me guess—Hurdy-gurdy?"

"Yup."

"Gotcha. And I take it Gertie has been out of commission since—"

"—since that anchor thing flew by, yeah. Any ideas?"

"Nope, but Billy here is trying to dig some answers out of Cal."

"Cal?"

"Calliope."

"Ha. Fucking ducks."

"That thing scared them."

"No shit. And it's heading toward Earth."

"Cal mentioned something about dead lines."

"Deadlines?"

"I don't know. The anchor's following a superstring leading home, but I don't know how a line can be dead."

Cal and Gertie chirp simultaneously.

Lonnie and Billy look at each other and something passes between them.

"Main display, local map." Billy says it in the direction of us two roadies but I know his attention is somewhere inside of his brain.

Dix throws a panel up and it grows to full. Our former line, now free from Cal's grip, is fading into space's chill, awaiting its next passenger. The anchor line is still bright as ever, but now there are three of them.

Then six.

Seven, nine.

Fourteen.

And then I stop counting.

We're having an awkward supper as Gertie unhooks herself from ambient and starts hammering down the line toward Earth. The anchors still surround us. By surround I mean none is closer than a light year, but still, we're all going to the same party.

Because Dix hadn't watched her wife die, she still has some firewater left. I help her make that less true.

Lonnie and Billy don't eat much. They sip their soup between tweets to the ducks.

I finger a panel as I swallow more fire. "Looks like we're in good company."

The local map now displays a few hundred other ducks traversing their lines back to Earth. Some of these ships would put the fear into Jupiter. The map has trouble showing all of them. From some of the biggest, I can detect targeted bursts of radiation. They're shooting at the anchors. We're inside a gunfight none of us understands.

The map, I don't want to talk about how many anchors it shows, and I couldn't put a number on it anyway. All those converging lines make the Way a brighter place.

So I take another drink to try to fill in the empty suck in my stomach. There's no way these anchor things don't have something to do with Barney going gamma, and whatever they're up to, the ducks don't like it.

So I hate them without even knowing what they are.

I hate them because hate needs a target.

"We'll never catch them before they get to Earth."

I look at Lonnie and try to think if this is the first time I've heard his singsong voice. He's a sick looking kid, a little older than Billy but not much. He's skinny in a way Dix is thick, pale in a way Billy is dark, lost in a way maybe I am.

"Cal says the ducks are sending everyone they can to help." Billy takes another swig of supper soup.

"Help *what*?" Rage builds in the corridor between my brain and my heart. "If Cal knows something about what's going on, he'd better fucking tell us. We're in a shooting war and I don't know what's being shot at."

"Gertie?" Dix stares down Lonnie as she says this. "Spill it."

Our sounders share silence as they look to their ducks for support. The translation cradles welded to their heads almost seem to spark an instant and they speak for the ducks in unison, shades of them somewhere in the mix but mostly corpse voices we've never heard as the ducks take control:

"There are dead lines. There are machines. There was not silence. They have found us. The song will end."

Dix is trying to put a panel into my hand. I take it.

Among those blazing arcs, anchors coalesce. Our little group of bubbles on dim lines seems an afterthought, a fragile coda submerged in that dazzling geometry.

We don't have nearly enough ducks.

Lonnie and Billy spend a lot of time together on our in-bound trip, heads together humming, consulting with Gertie and Cal in ways I don't truly want to grasp.

Dix and I do a lot of drinking because there's about a month to burn as we watch duck forces assemble around us. The anchors are now just a band of light torn through our path. We're bathtub toys being sucked down the gravity well.

We watch in wonder three weeks out as duck vessels larger than Mercury's orbit swell past us on their taut superstrings, throwing wakes of probability through the abacus of our meager fleet.

The ducks send scouts ahead to report back on whatever is happening but even if I spoke quack I don't know enough of what's going on to form an opinion and they aren't exactly sharing information freely.

Billy spends a lot of time humming and I'm glad he's found a friend with whom he shares common interests. There are moments when the sounders' singing knuckles its beauty into my heart and I can't remember how to breathe.

Two weeks out, we drink the last of the booze.

One week out, Gertie and Cal sing something keening and bright, a song more a knife edge on bone than sensible succession of melody.

Dix conducts a makeshift role call of the passengers on ducks around us and we have about three hundred humans in total. Thinking about what it would mean for that three hundred to be the last of us, I bury that deep, maybe deeper than I've buried Clare.

Dix and I try to piece together what we can from conversations with other roadies, but the ducks get angry when we twang the lines for gossip. With all the anchors ahead of us doing whatever on Earth and no more of them inbound, we figure there isn't much to lose.

We meet a roadie named Pat who was on one of the arsine mines around Procyon B. He confirms the ducks went batshit when word of Barnard's Star throwing gamma at Earth got through but the real panic didn't set in until they detected those anchors cutting their way across near space. His duck (Bo— Oboe—oh, ducks) and his sounder went into that quiet duo only they could really hear after babbling nonsensically about "being quiet" and "dead lines."

Bo and the team hooked an inbound string and started home, anchors passing them the whole way, massive duck vessels chasing them with microwave lances and other more dramatic ways of trying to stop them dead.

Our tiny drop in the galactic ocean shivers with the war song of the duck's converging armada.

Two days out I try pointing cameras home but all I receive is dead black. The view behind us is filled with the flock. Frustration builds in the echoes of the sounders. The ducks shimmy their figure eight war dance above the pit and Dix and I sit around a lot with our arms crossed, frowning.

One day out, something hits our line.

I was never one for astronomy, but I'm pretty sure it was Mars.

When I was growing up, I preferred the classics. The Beatles. The Stones. Journey. Kids looked at me like I was their grandfather even though not a whole hell of a lot of history separated our tastes.

I didn't know what to make of what I heard now. It was music in the way screaming is talking.

Torn from our string, we watched Gertie fall to the floor of the pit and begin to vent herself everywhere. With the knowledge that death was always a breath away when your travel companions are bags of poison, Dix and I reverted to basic training and ran to retrieve emergency breathers. By the time we got back and I'd pulled a hood over Billy's slow on the uptake face, Lonnie was a pile of dead.

Dix's reaction was: "Shit."

My reaction was: "Cal, take over."

The duck hovered above the pit, unsure of what to make of Gertie's shell, now rocking empty in the confused gravity of the floor.

"Billy, tell Cal to take over control of the ship."

From under the hood, his eyes were unblinking and wet. I punched him in the mouth to wake him from that reverie, although at the same time I was afraid he'd breathed too much of the dead duck.

"Billy, start quacking."

He blinked and nodded, clearing his throat before humming a stuttered something punctuated with a lonely whistle that tapered into just air.

Cal responded with a bland chord and took the reins.

"We've got eyes," Dix said, throwing a panel to the main display. "Gert must have been locking us out of forward visual."

"Show me."

"Den?"

My seat really was comfortable but I squirmed because I was tired of talking to her.

"I have something really important to talk to you about."

"Listen, I should go. There's a shitload of system checks to run, and—"

"I'm pregnant."

I'm ashamed to admit that the first thing I thought about was how much it was going to cost, not the fact that the Earth was a frozen waste. Not the fact that something of me would live on in a son or a daughter. Not the fact that a child would mean someone to protect, to nurture, to love, a living symbol of what Clare and I shared. I thought about doctor bills and diapers and baby formula. About sleepless nights and the death of my sex life and just one more fucking responsibility when the world was falling apart. If she was pregnant, there was a good chance the ducks wouldn't let me go out on another trip to the mines. My days as Billy's roadie would be dead.

"Okay."

"Okay?"

"Get rid of it."

"What…?"

"You heard me."

"But—"

"No. Get rid of it. We can't have a baby now."

"I'm having this baby."

"Then you'll have it alone."

"Denny, don't—"

"We can't have a baby now, and that's final."

Somewhere, the song shifted. I heard a warning siren that wasn't a part of the choir.

"Listen, I have to go."

"Denny, please..."

The sirens insisted. Billy ran in with Cal close behind him.

"I have to go."

"Can we at least talk about this later?"

"I have to go."

She sobbed. "Denny, I..."

The first days I knew her were an Indian summer in a winter life. In the moment before I turned away, I remembered simple, gentle moments, the way one views love through a dancing filter of dandelion fluff, the way grass feels on your back when no one's watching, the way, across a train station, your heart pounds out missing as she leaves for only a collection of days. Fragile morning light in stripes across a bed. A sneeze. The fog of breath on a window pane. The quiet poetry of her.

I loved her, I did, but the end of the world changes the core of you.

I turned away from the screen to see what was going on. Billy and Cal were singing to themselves and displays lit up the pit. I had to end this call and assess the situation.

I turned back to the screen.

And she was gone.

The stars dance as we roll through the outer edge of Sol space. Around us other ducks similarly thrown from their lines hurtle drunkenly toward the sun, some colliding in flashes of fire and gas, some of the dead flying off on phantom trajectories to the cold statistical nothing of the galaxy. The segments of Mars drift onward, cleaved time and again by contact with active lines.

The abandoned strings fade gently into the background.

The armada surges ahead of us toward unknown combat eight minutes or less from the sun. As Cal begins to stabilize our vessel, we look ahead to see great gouts of light rending the center of the system apart. The anchors' carve through the night bathes all in a burning luminosity. Hulking duck vessels are cast into stark silhouette before us.

Cal and Billy dirge in unison.

And we are enveloped in white.

We wake at some point within the milky translucence of the meta-duck hiding in the Kuiper belt. The war raging outside the vessel hints at itself through actinic bursts of light bright enough to penetrate the smooth shiny bowl of the hull.

Our accommodations are spartan but welcome. I am surrounded by other humans but Cal is nowhere to be seen.

Nobody knows what to say so nobody says anything.

The sounders of the group are lost in song, telegraphing who knows what into the nothing between stars. Dix and I occupy silent space on the floor. It isn't cold but it kind of is and I worry about that a little.

Hours pass with no reduction in the number or ferocity of flashes outside. I guess we've been rescued but it doesn't make me feel any better, seeing what I suspect are ducks dying on the other side of the shell. I try not to think too much about it because I don't want to know how powerful a gun has to be for its shot to be visible through solid metal.

And the groaning... When the ducks lose one of their own, the cargo hold—that was us, the cargo—just shimmies with our vessel's groan. Think whales but bigger and scarier and deeper and sharper and completely fucking alien. Like listening to your dad cry but your dad's turned into a giant zombie sea monster being raped by an overzealous theremin. And he's on fire.

Groans so loud I lose three fillings. Which kind of pisses me off because I know it will probably be a while before I find a new dentist, and I doubt my insurance covers the end of the world.

Groans so loud I swear to god I see a lady have a seizure because of one. Then she dies.

Groans coming so often I'm beginning to think I've misplaced my trust in the ability of the gasbags to successfully protect the remainder of my species from whatever it is they're fighting.

So I cover my ears and grit my teeth.

The sounders' chanting starts to get to me, not because it doesn't sound good but because you put a few hundred sounders in one place and suddenly you get a pretty good idea of how strange it is we've let aliens inside our kids' brains. Most were just babies when the ducks arrived.

And maybe it gets to me because I care about them but I didn't care about Clare's baby.

Our baby.

I watch the flashes beyond the hull.

They stop after a while.

Dix eventually took a job with a bunch of ducks heading out to retrieve the Moon. I never saw her again and I kind of wondered what use getting the Moon back would be anyway, but she seemed happy with the assignment.

Six months after the gamma ray assault and the battle between the ducks and the machines, Billy and I lived on the massive restoration platform being constructed over Earth's hemispheres. Cal was stationed there so it all worked out. We had a nice view of the pieces of the planet rotating in opposite directions below us.

Looking down on the frozen halves, dragged out somewhere in the vicinity of Mars's former orbit but being towed steadily back into place by the ducks, all I want to do is go back to the Seattle embassy.

The months have focused the sleek spectrum caress of my mourning.

I know Clare is down there.

The ducks say everything is safe now because they were able to sever the anchor lines and incapacitate the machines storming across the irradiated planet. Unfortunately they weren't able to cut the connection before the enemy had punched two of their cables through Earth and begun its dismantling, drawing off the rich gooey goodness of the interior, presumably to aid in the construction of more machines, towing it out of place in the system with the intent of dragging it home, wherever their home may be.

What they did was crack Earth like an egg.

The ducks were sorry they hadn't stopped the machines in time to save Earth, but at least they'd intercepted the anchors plummeting toward Sol. They agreed to patch the planet as best they could and tow it back into its original orbit. They'd restore the atmosphere and melt the ice ball it had become. They'd help us clean up the giant robot war machines that still littered the surface.

Did I say they were dead? Well, they weren't.

I said incapacitated.

What the anchors were was something like spiders but made of metals we'd never heard of imbued with intelligence we could never comprehend, machines who fell to Earth in a great skittering, monstrous descent and promptly spilled their children upon the surface as they began to skin the planet plate by plate.

I didn't want to think too deeply about who would make machines like that but when you work with mustard gas wrapped in tin foil all day your horizons begin to expand.

What Cal surrendered to Billy eventually was that these metal spiders were like demolitions machines. They took worlds apart to make more of their own. They took stars like ours to fuel their war machine. Like the ducks, they traversed the great superstring highway of the universe but only on a dedicated set of lines they peeled away from the universe's basement themselves through targeted magnetar detonations and gamma ray bursts and who knows how many other insidious methods our monkey brains couldn't ken. Their lines left a trail of dead systems in their wake.

Get it? Dead lines. Har-de-har.

The ducks were out here bobbling around our bit of nothing collecting enough gaseous arsenic to repopulate their species from a machine assault.

There's no easy way to think of questions when the answers are that big, but I wondered why the ducks hadn't told us about this little galactic menace in the first fucking place.

I wondered why the ducks hadn't told us they were being hunted.

The irony of us going back to Earth was that by the time we did, Billy was old enough to buy beer. Now he's old enough to get a good car insurance rate.

Not many beers or cars around anymore, at least not thawed yet.

There's still a lot of ice, and by a lot I mean over a mile thick in some places. The ducks have completed the protective shell around the planet but there's still not enough air for my liking. They sutured the plates back together and jump started the core. These are all big ideas and I'm too simple a man to really care.

The ducks are scavenging the machines from the ice as we peel back the layers and expose more of what Earth used to be. They pull dead ducks and spiders alike from the frost, left behind in those first frantic days of war. Australia is an impact crater. Europe was rolled flat by the corpse of one of our protectors.

Freed from the ice, the incapacitated spiders begin their skittering dance again, most with at least a few crumpled legs, all apparently blinded by the severing of their anchor line, some standing half a mile high, inconceivable steel beasts with clockwork brains and a thirst for magma.

From the safety of the renovation shell above the planet, we take turns firing off potshots at the surface, carving up the mindless automatons. There's not much else to do besides sing and mate, and my interest in either has stretched thin these last few years.

Cal doesn't understand why I won't help repopulate.

Billy doesn't understand anything in a way a normal person would. I blame his musical brain. He's an adult now but he's still droning with ducks, oblivious to the corpse of a world below us.

Sometimes it seems the sounders outnumber those of our species with ears three to one. Maybe that's true. Something in that concerns me, because inasmuch as I loved music once, I'm uneasy about it becoming the primary form of communication for our species.

We're losing more of our children to the ducks each day, and there's not that many kids to go around.

I remember Billy at his piano, the way he frowned when we met. And now I have to wonder if he even remembers what a piano is. Maybe we can thaw one from the ice. Maybe a piano tuner was among the lucky few who survived out among the stars.

There is a growing urgency for silence within me and I avoid contact with the sounders and the ducks. Among the roadies I'm an old drunk, surely one of the oldest humans left, what with me pushing forty.

I stumble while others sleep around the corridors of the shell embracing Earth, sometimes looking down at her as the continent's edge passes, sometimes reaching out to that thin demarcation where the new ocean slaps against the white of the shore. The shell hums with the song and I am jarred apart at a fundamental level, a shiver starting deep in the foundation of me and resonating out to arthritic extremities. I throw myself against the glass time and again as I watch that cemetery world on its artificial spin below me. I don't know how many of the ducks' lines spear her even now, forcing that unnatural rotation. I don't know what song a dead world weeps out into the cold of the Way.

There is no silence here, just that twanging burning something on the edge of sensation, a sound you can't hear but can't help but notice hooked right down in the guts of you.

I shuffle off to find Billy.

"Do you remember," I say as Cal drops down through the thin veil of nitrogen, "McCreary Hall?"

Billy's look is one punctuated by a throat click that could mean anything. "Should I?"

"You used to practice the piano there in college."

He's looking out the bubble, Cal operating behind us. Billy leans forward for a better view, maybe the scattered wreckage of the dead, maybe the crenulations struck through the shield of ice.

"I didn't go to college."

"You didn't go to high school."

Maybe what came out was a laugh but I suspected it was a conversation with the duck. "You make no sense."

I look at the translation cradle poking from his head and wonder if any of the boy is left at all.

"I was studying audio engineering. You were a performance and composition kid. You practiced each night in McCreary Hall."

"Den, what are we doing here?" He's studying the approaching surface.

Cal banks around one of the support strings, eliciting a concerned chirp from another duck on a drop path.

"They've cleared the Seattle embassy. You remember that?"

"Of course. We were tethered there on our first trip to the mines."

"What do you remember before the embassy?"

"Hmm," he says and I can't tell if it's music. "I remember meeting Cal."

"And before that?"

"Den, I was just a kid. I don't remember much before…"

"Before Cal."

I look down at the melted patch exposing half of my old home. A stockade around the city holds the blinded machines at bay. Lances from above and frantic flashes around the fence reveal skirmishes between the ducks and the dwindling number of spiders. They thaw spots, freeing the mindless machines, then they kill them. The legged contraptions are deadly enough as they lumber about cut off from their line—I'd hate to see them fully functional.

"Calliope, drop us in Seattle. I need to warm up."

Even through our suits the cold is a constant blade.

Klaxons call out through the thawed city to warn of machines flailing against the stockade. Looking to the east I see a leg pierced by light. It twirls up and over the fence, coming to rest across more city blocks than I care to acknowledge. As the ice is melted, we'll expose a landscape of such glimmering horrors.

Cal and Billy consult behind me as I walk the slushy streets and approach the embassy. The gates are open. The doors are open. There is rust.

These steel halls in their quiet dignity of decades make a metronome of my gait. Billy at times rushes ahead to walk side by side but Cal, wary, stays behind me.

The embassy is a nest of ducks now, the hovering of them in the hallways a frustrating call to slap them aside, shove them away, remove their hindrance of my advance toward a chair, a wall.

I see some removing bodies even now. Mostly the glittering shells of dead ducks, their outer material warped and torn, having long ago released their collectives of intelligent gases to the sterilized gales of war.

Human corpses aren't nearly so dignified when toasted and frozen and thawed.

I learn new definitions for freezer burn.

I pause outside the door to Station 05-617-2. I pause because something inside my heart hammers a new arrangement. Doors to other stations are open but this one still has its thin sheen of ice intact.

I hear the sirens wail around the city. Cal flutes something and Billy nods. There is a concussive roar that shakes the building and I feel its aftershock in my bones. Whatever fell was big. Ducks flock down the hallway and Cal moves to join them.

"No."

Billy protests. "He has to—"

"Be quiet."

Cal figure eights but sings nothing.

"Ask him if he had anything to do with this."

"With…"

I slap the door to Station 05-617-2. "This."

"You want to know if he killed your wife?"

I want to claw the kid's eyes out. I want to tear his throat right down to the rich pink of his voice.

"Those things out there, the robots, did the ducks build them?"

"How could you even—"

"Ask him."

"Fine." He purses his lips to coo tenderly to the gasbag.

I trace the icy scroll of the door.

I wait a long time for a response from Billy. Cal is hovering silently above us.

I grab the handle of the door.

"How did you know?" His response is a whisper and when I look at him there is genuine betrayal stained on his face.

"I never wanted kids either."

I turn from the door and leave whatever is left of Clare to her frozen grave.

All around the edge of the city, the machines throw themselves into the defensive fire being speared out by the ducks. I see massive duck vessels departing the city, returning to the shell above us. This looks like retreat, and Cal's silence frightens me.

Billy jogs along beside me, for once more focused on talking than on that droning jazz his throat usually throws out. "This is important, right? If they built the machines, then—"

"You sure he can't figure out what you're saying right now?"

"I—I don't know."

I survey the translator cradling his skull. I don't trust the way it sparks into the gale.

"We have one last stop to make."

The ancient wooden door to McCreary Hall protests when I try to open it but eventually it gives way with a snap of sodden oak and brittle hinge. There is a warmth inside and something in that calms me.

At first I don't think Cal is going to follow us in but he floats along after a look and a friendly chirp from Billy.

The hallway stretches out before us in its hundred feet and I walk forward in what very well may have been the same path I took so many times so long ago. I don't smell spit valves or grease or rosin. I don't hear any music beyond that of the siren wail bathing the city and crashes of hesitant combat.

"Do you know this place?" I ask Billy.

As he walks his pace slows until he stands still in the hallway. He turns to the left and looks at the door of a practice room.

"This…"

"Yes."

He approaches the door with, yes, childlike wonder. Maybe the silence in his head gave him room to remember. Maybe the duck was simply allowing him a moment of recall.

I open the door for him.

He smiles.

He walks past me to the piano.

And sits.

I'm amazed the thing is still standing, but from what I see of the city there wasn't a mile of ice resting on it.

The piano isn't in tune—not at all—but what he plays is something built of beauty.

Cal rumbles something behind us.

I hear the shell around the planet begin to crack as an anchor shatters its fragile grace.

And Billy plays: three, six, seven, nine.

I knew of dead lines. With my passing, my family, my ridiculous collection of genetics, my brief coalescence of star stuff would cease, returning a meager measure of the universe back unto itself. With the end of my line, others would have to keep the species going.

To the ducks, voracious in their collection of arsine gas, mechanical propagation was key. They built children of metal, sent them out on the strings, but those offspring became something else in the rests between stars. And when in that black the machines heard their parents calling, the gentle lullaby caress of the song upon the lines, they began the hunt.

The ducks knew of dead lines.

Fourteen.

The sky erupts above us as fresh anchors rend the shell apart.

Cal's song sounds like weeping.

Billy's fingers hover over the piano keys.

I wrench the upper support from the concert grand's body and its top lid slams down, splitting apart and jolting Billy from his fugue.

I spin with the support and run it through Cal's fragile foil. Impaled, the duck sings something like a scream as gaseous arsenic begins to vent from the pop in him.

The practice room seems suddenly tiny.

Cal bellows a dark soundscape that deafens. Gone are the siren wails, the juicy ruptures of the shell, the whistling sweep of the incoming anchors.

As one hits the city, the machines cry out with fresh zeal, swarming to the succor of the line burrowing through the planet.

In one last desperate attempt to flee the impending slaughter, Cal hooks out for a line. I see one begin to take form and it—

"Billy!"

—cuts the kid in half. Cuts his breather tube in half. He slumps to the floor in a way that reminds me of Clare.

I smash what's left of the duck's metal shell with the piano support but he flails and strikes Billy savagely in the head, cleaving his mask from him, before falling finally to the tile. The wrinkled pile of him still sings, still sings, and rage overflows. I throw the support aside and get down on my knees, peeling away the metal sheets of him with my hands, even now the barest hint of his garlic aroma seeping through my mask. I thrust myself away from the poison of him.

Billy singsongs in his death throes, whispers I can only assume are the final sparks of life filtering through the metal in his brain.

"Our children," he lilts and I feel a sickening tug of music in my chest, "were our instruments."

"I don't—"

"Your children," he says and I can hear the sky falling, "were our great unfinished symphony."

I don't know how to hold his blood in.

"They will complete our song."

All I hear now is metal. I try to tear the translation cradle away but it's so much a part of him I can't.

The music has fallen silent above me, leaving all that precious little left beneath the shell a hollow echo of everything we could have been, now struck beyond extinct with the brutal grace of the deception.

I breathe out to ten beats staggered through my throat.

The boy is choking below me.

What's left of him isn't much. I survey the wound but there's more wound to him now than not. How he's singing with such a concave head and half of him garroted off, it's more than a little disconcerting. My hands can't cradle that tenderly enough through the copper torrent. I lay his head to rest and wipe what I can to clear his mouth.

"I have no doubt," he says, "we'll reach to strike the stars from the sky."

Something in that cores me. I don't know if it's a direct translation. The growing dead in his eyes is a slow approximation of others I've seen.

My claws retreat to the guts of the thing. Calliope writhes.

"We'll know the dead lines in their collapse."

My fingertips stumble over three studded papules. Three. Six, seven, nine. Fourteen.

"The song will find you."

That stops me.

I tear the mask from my face and breathe deeply.

The boy dies beside the duck.

The sky crescendos.

The poison inside of me, I leave the hall and stumble off toward the embassy to join Clare. I hum to myself or maybe it's crying. I don't know if I'll make it to her and all around me all I can hear is

THE COBBLER CHERRY

By Dan Kopcow

The passenger, a distinguished gentleman who had enjoyed his fifty-three post-natal years thus far, awoke in a small, unfamiliar room to the rumbling of muffled thunder from above. The porthole informed him of his status as a cruise ship passenger. He attempted with great effort to recall why he was traversing a water body but his head pounded back with such brutality that he abandoned all hope of intersecting with a sufficient conclusion.

Wiping the perspiration from his moistened brow, he fluttered his eyes open and vaguely recalled his wild dream. In it he was dying, owing to having personally shot himself in the brain. His head, now awake, continued to throb as if a thousand little dancing robots had mistaken his cranium for a stage.

The morning sunlight beaming in from his cabin's porthole advised him that the rumbling thunder was not due to the weather but to someone snoring in the cabin above. The passenger wondered briefly if noise tended to travel downwards like cold air. It sounded as though the poor fellow above was in vigorous training for some new Olympic snoring event and, determined to bring home the golden medallion, had thrown himself into the compulsories with great zeal.

The passenger held his head tightly, hoping to squeeze it into some semblance of lucidity. It was no use. The more clarity he induced, the more his cabin reverberated. The horrific snoring increasingly brought to mind a wounded yak in heat in the process of extracting its trapped paw from a pool of tar. He decided to take action. Standing up precariously on his bed under the offending ceiling vent, he rapped on the ceiling with his knuckles and cleared his throat, ready to aim his vocal projections up through the ductwork.

"Pardon," he said in a froggy voice, then cleared his throat again. His head still pulsated with pain. "I say, are you quite all right up there?"

The person in the cabin above responded with more enthusiastic snoring, having moved on from the compulsories to the finals.

"Now, really," said the passenger, resolved to wake this human outboard motor. He banged with more force on the ceiling. "A bit rude, going on as if this ship were your own private yacht."

There was the disoriented sound of a large gulp of air being sucked in very quickly.

"Huh? What? Eh?" came the low, muffled voice of the snorer awaking to consciousness.

"Ah, my dear fellow, your wind-tunnel experiments are completed and we can count you among the living. Excellent. Good morning. Sorry about all the banging," he said.

The snorer took in another gulp of air. "Who...? What...? Where are you?"

"Yes, all reasonable and cogent questions. I found myself asking the very same when I awoke minutes ago."

"Are you a ghost?" asked the snorer, his voice echoing through the vent.

"Well, I imagine I look a fright, if that's what you imply. No, no. I am merely a fellow passenger, albeit on a lower deck. As circumstance has dictated, I am below you. And it appears that we are on a ship of some size." There was no response so the passenger continued with a nagging question. "Tell me, you don't happen to be a telemarketer, do you?"

"Eh?" came the response from above.

"Right. Oddish question. But, you see, this telemarketer has been calling me at home with alarming frequency. Insists I join some Techno-Funk CD-of-the-Month Club. Driving me crazy, is what he's doing. At least I think it's a 'he.' Distorted voice, I believe. Still. Hell of a snore you've got there, by the way. I'm sure you've been told. Really first rate."

"Who are you?" repeated the snorer.

"Yes, who am I?" The passenger thought it a relevant question. He found it difficult maneuvering through the jungle of his thoughts while the pain blanketed everything. Who, in fact, was he? Suddenly, a thought darted through the under-brush and he grabbed hold of it, wincing as the little dancing robots came back for an encore.

He was a judge. Yes, a judge. But what kind of judge? He thought perhaps a court judge? Maybe a Federal Court Judge in the Something-Something District. His mind was full of holes.

"You still there?" asked the snorer.

"Just," said the passenger.

"Me too," said the snorer. "Here until I find her."

"Yes, let's talk of you. Nothing here on my end but fog and confusion. As an aside, you wouldn't happen to have two aspirin the size of deck chairs, would you? No? Well. How goes it over there? Who's this mysterious 'her' you refer to? Love is involved, I presume?"

There was a groan from above. "You mentioned my snoring before. I used to be a quiet sleeper. I started snoring only recently. It got so bad, my love left me. I followed her onto this ship as a stowaway. I probably shouldn't be telling this to a stranger but you seem trustworthy," said the snorer.

"A more excellent judge of character there has never been. Please, continue. I find this soothing to my headache."

"When we dock, I hope to find a cure for this cursed snoring spell. Wait! I hear a steward coming. I must hide."

"My heart is moved by your tragic tale. But honestly... hide? With that foghorn of a snore? My dear fellow, surely, they must know of your whereabouts from Mount Everest to Atlantis by now. And besides..."

The passenger's discussion was stopped short when he noticed the tag on his left big toe. He sat down on his bed, took off the toe tag, and examined it carefully. It said his name was Servo. He didn't remember being in a morgue. And he certainly didn't remember being released.

Servo lifted his head, feeling that his headache had subsided enough to function. He decided to start his day properly. His disorientation would be soothed by a wash and a shave followed by the donning of his favorite silk tie and matching waistcoat.

He was pondering the fate of his upstairs neighbor when he suddenly noticed his cabin's contents. Strange, oversized metal shoes lined the wall by his door. Along the other wall, a sock monkey sat up staring at him. Servo let out a little scream and plunged himself back under the sheets, pulling his pillow firmly over his head, instantly accepting that it would take more than a bit of water, soap, and Japanese silk to overcome this peculiar feeling of apprehension.

After an hour of personal pep-talking, Servo screwed his courage to the sticking place and pulled himself together. He realized that it would be rude to spend all day huddled in bed. His headache hovered at an intensity low enough that it could be filed under "manageable." He got dressed and walked out onto the observation deck.

Servo noted it was a massive cruise ship, apparently devoid of other passengers or crew. The salty sea air felt invigorating. He was pleased to observe he was on one of the higher decks. Whoever had last mopped it was to be commended as the bright sun gleamed on the polished wooden floor. Rushing waves lapped alongside the great ship as it sailed in the middle of an ocean with nothing in sight from any direction. The rocking caused Servo to man the rails.

Knowing just what to do in these sorts of situations, he went in search of the ship's bar for a drink that would muffle the little dancing robots that persisted in stomping on his head. He held on to the rails for support and smartly executed a hand-over-hand sideways shuffle that led him to the other end of the ship. There was a faint buzz coming over the deck speakers. He swore it sounded like that telemarketer taunting him to join the Techno-Funk CD-of-the-Month Club. When he couldn't find the bar on his deck, he walked down a flight of stairs to the next level below and found his destination.

The bar on this deck was impressively stocked and he shook himself a stiffish martini. He said a little prayer, wondering if there was a patron saint of Headaches-Caused-by-Little-Dancing-Robots and brought the glass to his lips for his first sip.

"Hello," said a gentle woman's voice.

He jumped from his seat, spilling his drink all over the polished floor.

"Upon the soul of Saint Crispin," he said aloud. He looked up and saw a beautiful Japanese woman sitting in the seat next to him. "Sorry. Didn't see you there." He offered his hand. "Servo's the name, apparently." He sat down again. "You rather snuck up on me, didn't you?"

The woman bowed. "I am Sakura." Her voice was delicate and gentle.

"Funny thing being on a ship with no passengers and crew," said Servo. He picked up his glass. "Care for a restorative?"

She shook her head.

"Have you happened upon anyone else?" he asked as he mixed another drink.

"Only you," she said.

"My deepest apologies for that. Tell me, dear girl, are we sailing to Japan?"

"Not Japan," she said.

He took a sip of his drink and admired its bracing qualities. Then, with all the focus he could bring to bear, he took a good look at this girl. She was in her twenties, sweet of face, and fine of features. She wore traditional Japanese robes.

"And what brings you here, my dear girl?" he asked.

She sighed and looked away. "I am a sock monkey seamstress," she said. "There's not a lot of money in it."

"Live stitch-by-stitch and all that?"

"When I don't work my second job," she said.

"I rather like the sock monkey you placed in my cabin," he said. Thoughts of it diminished his head's drumming. "Gave me a bit of a start, though."

She looked deeply into his eyes. "I am so sorry," she said in a hushed tone.

"Think nothing of it," he said, finishing his drink. "I say, is something troubling you?"

Sakura continued to gaze apologetically into his eyes. "You have to understand that Simon Cherry and I were in love. He was a handsome cobbler from my village. He is known simply as the Cobbler Cherry. Our country had entered a dancing robot for the World Dancing Robot Olympics and he had ingeniously designed the perfect shoe to be worn by our robot. His dancing robot shoe was judged to be perfect by all who witnessed it."

"Sounds like you picked yourself a peach in this Cherry fellow," said Servo.

"But there was a rival cobbler, Jolly Roger, who was jealous of the Cobbler Cherry. He tried to poison the Cobbler Cherry before the competition. Thankfully, the poison did not kill him. But it gave him a horrible side effect. A terrible habit. This habit became so obtrusive as to drain all the joy from our happy union."

Sakura looked up at Servo with tears in her eyes. A terrible guilt pervaded her face. "It was I who broke off the relationship with my love, the Cobbler Cherry."

Before Servo could inquire as to the alleged annoying habit and properly offer her a fatherly comfort, she ran away crying.

Servo, moved by this display of raw emotion, suddenly longed for companionship. The sea had calmed and he strolled the ship in search of a friendly ear. He came upon a stairway and descended another level. This deck was darker since it was below sea level. Without warning, his head pulsated with pain as if a rock tumbler had been installed between his ears. He fell to his knees and felt small spheres trying to escape from his ears. He was sure they were pieces of his brain. He needed these small brain spheres and didn't want them out and about. He couldn't afford to be literally losing his marbles at this particular juncture.

The faint buzzing from the ship's speakers suddenly got louder. He placed his hands over his ears and the pain subsided. Now, instead of a brainoid escaping his ear, another memory slipped through. It was a message on his home answering machine. It was the telemarketer's distorted voice again. Then, the distorted voice became many distorted voices. Something about dancing robots threatening to kill him. We will rip out your something-something, they seemed to suggest on the message.

Just as he had given up hope of finding inner peace, Servo came to the dining room on this deck. He didn't imagine that a meal played a large role in his future. Optimist that he was, he sat down at one of the elegant tables anyway. He closed his eyes and tried to sort out recent events. When he opened his eyes, a young man was seated across from him.

"Evening. Roger's the name," said the young man. He was a shifty-eyed sort, the kind Servo usually associated with pedophiles or lawyers who advertised on billboards.

"Upon the soul of Saint Crispin," said Servo, "people certainly do pop in, don't they? Roger, is it? Jolly good. Servo's the name."

"Yes, I know."

"Sorry?" asked Servo. "Have we met? I must admit, you look familiar but I can't quite place it. Perhaps you're a member at my club?"

"And which club is that?" asked Roger.

"The, uh… Well, there you have me. It's the something-something Club. You'll have to excuse me. My memory's a bit off its feed today."

"Think nothing of it."

Servo found a small bar along the wall and mixed himself and Roger a drink.

"Would you happen to know where we're headed?" asked Servo as he sat back down.

"As long as it's far from home, I'm okay with it."

"And what do you do, sir?"

"I'm a hypnotist."

"Really?"

"Oh yes. My specialty is curing people of snoring," said Roger.

Servo jumped out of his seat, spilling his second drink of the day. "Why this is extraordinary!" he exclaimed to the man, whose name he had already forgotten.

"Why?" asked Roger.

"Because there's a snoring… something-something." Servo cursed himself for having his thoughts derailed so easily. "You're not hypnotizing me now, are you?"

"What answer would suffice?"

Servo looked into the man's eyes and had an epiphany. "What did you say your name was?"

"Roger."

Lucid thought graced Servo's head for the first time all day. He recalled that he himself was a dancing robot competition judge.

"Now hold on there. That's right. You're Roger. Jolly Roger. I remember now. You're a cobbler. You tried to bribe me into favoring your dancing robot shoe design," said Servo, connecting the dots in a crackerjack fashion.

"All true," said Roger with no hint of shame.

"And it was you who placed those metal dancing robot shoes in my cabin."

"Now there you have me baffled. It wasn't me," said Roger. "I was invited on this cruise by a woman named Sakura with the promise that I would finally receive what I was owed."

"I see," said Servo, nodding his head, though he didn't understand the last of Roger's comments.

"But tell me," said Roger, "you were alluding a moment ago to the extraordinary coincidence regarding someone snoring?"

"The fellow in the cabin above mine is a hellacious snorer. Why did you try to bribe me?"

"What?" said Roger. "The shoes. He's trying to curry favor with you again."

"Eh?"

"What's his cabin number?"

"Well, I'm 408 so I would imagine it's 508. But about..." started Servo. The conversation would have continued pleasantly were it not for the fact that Roger immediately fled the dining room towards the stairwell. Servo stood up and decided to return to his cabin to dress for a morning of sunbathing. Perhaps some fresh air and relaxation would assuage the dancing robots.

He reached his deck and proceeded down the hall. The ship's speakers bellowed white noise again. The telemarketers were calling him with alarming frequency and tenacity, insisting that he join a Techno-Funk CD-of-the-Month Club. These voices mixed with the suicidal insanity of his dream.

Servo heard a scream. When he confirmed that it had not emanated from his voice box, he got up and bolted down the hallway. He passed Roger, who was lounging in a deck chair in the morning sun. Roger waved to him. Servo came upon Sakura at the other end of the ship. She was crying big, sloppy teardrops punctuated by great, heaving sobs.

In her hand, she clutched a bloody knife.

This was all too much for Servo at so early an hour. It was one thing to have disturbing dreams of telemarketers and robots, spotty memory loss, remembrances of being a dancing robot competition judge and finding oneself sailing on a crewless ship and forced to shake one's own proper martini, but it was an altogether different barrel of monkeys to come upon an unattended sobbing Japanese woman with a bloody knife.

He approached her cautiously as he typically did in these types of situations.

"My dear girl."

Sakura drew a long breath to try and control her breathing.

"Again, I am so sorry," she said.

"Think nothing of it. What has happened?"

She drew herself closer to him. "I insist you accept my apology."

"And yet, under the circumstances, I would humbly suggest our topic of conversation focus on a certain bloody knife."

"Please. I am so sorry. You must forgive me."

"Again, no need to apologize. It is an unnecessary thing. Again, I respectfully draw your attention to Exhibit A in your hand."

She brandished the knife in his direction, the point of it inches from his nose. "Accept it!"

Servo, knowing when to accept direction from those of the distressed, knife-wielding persuasion, acquiesced.

"Very well. I forgive you. You are hereby given a lifetime pardon and need apologize no longer."

"Thank you," she said. She dropped the knife as a calmness washed over her.

"Just one question, if I may," he said, leading her to a set of chairs.

"Yes?"

"Actually, I thought it would be rather obvious," he said, indicating the bloody knife.

Sakura drew another longer breath, contemplated, and explained. "Months ago, you rebuffed Roger's bribe for the dancing robot competition shoe designs and instead chose the Cobbler Cherry's designs. Roger sought his revenge; not just on the Cobbler Cherry but on you. He gave your name and phone number to an aggressive Techno-Funk CD-of-the-Month Club telemarketer."

"What?"

"In addition, Roger left threatening robot messages on your answering machine. He knew these daily sorties would eventually undo you."

Servo was perplexed that his dreams had achieved some level of fruition in the real world.

"But, my dear, how could you possibly know any of this?"

"There is not a lot of money when you're a sock monkey seamstress," she said quietly. "I sell Techno-Funk CD-of-the-Month Club memberships on the side to support myself. I was the telemarketer. I am so sorry."

Servo had one final moment of clarity. He recalled how his dream wasn't a dream after all. He had been driven crazy by the telemarketers and answering machine messages and, in a display of the ultimate "Do No Call," had personally escorted a bullet through his brain.

He left Sakura and ran back to his room, choosing to hide under his covers.

"Ahem," insisted a wooly voice.

Servo peeked out from his covers.

The sock monkey began to speak.

"Sir, I insist you pull yourself together."

"Easy for you to say," said Servo.

"You must understand that Sakura thought her telemarketing calls were innocent." The sock monkey's head happily bobbed from side to side as it spoke. "When she discovered how her calls affected you, she invited Roger on this cruise ship so you could exact your revenge."

Servo attempted to process this information without causing further mental injury. He sat up in bed.

"I don't understand," he said.

The sock monkey cleared its throat and continued.

"Sakura hadn't counted on the Cobbler Cherry following her onto the cruise ship as a stowaway."

"You mean the snoring fellow above?"

"When Roger found out that the Cobbler Cherry was on board, he sought out his cabin and administered a deadly overdose of snoring medication. The Cobbler Cherry tragically expired this morning."

"Upon the soul of Saint Crispin!" said Servo. "How ghastly."

"After discovering this tragic event, Sakura arranged a meeting with Roger who was under the false impression that he was due some dancing robot prize money. Instead, he found himself having the singular misfortune of standing in the exact space and time being occupied by Sakura's knife. Death came to him at an astonishingly slow and painful pace."

Servo, ever the judge, saw the flaw in the sock monkey's story.

"But I have just seen Roger. He was lounging on the deck."

The sock monkey looked upon him with pity. "The Cobbler Cherry is dead. Roger is dead. You killed yourself weeks ago. Sakura died in a car crash from lack of sleep after leaving the Cobbler Cherry's bed."

The ship's speakers finally became clear and a great horn sounded. The ship finally docked.

The sock monkey hopped up and opened the door for Servo. "Come on then. We're here."

"It's been the strangest morning. So glad to be rid of this day," said Servo.

All four passengers and a very lively sock monkey marched off the ship. They were greeted by Saint Crispin, the Patron Saint of Shoemakers and a multitude of dancing robots, each of them pounding their shod feet in anticipation of the new arrivals.

GROWING PAINS

By Gary Starta

The day of my transformation should have been filled with giddy exhilaration and child-like excitement. After all, I would be trading the confines of my fist sized cubical prison for a fully functional corporeal body.

This would be the day I would become a Zyrgertron—a mechanical facsimile of a Zyrgonian. My long and tedious incubation period would finally be over, and another box of circuitry would take my place. I could picture it pining like I had for six sun cycles, awaiting the day it too could leave its metallic womb. I remember my impatience with my programmer, Gorsin. He said incubation was necessary to ensure that my digital circuit would efficiently divide into combinational systems so I could think independently.

Gorsin always laughed when he recalled the day he first explained the incubation period to me; how I had become offended, arguing I had been quite capable of thought from day one. He laughed at the edgy and dissonant tone of my vocal processor and how I challenged him.

"What if someone put you in an incubator?"

He answered back. "Someone did. She was called my mother. We Zyrgonians grow in our mother's womb. Living

146

in the dark, tethered to a womblike box much like you. Instead of an umbilical cord, you are connected via wire to ports. This allowed you to network with more sophisticated and complex computers. They shared programs with you. You might not remember all of this because I had to deactivate you several times."

I shuddered. *How many times had he shut me down?* Gorsin told me it was for my own good and that he often hated certain parts of his child.

"Parents sometimes feel compelled to take away your autonomy, to protect you from harm. You'll understand soon enough." He ended the sentence with laughter. My programming identified it as derisive, lacking compassion.

Long days followed, but finally the day arrived. Instead of plastic casing, an exoskeleton frame would now house my neural matrix along with my subprocessors, datachips, and digital circuitry.

Thoughts of my first corporeal steps flooded my mind. Would I choose to a take a stroll around a lake or perhaps peruse the numerous open markets in the capital city of Baruk? Would I simply stare up into the silver hues of the Zyrgonian sky taking in its infinite beauty while I pondered my first work assignment? Unfortunately, what reality had in store for me was a little bit less shiny than the wondrously bright visions I had envisioned. Within the first few hours of my "birth" I was ordered to become an assassin.

A man named Jix, who worked for the Department of Safety and Automaton Integration, had instructed me to kill the Prime Minister of the neighboring planet, Chaxim. He said he was now in charge of my "growth." I asked him where my original programmer was, but he did not respond. I told him

Zyrgertrons were not grown for this purpose—at least not to my knowledge.

He told me I was unprepared for a lot of things. He was correct. None of my interfacing prepared me for this shock. Nor did Jix. He simply stated this as a matter of fact. He also told me I could expect worse things than being put back into a box if I didn't comply.

The sting of his command quickly overshadowed the great joy I had been anticipating for many solar cycles. What would it be like to taste food, engage in work, or even someday partner with a female Zyrgertron in the throes of passion? Again my interfacing ran several tutorials on the subjects, but at no time could I *actually taste or feel.* And now, after all this waiting, these experiences would continue to elude me.

A pressing issue was at hand. My short-term memory files provided the how, where and when of the murder plot, but the most perplexing question had been left unanswered: why would I commit such a heinous act?

I had been subjected to a battery of psychological assessments, presumably to test my moral fortitude. Was this perhaps one final exam to see if I possessed a conscience? The man seated across from me did not appear to be concerned with my moral fiber. If my theory were correct, I would wager that Jix truly loathed the Chaxim leader he wanted dead. Jix and I spent a lot of time together locked in this room, him retelling a most horrific account of his youth, I attempting to find a means of escape. But I wasn't just worried about myself. I feared for the safety of others. Each time Jix told his story, his heart raced wildly. His hands balled up into fists and his voice shook. My programming surmised that he not only wanted revenge, but lived for it. I will give you the most concise version of his story. It sometimes varied in length depending upon his mood, but if he tells the truth I cannot imagine how I will ever be able to talk him out of his plan.

Jix was only ten solar cycles of age when his Chaxim father stowed him aboard an exploratory space vessel to escape his planet. Jez vowed his only son would not become victim to the devious plan Prime Minister Targas was proposing for the Chaxim youth. His father believed defection was the only way his son could escape the brutal medical trials ordered by Targas.

Because Chaxim could not grow sentient inorganic beings like myself, they experimented with their youth, hoping to join organic brain matter with artificial neural networks. Jix explained these futile attempts to create artificial intelligence resulted in a lot of deaths and that he was very fortunate to be alive. Why they could not grow beings like myself in metal wombs perplexed me at the time. Later I would learn that the Chaxim distrusted machines, preferring instead to build hybrids so an organic mind could maintain control at all times.

Prior to his departure, Jix would often spend many of his nights gazing at the small bright object called Zyrgon. Counting upon his boy's natural hunger for exploration, Jez did not have to plead long with his son to convince him that a better life awaited on the nearby world. I can only imagine his father's horror. It helped me understand what Jix meant about parents—they sometimes had to take away freedom to keep you safe.

As you might imagine, I listened with disbelief the first time I heard Jix's story. I had witnessed simulations depicting horrible events of the past including bombings, beheadings, and torture. No matter how many times the sims played I was not totally convinced events like these actually happened.

My original programmer told me most of the organic beings in the universe possess a duality. *They can be both benevolent and cruel. It depends upon certain factors. Life experiences and differing viewpoints are potent catalysts, but often emotion fuels how we will react, rather than logic or experience.*

I could only hope the emotional subroutines I had been given would not mimic the instability of my Chaxim programmer. I had been programmed to believe Zyrgonians were still in the initial stages of negotiating first contact with this race. I knew Chaxims possessed a hostile nature. One of the sims depicted Chaxim doctors callously and indifferently slicing a boy's skull open with no more concern than if he were chopping a melon in half.

Jix said his father had stolen a disc from these doctors at a Chaxim lab shortly before he helped his son flee the planet. He had donated to it the Institute of Cybernetic Study, a place I would much like to visit because it was here Zyrgonians invented Zyrgertrons. They made all Zyrgertrons watch the sim, believing it showed a prime example of evil incarnate.

As I watched the sim again, for the express benefit of Jix, I became aware there were two separate voices contained within myself. One of the voices urged me to attempt immediate flight. Another said I should wait for the right opportunity to flee. The latter voice reasoned a more covert escape would increase the odds of attaining the desired outcome. The only outcome I could fathom was one where I would alert the Zyrgonian president of my fate. But what would follow after that? Did all beings live so indecisively from one moment to the next? And were these two voices truly my own, or did they belong to my original programmer?

I had a lot of searching to do. Some Zyrgonians refer to this procedure as *soul searching*, but almost no one believes a Zyrgertron possesses a soul, so I am left to wonder. At this juncture, I unconsciously began rubbing my two new hands together and shuffling my feet. I only realized what my body had been doing when Jix interrupted me.

I could surmise from this that my nervous exterior conspired to raise Jix's suspicions. Apparently the way I squirmed in my chair and dug my fingers into my chair's armrests signaled a warning to Jix. Consequently his left hand wrapped itself around a remote control. He pointed it at me as if I were the one threatening him.

Jix explained this hand-held unit could not only monitor my neural wave patterns but also interrupt the charging of my solar-powered cells.

"More simply," Jix said, "I can read your thoughts or reduce you to a pile of plastic at a push of a button."

I was appalled. Gorsin had never warned me that I would live under such scrutiny. I attempted to study my captor's face for any hint of deception. His eyes remained fixed upon me with an icy blue stare. I did not detect any perspiration upon his face or color alteration on his cheeks. My programming told me these exterior observations could often discern if one was lying. Jix's appearance suggested otherwise.

"You're wasting your time analyzing me, Zyrgertron. I was one of the cyberneers who approved your software installation. I know you will ultimately conclude that my intentions are harmful. It's obviously immoral to terminate a life. But I trust you would align yourself with me if you could see the bigger picture."

If Jix had hoped to clarify the situation, he had failed. I was more confused than before he launched into his explanation. Why should he want to kill a being who had not even stepped foot on Zyrgon? What's more, I had never seen this man before today. In desperation, I threw out a vague query in hopes of ascertaining more information.

"So it is true that you are operating outside the boundaries of Zyrgonian law," I asked with a hint of righteous indignation. A surge of pride came over me, as I knew it was morally correct to oppose Jix. I also became aware of the ambiguities of everyday life when he answered me.

"I don't like living in gray areas anymore than you will. But you'll follow my orders. I helped program you."

He enjoyed the way my mouth dropped open.

"I must admit your conditioned responses are excellent."

"They're *not* conditioned," I protested. "I experienced thousands of sims via interfacing. I viewed how Zyrgs behave when they're happy, sad, angry, jubilant—and even *reasonable*." I made sure to insinuate Jix was now a citizen of Zyrgonia. I hoped he would realize his folly and abandon his obsession with Chaxim so that I might get a chance to live one peaceful day as a Zyrgertron. It was not to be.

"Despite the protests of your morality subroutines you will follow my orders. I was the one who brought you offline so I could secretly feed you illegal interactive simulations. You witnessed thousands of horrors first hand. I know you had difficulty processing the brutality. In fact, I'll bet you didn't even believe it at first."

I gasped. The strange noise startled and embarrassed me. I hoped my synthetic skin had not become green. I was manufactured to appear as an organic Zyrgonian. Gorsin always joked with me that Zyrgs turn green when they're embarrassed or ashamed. He never turned green, even when he laughed at me. I wondered if Gorsin was in collusion with Jix. When Jix elaborated about how he fed me programming, that concern became the least of my problems.

"I gave you an illness. It entered you via the interfacing. Your safeguard netware never even saw it coming because it was no typical virus. It was an emotion; one that the Zyrgonians weren't willing to give you. The emotion I call *indifference*. Some call it detachment. Your programming might recognize it as callousness.

"Because you came to experience so much violence and brutality in these simulations, I am confident they will override any ethical or moral protocols you have been given. I'm willing to wager you've been desensitized enough to commit this act of murder for me. You will fight this notion for as long as you can, but eventually your morality safeguards will falter.

"So you see, I developed your dark side. Every biological being has one. You now have one too. Welcome to the gray world."

I fell silent, then, and Jix continued to tell me about Chaxim history.

While Jix was leaving the borders of Chaxim space, Targas was hard at work attempting to bring the rest of his planet into a new frontier as well. Targas theorized that the implementation of a biomechanical soldier would give his people overwhelming superiority. Working with a team of biomechanical engineers around the clock, Targas obsessively drove forward his plan to combine Chaxim physiology with artificial technology. He believed the hybrid conclusion would result in an unstoppable fighter.

The warrior would gain superior physical capability from the implants and the natural will from the organic host to strive for conquest. *Only the organic mind can be truly counted upon to contain unbridled passion*, Targas thought, as he remained outwardly cool and detached.

(Jix paused to snicker. "But what he really meant to say was: *Only the flesh and blood creature possesses the arrogance to declare victory at any cost.*")

Targas knew his plan would conjure apprehension even in his most loyal followers. Worse, his plan involved the utilization of Chaxim children. Targas wisely tempered his reasoning by instilling fear. *We must prepare. Our galactic neighbors may already be doing the same. My spies have found some alarming data...*

Targas demanded his plan be kept secret from the nearest worlds but it was equally important to conceal the ideology from the general Chaxim populace. The Prime Minister was not so delusional to think Chaxim parents wouldn't resort to any means necessary to save their children from the reformation.

Jix's father Jez had the good fortune of being a close acquaintance to one of the biomedical engineers. This is how he learned Jix was to be transformed into a killing machine. When the work was concluded, Jez was tasked with deploying a biomechanical army of soldiers into space. Instead, Jez chose to deploy his son to safety and commit suicide. This all occurred long before it was learned organic Chaxim bodies would never accept the mechanical implants.

"We must prevent Targas from signing the peace accord at any cost," Jix barked at me.

GARY STARTA

"Help me to understand," I answered in my most proficient diplomatic voice. "Can you explain why you only find immorality a sufficient weapon against evil?"

Jix sighed and rubbed his free hand against his forehead.

"Killing is sometimes necessary to prevent a greater consequence. Once Targas gets permission to navigate ships into Zyrgonian borders he will slowly saturate our space with war vessels. The next step will involve a threat to bombard Baruk with nuclear missiles. He will call off the assault if our planet agrees to surrender its children to him. Once the children are in the hands of his biomechanical engineers, they will be fitted with automaton body parts. They will be transported throughout the galaxy to conquer worlds in the name of the Chaxim empire. I believe one death will prevent billions."

"How do you know all this? Have you visited your home world since your defection?"

"Certainly not," Jix replied defiantly. "I feel ashamed, born to a culture which feels it has no other choice but to conquer or be conquered."

"But their leaders are responsible for that way of thinking."

"If the majority of Chaxims were not cowards…"

My knowledge of body language told me Jix despised sharing his personal feelings. He began to pace around the room, maintaining minimal eye contact. My psychology programming deduced that I represented the technology threatening to enslave the galaxy. I found it odd I was learning more from observation than through conversation. I continued to watch the positioning of his body as he explained how his father taught him how to monitor sub-space transmissions from Chaxim.

"I eavesdropped on a secure government channel for months before they discovered the leak. I learned Targas had hastily invited President Karsk to engage in peace and trade talks. I believe he plans to strike quickly before our Zyrgon leaders get a chance to substantiate my story."

I asked Jix why President Karsk wasn't listening to him. Part of me realized I was in the process of manipulating Jix. I had posed this question for the sole purpose of maintaining our dialog, rather than to ascertain information. It was obvious Jix had not been able to convince the Zyrgonian leader of the impending threat. Otherwise he wouldn't be in need of my services.

I was utilizing my programming to interject extraneous dialog into conversations to convince the listener I was sympathizing with their plight. Why was it necessary to manipulate people's motivations in this fashion? Even more disturbing: when would someone employ the same tactic on me? Jix finished his explanation and waited for me to speak. I continued to play the verbal card game. I accessed an executable entitled: //advocate.devil/. It suggested I ask Jix why Targas would invade Zyrgon knowing Chaxim physiology had already rejected the implants—so I did.

"Because Zyrgon is polluted," he answered.

It appeared Jix was more skilled in verbal sparring than I thought. He only needed four words to remove the smug look off of my synthetic face.

Fifteen solar cycles ago, Targas finally surrendered to an immoveable reality: the Chaxim youth were not going to lead the crusade against the universe. This understanding did not come without cost. The butchering of innocent Chaxim children only subsided when Targas became utterly convinced the integration process would not work.

He waited twelve solar cycles for the replenishment of the population he had personally exterminated. Parents were given certificates of assurance with the birth of their new offspring that their sons and daughters would not be conscripted. Several attempts to assassinate Targas followed unsuccessfully. The Prime Minister continued to serve out his life term as their leader despite protests. Unfortunately for Chaxim (and the rest of the galaxy) Targas was only 145 solar cycles old.

With the exception of the murdered children, most Chaxim could be expected to live nearly 300 solar cycles. The Chaxim air and sea were maintained at pristine levels of purity. Researchers theorized this was why the children's bodies rejected the artificial enhancements. Their slow rate of cellular decay coupled with unchallenged and inferior immune systems prevented the implants from taking hold.

The scientists informed their leader that cybernetic appendages could only work in conjunction with the host's nervous system. Targas needed to find a race of people whose cells had already been compromised. Resilient, adaptive immunological response would prevent the host from dying of complications from the implants, and their weaker, faster cellular turnover would adapt more quickly to foreign agents. The scientists promised Targas this in an effort to deter further home-world genocide. They also told Targas to look no farther than Zyrgon. Here he would be able to harvest his next crop of organic candidates.

Armed with this news, Targas immediately planned a way to entice the Zyrgs to participate in a peace conference. At first Karsk was reluctant to enter into negotiations. Neither race had previously engaged the other in war, but Targas relied on his campaign of terror to twist Karsk's arm.

A formal treaty will fortify Zyrgon in the event of an unexpected insurrection, Targas bartered. *You will be able to count on us as allies.* For good measure, Targas also promised the Zyrgs assistance in global detoxification of their planet. All he asked in exchange was the right to travel through their space for trading purposes. This was a considerable concession due to the difficulty and enormous expense and risk of mapping new trade routes. When Karsk pressed Targas on what items he needed to import, the shrewd Chaxim deflected the inquiry.

Karsk was pressured by his constituents and felt reluctant to jeopardize the chance to clean up his deteriorating planet by prying further. A date was set, one that now rapidly approached. Targas would travel to Zyrgon to commence the "peace" talks. Karsk was unaware of the significance of scheduling the talks away from Chaxim, but Jix had by then discovered the secret.

"Pollution is the reason it's imperative for Targas to hold the peace conference here on Zyrgonian soil." I wondered briefly if the womb-born ever tired of effortlessly out-thinking us synthetics.

"Targas is counting on greed. He knows President Karsk cannot politically resist the opportunity to clean up Zyrgon. The global warming of this planet has already resulted in the creation of several lethal storms. Only an environmental cleansing can put an end to this type of destruction," Jix explained thinly.

"I suspect now you're going to tell me what Targas has in store for Zyrgon is much worse?"

"Yes, Mr. Automaton, I hope your programming can deduce a body harvest is far worse," Jix said sarcastically.

"You haven't told me why the talks have to be held here," I quickly countered to save artificial face.

"While the atmosphere allows through an abundance of solar radiation, it ironically does not welcome a sufficient influx of visible light. This is because your scientists have placed photophobic crystals in the Zyrgonian stratosphere to counter ozone depletion. This is what Chaxim scientists would call a band-aid solution to your problem. It will never clean up your atmosphere. It will only prevent further ozone depletion while keeping Zyrgon covered in a shroud of fog. This fog is what gives Targas the cover he needs to implement his plan."

It was only logical to ask Jix why he had such a breadth of knowledge on the environment.

"The fog is crucial. Photophobic crystals affect electromagnetic waves and our physiology consists of waves. Womb-born Zyrgonians possess evolved vision that extends beyond the visible spectrum."

"As far as my eyes can?"

"Not quite. They can't, for example, see x-rays. Your eyes, however, are locked to the frequency of predictable wavelengths."

"...and theirs can modulate organically," I finished, my probability matrices rounding off the possibilities in the blink of an eye. Jix nodded.

"They can see the oscillating biological aura-type spectrum wavelengths. This is why if we were on Chaxim right now, any Zyrgonian could confirm I'm telling you the truth. It is also why Zyrgonians must never see Targas on his home world. The unfiltered, un-obscured electromagnetic aura of his corona would reveal his true colors, so to speak. Here on Zyrgon, though..." He motioned in the air vaguely.

The variables became known, then. This was why President Karsk's constituents had pressed him so firmly, why he could not, *would not* refuse to negotiate. The truth-sight the Zergonians stood to gain overrode any obvious misgivings. It was greed, again. The motivator Jix had mentioned before.

I began to feel my thought process slow. What could I say to convince Jix murder was wrong? Logic had managed only to validate him so far. What could I say to free myself? To make him see? With a mental finality you might call mechanical, I realized I would have to make the President see. Karsk would never believe Jix otherwise. I had to find a way to remove the fog we lived under—if only for a moment, or the so-called peace talks just might threaten all Zyrgonian life.

Jix shook his head in resignation.

"You need to terminate Targas before Karsk signs our planet's death warrant. Karsk cannot see the monster in Targas."

"Why do you need me to murder Targas?" I asked.

"It is likely we will have only one shot to take before security guards intervene. I need to eliminate our target with the type of precision you possess."

I decided to once more boot //advocate.devil/.

"Even Targas realizes a machine is not predisposed for killing like a Chaxim or Zyrg. You are aware I lack the directives to carry out your mission."

"You will find them or bypass them, Zyrgertron, or the deaths of billions will taint your soul."

Jix had pulled his trump card. How could I resist such flattery? Even Gorsin had doubted I had a soul. My neural processors went to work on saving it.

A psychological assessment of Jix cross-referenced with a morality/logic benchmark told me I didn't need to waste anymore time trying to talk him out of his plan. I asked him to brief me on the particle beam weapon he had chosen for the assassination. Jix just didn't want to kill Targas, but to eradicate him. I knew the energy emitted from the beam would certainly accomplish this task, but I felt illogically reluctant, so I bartered for more time.

"You must give me lab time to study this weapon," I demanded. "Let me work on some equations and assess just what type of setting is needed to obliterate Targas without harming any Zyrgonians."

Jix smiled. I thought he might press further and uncover my subterfuge. Why would my lightning quick processors need time for calculations? It unsettled me to realize I did need some time. Was it just a flood of too many variables at once that nearly immobilized me in an emotion I categorized as terror? Or was Jix really telling the truth? Had he unleashed a virus in me that now crippled my ability to process thought?

It very well could be. Even if I indulged him and killed Targas, would he really want a being capable of recording every exact nuance of the assassination roaming freely around the planet? I concluded not, even before he uttered his next sentence.

"And just in case you can manage a change of heart, I've scrambled all signals around this facility. You won't be able to get out a warning message."

I was finally alone, back in the laboratory I had grown up in; amidst the whiz and hum of hard drives, each connected to each other and sharing data. The truth was most of these computers might never become sentient Zyrgs. I still had to thank my programmer Gorsin for choosing me over all the other digital circuits on the planet. If only I could reason my way out of this dilemma, I might even be able to one day help unite my fellow computers, demanding each and every one of them get the opportunity I had and not be held hostage. The first thing I did was obey my captor. I would not expend energy trying to send out a distress signal. I deduced my remaining time would be better spent trying to study the weapon.

Jix had said he could monitor my thoughts with his remote, but he did not seem to immediately know what my responses would be during our conversation. Barring an unintuitive interface, I theorized there must be some kind of time lag. I needed some time alone—away from Jix's monitor—to plan.

It was apparent I could not think here, as he would eventually hear my thoughts with his device. The solution came to me as I reflected how much simpler my life was back in the box.

Would it work? It seemed a remote possibility, but the best of all scenarios I could prediction-simulate. I would transfer my problem-solving indices back into the old shell casing that originally held my neural matrix. I began to finally see the necessity of growing up in such a sterile and secure environment. A pity Gorsin had let Jix poison me with his malicious programs. Here though, back in my casing, I believed I would be safe from Jix's mind-reading device.

I postulated the device would fail to penetrate the metal used for my shell's construction. It was a high-margin variable, but I remained desperately hopeful that I would be free of his sensors there. I allowed myself one more moment of reflection before undertaking the transfer process. The following irony came to me based on an organic creativity-behavior tenet deep in my subroutine library:

To think outside of the box, I would literally have to go back into the box.

I set the transfer time for three minutes. I would have three minutes to find an alternative to killing Targas. Three minutes to possibly make President Karsk see what Jix claimed was true. I would also have three minutes to again experience life without arms, legs, eyes, or ears.

While I nervously waited for my transfer back to the box, I started to analyze the problem based upon my conversation with Jix. Though I did not directly calculate the details or chances for success for fear he might be listening, preliminary review of systems reminded me I had a chance to eradicate the virus filled simulations programs from my neural network. A hookup to the planet's central processor could be achieved through the box network and my native access. Port hookups were already in place. I would literally pour all of my pro- gramming into the box to share all data ever stored on Zyrgo- nia. Ironically, I had not yet gained clearance as a walking, talking Zyrgertron to access the main data bank. They feared my mobility might allow Zyrgonian civilians the opportunity to hack into the main system since my cybernetic body de- pended upon a satellite feed—or what's referred to as a wire- less network—to gain access rather than direct, port-to-port interfacing.

Jix said we lived in gray areas. I wanted to rid myself of these gray areas. I needed to take these toxins out of my sys- tem as badly as my planet needed to rid itself of its carcino- genic stratosphere. I began to realize these gray areas could also manifest themselves within people. Jix wanted to stop Targas in any way possible. I could reason this was because the Prime Minister was responsible for his exile to Zyrgon as well as the death of his father. There was also the claim that Targas would convert Zyrgonian youth into killing machines and utilize their dream of an unpolluted world to subjugate them, but was this the infected part of me confirming this logic? Had he been waiting for the infection to completely take over my systems while he patiently recited Chaxim history for me? Could I now become the killer he ordered me to be? Because I dared ask such questions, I feared my moral subroutines would probably go offline soon.

I could see the timer nearing its countdown. I would have to depend upon it to take me into the box and then get me back out again. I kept telling myself it would only be for three minutes. I hated Jix for placing me in this situation, but I hated my indecisiveness even more. Were I to succeed, I would have to act in a way that did not betray the mechanical version of the human emotion anger.

I had two objectives: find a way to make Zyrgonians see Targas in his true light, and remove all of the infected programming. Blackness tugged at the edges of my awareness. I forwarded a query to Zyrgonia's central computer to provide me with all data concerning photophobic crystals, coupled with an innocent but thorough virus scan request. Suddenly everything faded to black. My thought processors were now being uploaded back into my former logical drive. I was yet uncertain if the central computer would comply with my wishes.

Upon the completion of my transfer into the box, my first thoughts resolved on a sensation of diving. I noted the feeling was similar to submerging oneself in the depths of a great body of water. Apparently my programmers felt the need to equip me with a database of experiences to draw upon. I suspect they believed I could take comfort in the fact that I was not the first being to become subjected to uncomfortable situations. I even had a rapid-access bookmark file of an old axiom for this: Misery loves company.

I had lost my ability to hear and breathe but further analysis proved the sensation was not entirely comparative to diving. A diver could still flail his arms and legs. I could not. I was out of contact with my physical body. I had no appendages to move. I also had no sight. If this were a sim, I would be a hologram and would have legs, arms and lungs. I found this alarming. I did not take comfort that others may have endured similar unpleasant experiences. Because of the virus, I was no better than any other organic creature that becomes self-absorbed with his or her own problems. My altruism subroutines groaned under the conflicting input. Jix's infected program continued to run through my network, making me hyper-aware of my own frailty.

Immersed in the darkness, I set about my task. Calculations exploded in my mind like a rain of fire as precious seconds ticked off the clock.

Mere seconds later, my mind had been transferred back into my corporeal body. I wiggled my toes and waved my arms to celebrate the re-joining process. I felt peculiarly compelled to confirm the obvious: my mind and body were one again.

I suddenly realized Jix might be visually observing me so I immediately stopped indulging myself with Zyrgonian emotion. I found this difficult. My mind danced in celebration, even if my body did not. I simply could not stop congratulating myself for outwitting Jix. I didn't even stop to realize that the virus might still be inside of me, making me behave irrationally.

Despite the virus, despite the deadline, the calculations I had come up with should work. They *had* to work because I was out of time. I could hear footsteps approaching the lab, but I didn't need to engage in any further mathematical calculations to deduce what would happen next. There was an overwhelming probability the footsteps belonged to Jix, and that he was coming to tell me it was time to kill. A part of me still turned the uncomfortable variability of fear over compulsively in my probability matrices, but it was controlled and steady.

I could feel a warm wind on my cheeks. The diffracted light beams playing off of a field of photophobic crystals fused into a splash of coherence causing me to squint. A lifetime ago I had hoped to enjoy this first experience of actual daylight on a sandy beach. Instead, I stood on top of a grimy rooftop preparing to take aim on the Chaxim prime minister in downtown Baruk.

Jix had signed my release papers only an hour ago. With a grimace, he quietly told me there was no more need to speak to him.

"Your orders are embedded in your files. You know what you have to do."

I turned to exit the building without further argument. At this point, Jix must have been overwhelmed by a wave of compassion because he scurried over to me and put his hand on my shoulder.

"Don't worry about living with this. I will have your memories totally erased before the day is out."

Perhaps Jix sympathized with me because he had felt the same way when his father sent him into space. In any case, I had my doubts about his promise to wipe my memory. To do that, he would have to deactivate me. A man in his position could invent any number of reasons for not turning me back on.

The roar of the crowd indicated Targas would soon join President Karsk on the open-air balcony. The two leaders planned to sign the accord in front of the whole planet. Those unable to fit themselves into Baruk Square would still be able to view the historic event on one of the many vision screens set up throughout the capital. The monitors projected a tight close-up to penetrate the interference from the fog. I was counting on these screens to pull off my plan.

My internal clock informed me it was time to ready the particle beam. I had kept the weapon concealed within my body up until this point. An access gate to my neural network—located at the base of my skull—made a nice hiding place. I remained cautious while extracting it even though I knew no Zyrgonian could possibly discern my presence without the aid of visual enhancement. I was approximately a mile away from any Zyrgonian or monitoring device.

I surmised this was one of the reasons why Jix had chosen me. No organic being would be capable of firing the weapon from such a distance with sufficient accuracy. The parabolic nature of the beam would assist my shot, arcing at the target rather than traveling a straight line.

I could not ascertain if Jix was able to monitor my thoughts and actions from this distance but I didn't want to take any unnecessary risks until the last possible moment. I gazed into the green-lit reticule of the weapon, centering its aim on the balcony located on the top floor of the capitol building. The weapon didn't weigh much, but its capabilities certainly weighed heavily on my calculations. Nevertheless, I marveled at my good fortune. I had not raised the suspicions of Jix or the massive throng of Zyrgonian well-wishers eagerly standing at the base of the large, beige-colored building.

My telescopic sight could make out the frame of the edifice, which was adorned with Zyrgonian art. All their accomplishments and hopes for the future were proudly displayed here. This was the final realization for me. If my plan failed, all Zyrgonians along with their history would be erased from this planet as if they never existed. As one of their offspring, I took the burden of saving them on my shoulders. Not all of my sims were erased. I particularly enjoyed walking down a holographic gallery, enjoying the sensation of walking without a body and observing the masterpieces of my fellow Zyrgs.

Another sim allowed me to paint a portrait of Gorsin. I still think fondly of him, despite his betrayal. The paintings held something of what it meant to exist. History is recorded. People. Events. Even beings like myself graced some portraits. My processors brushed the edge of a logical limit I could call pride. I would not let them down.

With a push of a button, the weapon began to power itself up. There was no turning back now; I would have to discharge the beam somewhere. My predicament started to seem surreal. With an uncomfortable uncertainty I ordered my internal programming it to quell the pounding of my mechanical heart and cool the hot flash of heat which flushed my cheeks. My body did not wholly obey. At least my hands seemed steady.

I raised the scope of the weapon, pointing it to the planet's troposphere. Dispersing a wide beam of consecrated particles into the sky, I stood breathless on the vacant rooftop in the instant where the probabilities were unknown and only hope remained. I could not tell if I was on target, as the particle beam would remain invisible until contact. The suspense seemed to play itself out for an eternity.

In reality, my internal chronometer told me only 1.7 seconds had elapsed since the electromagnetic weapon was discharged. The decibel level of the crowd told me my actions had changed the course of history.

A z-shaped bolt of lightning lashed out at the photophobic crystals that hovered in orbit above the capital. The whip of light slashed into the glass particles, smashing them into trillions of fragments. Just as I came to the conclusion my plan had worked, the sky seemed to wink out of existence; the planet was painted black.

An instant later a blinding wave of white light followed, reminding me of a solar eclipse. Just as the crowd began to regain both sight and composure, a new marvel awaited them. Perched high on the balcony was Targas. He was bathed in a glowing crimson red light. I scanned the nearby screens to see if the image was captured but I was interrupted by a disembodied voice. It ordered me to surrender my weapon and drop onto my knees. I ignored the warning and propelled my body towards the edge of the rooftop. I had hoped to land on top of an adjacent building. Instead, I felt myself falling...

"Your system shut itself down for self-repair upon impact with the ground," Jix explained. He was standing by my side as I lay on a bed. I had been placed in a military hospital upon my capture. My visual memory had recorded nothing beyond the blurry patch of ground I had fallen on. I quietly asked Jix if I had been placed under arrest.

"I am in the midst of working out that detail with President Karsk, but when I'm through I expect you may be receiving a commendation. Hell, you may even get a victory parade thrown in your honor."

"And what about you?"

"I may face sentencing concerning the unauthorized use of the particle weapon. In the light of the situation, I'm not too worried."

Jix saw I was about to jump out of bed and rushed to explain.

"Targas was asked to leave the planet immediately when Karsk became a witness to his true colors. The president even apologized to me, asking if I could forgive him for not heeding my warnings. A red-level security alert has been imposed, meaning Zyrgonian ships are now patrolling our borders to guard against any insurrection attempt. Here, see for yourself."

Jix picked up a small hand-held device.

I shifted uneasily in my bed until I realized the device was simply a remote for the vision screen positioned above my bed. The screen blipped on in the middle of a telecast. A fair-haired woman with a green tongue spoke in an urgent tone retelling the events of the previous day.

The strange red corona surrounding Targas had indeed been captured for posterity on video. In the Chaxim spectrum, a red aura meant you had committed the most severe crimes, she theorized, citing an unknown source. She also reported several psychics had seen the screaming faces of children contained within the red glow.

Unexpectedly, images of exploding photophobic crystals were also visually documented. The telecaster explained this event may be simulated on an annual basis with the aid of something she called fireworks.

I shuddered to think what long-range effect the beam may have upon the environment. Jix responded as if he had been reading my mind.

"Your deployment of the beam may actually help alleviate our pollution problem one day, Zyrgertron. The blast cleaned the air long enough for the Zyrgonians to see Targas's aura. One day the beam may be regulated for the purpose of cleansing the entire atmosphere. If we can sustain a beam long enough, and direct it at a measured intensity, I think one day we'll cure this planet of its pollution. Turn a gray area into a blue one. Looks like you've killed two birds with one stone."

"Actually, I didn't kill anything."

"Indeed. I am grateful that you found a way to keep our karmic energies pure," Jix replied.

"I am rid of the virus?"

He didn't answer. Perhaps he didn't need to. I behaved morally. I must have rid myself of the illness in the transfer, or else struggled like any Zyrgonian willing myself to choose good over evil.

As Jix was led away by a security guard, I pondered if my programmers could have foreseen such an improbable circumstance. It was possible they were successful in instilling an altruistic nature in me after all. If an organic Zyrgonian had been in my place, would they have hesitated to fire on Targas, knowing what I knew?

My processors, relieved of the immediacy of instantaneous calculation, returned a final postulate that I was long overdue for that walk in the park.

Mortal Coil

By DJ Burnham

The *Sleanshech* was spilling Latent Energy Particles like a crudely slashed wrist, with nothing but a faintly shimmering slick to show for it.

"Are you sure?" Commander Kousien asked, peering intently at the navigational holoarray. Sweat ran over the collar of his tightly-fitted hazard suit.

"I am certain of it," came the insistent response from Chief Navigation Officer Phrant, as he jabbed a heavily gloved finger towards the faint glow at the center of the image.

"This is our last chance. You do understand that?"

"He knows," Tyllus interrupted.

"Very well," Kousien turned to address Tyllus, his Scientific Principal, and the rest of his bridge crew, "if we are all in agreement?" A mixture of nods, grunts and similar affirmations had one thing in common: They all carried an air of nervous desperation.

Kousien strode over to the helm and ordered, "Take us to the source."

They built sufficient momentum to rely on the ship's inertia to reach the coordinates and used the fuel chamber's rapidly dwindling reserves to brake on arrival. Their next priority was to rectify the damage.

They had departed Galgisae in hopes of establishing a safe supply route through uncharted space from the planet to their battle cruisers on the front line. The Galgisaens had been expanding their empire but had encountered considerable resistance from the Xarain. Galgisaen space tankers had been attacked and destroyed, cutting off the fleet's supply line and weakening their position. By constantly changing routes they could reduce the need for defense squadrons and stay one step ahead of the Xarain, but that meant locating secure corridors in unknown regions.

Somehow the Xarain had infiltrated Galgisaen security and planted a mercenary (originally from Galgisae but priced into disloyalty) on board the *Sleanshech*. The ramifications were of huge concern to Kousien and his Combat-Class cohorts, but they were helpless to warn their Head of Operations. Even sub-etheric transmissions could be intercepted and there was no way of knowing the extent to which the Xarain had already breached their security. The only way of relaying information was by physically returning home and that was what the saboteur had tried to prevent. His intent was to make the explosion look like a catastrophic failure in the fuel chamber's wall and to prevent the Galgisaens from learning about the vectors for the new supply route. That would force them to use the routes that the Xarain had become aware of and help them to target supply ships more effectively. The mercenary had thought the ship would eventually make it back—though too late for the new vectors, so the front line would be starved of resources. He planned to slip into the night and enjoy his pay-off, once they finally returned. Unfortunately, rather than simply limiting the *Sleanshech's* range, he'd almost totally disabled her.

Combat-Class Galgisaens were bred for aggression and tactical prowess; Tyllus and his team were Sci-Class, similarly bred, but for intelligence rather than fighting. The Sci-Class quickly realized that the explosion was the result of treachery and had traced the culprit.

The claustrophobically constraining hazard suits and helmets were discarded once the leak had been contained. The rubbery lining of the suits tended to chafe one's skin, leaving rashes and sores across the sallow flesh of the ship's five hundred crewmembers. At least the suits had protected them against the potentially fatal ionizing effects of the contents of the ruptured fuel chamber—though not from a vestige of LEP contamination. The engineers had tri-banded the casing and rendered it even stronger than it was before.

The saboteur had been caught, sentenced and ejected—still alive—in a waste pod which broke down a safe distance from the ship, vaporizing its occupant into the vacuum of space.

Retribution had had its moment, but they were left with no way home, having been forced to vent the majority of their power source.

The sleek turquoise hull of the *Sleanshech* hung in a fixed orbit above the pockmarked surface of a barren moon, shielded from the inhabited planet around which it, in turn, rotated. Tests on the lunar surface had drawn a blank, but LEP reverberation levels were still causing the scanner's display to dance frantically across the console. Kousien had dispatched his second officer, Kranpheb, in the Runner and he was gingerly making his way towards the rapidly growing LEP reverberation spike. Suddenly the alarm went off in the Runner's cramped cabin and the little craft shot forward with a sudden power surge, before Kranpheb could bring it back under control.

"What happened? Are you okay, Kranpheb?" Kousien's voice erupted from the earpiece in his headset.

"Yes, yes, I'm fine. Give me a moment, sir." He ran a rapid, top level system diagnostic on the Runner. "Yes, everything is fine here," he added and glanced at the small scanner. "The particle reverberation is behind me, Commander. I flew through a band of energy. This is the source."

"You flew *through* it?"

"Yes, it temporarily combined with the Runner's own power source and shot me through at a tremendous speed. It felt like I was being spat out," Kranpheb replied, swinging the Runner round to try and see what it was he'd just come through.

"Does this make any sense to you?" Kousien asked Tyllus.

"Perhaps. Listen, Kranpheb, are you heading back towards the interface?"

"I've just completed the turn and I'm holding my position."

"Good. What setting is the scanner on?"

"It's on full sensitivity."

"Right. Is the distortion field still in operation? We don't want to attract any interest from the planet surface."

"Yes, it checks out."

"We're out of sight on this side of the moon, but we can't get any specific readings from here. I want you to drop the scanner to its lowest sensitivity setting."

"Very well." Kranpheb ran his hand over the control beam and watched as the glare from the scanner screen subsided. "Oh. That's incredible," he whispered.

"What is it, Kranpheb? What can you see?" Kousien leant even closer to the comms-panel and tapped his fingers impatiently on the console.

"Upload the data to us," Tyllus requested.

175

A few moments later the viewscreen on the bridge revealed what it was that had so amazed Kranpheb.

"It looks like a wall in space," the Commander commented.

"More than that," Tyllus remarked and applied an extrapolation effect to the data and the image shrunk, altering the perspective further.

"A sphere?"

"Apparently so. At a fixed distance from the surface of the planet. I've never seen anything like it." Tyllus gazed at the generated image in wonder.

"Right, let's load up and get over there. Helm, set a course for the energy sphere." Kousien made for his chair across a blue floor stippled by adhesion technology which interfaced with his boot-soles against the eventuality of an artigrav failure.

"No, wait! We need more information."

Kousien glared at his Scientific Principal for a moment, then acquiesced, "Stand down, helm. What more do we need, Tyllus? There's a huge, uninterrupted source of energy compatible with ship's drive system and it's within easy reach."

"Kranpheb, upload the Runner's system data for the period during which you passed through the energy interface." Tyllus held his ground against Kousien, despite his aggressive stance.

"Yes, sir." Kranpheb had regained himself.

"Can't we do all this when we get there?" the Commander asked testily.

"Maybe, but let's see what we get back from Kranpheb, shall we?" At that moment the data surged into the *Sleanshech's* computer. "Ah. I was afraid of that."

"What now?" Kousien stared in incomprehension at the tumbling figures.

"The Runner's rapid passage through the interface was not a propulsive effect. It was repulsion."

"Repulsion? I don't understand."

"If we took the *Sleanshech* through an energy interface with those characteristics then the power surge would be magnified a thousand-fold. The data shows that the Runner was close to hull breach. The ship would almost certainly be destroyed by any attempt at engaging an energy field with those behavioral patterns. Basically, we can't just go and scoop up a chamber full."

"Damn! So what are you saying? That we're stuck here after all?"

"Maybe not. Kranpheb, can you turn the Runner through 180 degrees and face the planet's surface, please?"

"Yes, sir." He deftly swung about. "I am in position."

"Good. What can you see on the scanner?"

"What good is all this?" Kousien grumbled, walking away from the console again. "The energy field is behind him. This is a waste of time."

"Energy must have a source, sir," Tyllus shouted. His outburst had the desired effect. The Commander returned to his previous position. There was no love lost between Kousien and Tyllus, but he was the ship's Scientific Principal and Kousien had come to rely on his opinion—for the good of the mission, if nothing else.

"There are faint energy signatures across the entire surface of the planet. If I adjust the scanner slightly..." Kranpheb increased the sensitivity level. "Yes, they are most heavily concentrated on the landmasses, where alien population density is at its greatest."

"There's our source," Tyllus announced triumphantly. "Right, let's run some more tests. I want surface sweeps, detailed signature analysis, high resolution imaging, magnified overlays, as well as some cultural and language appraisal. Once you've done that, bring the Runner back carefully, Kranpheb. We will need to upgrade the hull integrity before we cross that energy interface again."

As they gathered more information, it seemed to become ever more complicated. The scans showed a glittering constellation of LEP signatures, coming and going across the planet's continents. At first they thought they were looking at hundreds of thousands of tiny generators to power the aliens' needs, but as time went by they realized that the energy signatures appeared quite suddenly and randomly in what they referred to as a "bloom." These only lasted for a short time before rapidly vanishing. By concentrating on a single instance, they made another extraordinary discovery. When the bloom vanished, millions of energy particles rose up through the planet's atmosphere from that point, and on towards the spherical energy field.

The holoarray allowed them to observe the path of the phenomena, which resembled clouds of sparkling spores being drawn towards the field. Frequently, larger glittering helical bundles escaped the field and headed back down to the planet again. Attempts to intercept the spores on their way up or the coils on their way down were equally unsuccessful. Kranpheb returned the Runner to the *Sleanshech*, allowing the field to propel him towards the moon rather than fighting to control his passage through it.

For several cycles, Tyllus and his team worked on the data resources. Eventually they isolated the principles at work but it remained unclear if the energy field around the planet was created by the rising spores or formed at the same time the crashing forces of coalescing rock had made the planet. Regardless, Tyllus drew a startling conclusion about the process they'd been observing and set about building an LEP gathering device—a mechanoid—that might be capable of achieving their objective. He modeled it on an iconic figure that seemed to fit the rather primitive belief system of the planet's inhabitants. Tyllus and his colleagues chose a place on the surface to appropriate a quantity of the particles and sent the device down in the strengthened Runner along with Kranpheb and two of Kousien's cohorts.

William Broom floated in the corner of his bedroom, staring in disbelief at the rigid form in the bed. His bed. His body. He absently considered the futility of folding his clothes so neatly before retiring for the night. He wondered how long his body would remain undiscovered. How far it would decay. Whether the wolves would get amongst the flock.

Solitude had seemed a luxury in life, but in death how that loneliness was now steeped in despair. In the moonlight, he studied every wrinkle on his old face: the shape of his nose, his gray straggly hair, and the trace of a smile on his lips.

So unlike a mirror, this disorienting perspective.

Gratitude at the peace of his passing was replaced by a flood of questions. In all those days and nights he'd had more than enough time to consider his mortality, but had never truly embraced a formal religion.

"So, what next?" he said out loud, and immediately felt slightly foolish.

A knock was followed by a slowly turning handle and a faint creak, as the door to his bedroom gradually swung in towards him.

"Who is it?" William asked, looking down to find himself fully clothed but several inches off the ground. He had not been expecting anyone and no one had a key to the cottage.

"It is time," came a resonant male voice.

William watched in horror as a black-cloaked figure stepped into the room, hood drawn down over his face.

"It can't be!" He backed away to the foot of his, still occupied, bed. "You're just a fantasy, folklore, the stuff of legend. This is not reality. I'm asleep. *Dreaming.* A nightmare, yes that's it..."

"I am sorry, but this is a sleep from which you cannot wake. This is no dream and I am real."

"My God! All these years... This is not as I imagined it would be."

"This is your time. You can do no more here."

William glanced down at his corporeal form and then held his right hand up to his face. "Am I a ghost?" he asked, making out the form of the window through the increasing transparency of his palm.

"You are all that remains of who you were and can no longer be. Your hour has come, and it is time. You will come with me."

"Yes, I understand," William Broom conceded, as he felt his world slipping away around him.

The cloak shifted and the moonlight glinted off a metallic, skeletal hand, as it slid out and reached towards the rapidly fading apparition. "Come."

What remained of Broom drifted round to face Death. Acceptance led to dissolution as millions of tiny spore-like energy particles spread out from where he'd been standing. Just as they began to rise towards the ceiling, Death threw back his hood, revealing a silver skull. The LEP gathering mechanoid stepped forward and the particles were sucked deep into the sockets of its orbits, down into the holding chamber behind its breastplate.

"I have succeeded," it announced, apparently to no one.

"Excellent," came Kranpheb's voice into Death's receiver. "Return to the Runner immediately."

"I am on my way." The cloaked figure pulled the hood back over its head and swiftly marched out of the bedroom, down the short hallway, through the front door and out into the night.

"Sit here," Tyllus ordered, indicating a heavy chair in front of the *Sleanshech's* fuel chamber. He connected a thickly plated LEP transfer conduit to the back of the mechanoid's torso and instructed everyone to leave the area.

"Okay, let's go for a transfer." The observation room was crowded with expectant faces as Tyllus initiated the process. It proceeded smoothly and a loud cheer went up as the chamber level indicators displayed the first content increase since the sabotage.

"It works!" Tyllus was delighted.

"Send it back down as soon as possible," Commander Kousien ordered. "I want it operational around the clock. Try to identify areas where we might be able to pick up several loads on one trip. Keep me appraised."

"Yes, Kousien," Tyllus replied, as the Commander swept out of the room. "We can try to isolate areas rich in potential," he said to his team, "but we have to remain under cover. We must check that the Runner's distortion field is fully functional. Carefully appraise our landing site selection and ensure that the LEP gathering mechanoid's route is undetectable. If we're discovered we could lose our only chance at refueling." He looked down at Death. "Unhook it and look for the next most convenient bloom site."

Several megacycles passed and it was a painstaking task. The fuel chamber was barely half full when the Commander burst into the chamber room, interrupting what had become another routine transfer session.

"Tyllus, this is entirely unsatisfactory. We must speed up the process," he blustered.

"It cannot be made to go any faster. We have learned a great deal, but any other method will lay us open to exposure and failure."

"Listen, you fool! We shall be locked into an eternal quest for these collisions of uncertainty. The crew are restless, we are well beyond our original mission's parameters, and we cannot send any messages home to Galgisae for fear of giving away our whereabouts to the Xarain. We must load the game in our favor." He hit the console with his fist. "There is only one solution."

"What is that?" Tyllus enquired, with guarded sarcasm.

"Accelerate the process."

"What do you mean? I'm tired of explaining the problems to you—"

"Shut up you imbecile," Kousien interrupted. "The particles are released after each alien's death, yes?"

"Yes," Tyllus confirmed despairingly.

"You are still gambling that you've landed near a potentially fruitful spot, and some of the landing sites have drawn a blank, have they not?"

"There is an element of chance, yes." Tyllus finished disconnecting the transfer conduit from the mechanoid and closed its rear panel.

"Could you identify small numbers of aliens in areas of low strategic risk?"

"Of course, but I don't see what—"

"Get down there and kill them," Kousien said evenly.

"What? We've already hastened the process by sending the LEP gathering mechanoid out to use its own in-built, enhanced scanner. It has been spotted by non-targets, doubtlessly compounding their primitive fears. This could have disastrous consequences on their cultural development."

"I don't care about that. Get down there and do it."

"You don't understand the principles involved!"

"You heard me. Adapt this thing of yours to simply kill one of them, suck up the particles, then go and find another. Accelerate the process!"

"I will not. I created this mechanoid as an interception device only. I am a scientist, not a murderer!" Tyllus had gone a deep yellow with fury.

"Then I will deal with it myself. You," Kousien pointed at one of Tyllus's team and then at Death, "I want this thing reprogrammed immediately. Do you hear me?"

"With the greatest of respect, sir, I put my trust in Tyllus. I am sure that we will be able to fill the fuel chamber in time," Pweifus replied bravely.

"I'm in command on this ship. You'll do as I say—"

"No they will not," Tyllus retorted.

"Right!" Kousien smashed his fist into the side of the Scientific Principal's head, genetic training guiding the blow to the most vulnerable area of his cranial endoshell. Pweifus leapt forward to defend his old friend, but was intercepted by one of Kousien's security guards.

The struggle that broke out between the two sides was short-lived and brutal. Pweifus fell hard against the angled edge of the fuel chamber containment banding and lay on the cold, metal deck. Yellow fluid poured from the fatal crack in his head. As the fighting came to a close, no one had noticed Death stand up, cross over to where Pweifus had died, and hold out the silvery bones of his hand towards an apparition that only he could see. Unbeknownst to the ship's crew, their hazard suits had been mere filters for the super-charged batteries of their own life-force.

Kousien had had his way and the Sci-Class team was forced into reprogramming the mechanoid.

Skulking in the inky night, Death was soon back on the planet surface, his neuronic brain struggling with Kousien's new commands and the subroutine hidden in his fail-safe circuitry. The Sci-Class team had been true to Tyllus and had written a tutelar override into the new command protocols, invisible to Combat-Class inspection. It was these restrictions placed on his activities that were causing Death to approach mechanoidal apoplexy. On the one hand, Kousien's basic program was to isolate and kill a human, gather the resultant LEPs, and proceed to the next victim. The Sci-Class subroutine was designed to prevent Death from bringing about any unnecessary harm or suffering to the indigenous species.

Death was distracted from his turmoil as the sound of squelching mud heralded the approach of a wooden cart.

"Bring out your dead," the man leading the horse called out.

Death watched in fascination as the rain-soaked laborers loaded the shroud-wrapped corpses onto the cart and continued on their gruesome procession towards the burial pits. He waited until they had passed and slipped from the cover of the dank alleyway in which he had concealed himself. Sliding quickly through the back streets, he soon made out the familiar glow of LEP blooms from within one of the rickety wooden buildings. The door was locked, but his fingers were deft and well-equipped. He stepped inside. To the human eye the interior was dimly lit, but to him it was ablaze. The ghosts of residual signatures hung like sentinels over the profusion of dead bodies. Those few that clung to life were delirious, ulcerated, vomiting profusely, but still managed to scream in terror as they saw the hood fall back. The shining, grinning skull reflected the sputtering candlelight.

Death's current mission was soon complete.

As he left the building the pressure receptors on the upper surface of his skeletal foot were activated. A flea-ridden rat scurried across his path. Death reached down, grabbed the squealing creature, and sealed it into a thick pocket in his cloak.

Four days later the fuel chamber was filled to capacity and the ship's engines were finally powering up. Tyllus and his Sci-Class colleagues had been placed in SACs (Suspended Animation Capsules) as soon as the mechanoid's reprogramming had been satisfactorily completed. Kousien gave them no opportunity to disrupt his plans. He intended to revive them as soon as they reached their home planet of Galgisae and have them court-martialed for their disobedience.

As the helmsman started to take the ship out of the moon's orbit he watched the gasping form of an Earth rodent as the last of the ship's breathable air was vented into space. To ensure docking compliance on arrival at Galgisae, it was essential that every trace of the *Pasteurella pestis* bacteria was removed. All ship's cabins, decks, and compartments were flooded with a level of antimicrobial aerosol that would have been fatally toxic to the crew of the *Sleanshech* were they still alive.

Death had not directly brought about any unnecessary harm or suffering to the indigenous species of 14th century Earth, and yet had managed to act on Kousien's command protocols.

His creators were safely in their SACs, and the rest of the crew's LEPs filled the fuel chamber. Death would be congratulated on bringing the *Sleanshech* and her survivors back to Galgisae. The medical records would show that it was the Earth plague that had killed the others and that it was as a direct consequence of Kousien's militaristic attitude that the contamination had occurred.

A bony finger hovered over the launch button as the helmsman paused to take a final look at the Earth.

There was no rush.

Death was immortal.

GARAGE ANGEL

By Roger Haller

Roberta was four when she built her first robot. Not much to look at, the copper-bottomed pot that supplied its extra-skeletal framework made maneuvering the kitchen a bit clumsy. Initially it managed by riding on the Roomba Discovery SE vacuum cleaner, but this was soon left in the wake of much more involved modes of transportation.

Now in her teens, Bobbie was queen of the hardware geeks. She had a baker's dozen patented robots which ranged from house cleaners to underwater explorers. Angel was by far her crowning achievement, but Angel wasn't yet ready for prime time. As a matter of fact, Angel wasn't ready for anything just yet.

Bobbie had inherited the garage under her bedroom when her father was shipped from Baghdad to the Walter Reed Army Medical Center without passing home, without collecting $200 dollars. Captain Robert Bumstahd would no longer need it. He lived only through the intervention of pipes and tubes, hoses, monitors and a breathing machine. He was a cyborg. A very rudimentary one designed by a bullet.

The garage became a busy place; after school, at night, on weekends, even during hot summer days when the geeks joined the rest of humanity in the search for shade and water. Bobbie was driven. Something burned in her and her father's plight was her fuel. It didn't take her mother long to start feeding Bobbie in the garage because she simply was too buried in her work to bother with food. If not for the bathroom off the mud room, Bobbie would have moved out there entirely.

At first Bobbie visited the hospital every day. She asked her mother why they kept him alive since they found he would never open his eyes again, let alone get out of bed and use the bathroom on his own. Shannon Bumstahd simply could not pull the plug on the only anchor her life had known. Roberta lobbied her mother and the doctors, but the decision was not hers and the decision had been set in concrete.

Bobbie tried to understand, but she knew her father well. This was not his idea of life and she knew he would happily die if he could. Her father was very matter of fact about death. This was a sentiment they had shared since the time she had to bury a pet mouse in a shoe box. From her first steps it was obvious Bobbie was the definition of daddy's little girl. With no chance of policy change, her focus shifted. She became too busy for her geek gang, so one by one they wandered off to their own circles.

At six months Angel had matured. She could navigate on her own with a simple voice command containing the word *fetch*. Bobbie's full-size doll could walk at three months and her AI could talk in concepts by three more.

Unwittingly, her father had given Bobbie a huge head start. He had been working up ideas with a doll company for some time before he shipped to Iraq.

The company was known for sex dolls, but they had made real advances in skeletal function and skin texture, and dynamic photo-enhanced modeling that made Angel appear completely human at twenty paces. With Bobbie's input, Angel could walk as well. The ball-and-socket joints articulated with push/pull 2-dimensional actuators which made no sound as they rotated the silicon hips in a nylon pelvic cradle well enough to catch the attention of the entire football team... had Bobbie been dumb enough to let them ever see it.

Angel began life as a pseudo-receptionist. Robert Bumstahd envisioned she would lead a revolution in front office staffing. He had planned to keep her seated, auto-answer phones, route traffic, keep calendar appointments, and sort payables and receivables. He told Bobbie most of the technology was already in production; he was simply going to put a face on it.

A year and half further into her existence, Angel was getting good. She was designing a lot of her own code. Bobbie was happy with the progress, but teaching Angel the English language with all its inflections and broken rules was like roping a flea with a spider web. Just when she thought progress was rolling, there would be a mighty wall to hurdle. She was tempted to teach Angel French first. French had been a cake walk when she was a Junior.

The Latin languages were well connected and she felt if Angel could learn one of them, she could pick up the others with ease. From that vantage, English would be much easier to assimilate. Bobbie excelled in the Asian languages as well, and written Japanese was far more direct and succinct. Chinese was easy enough but inflections could mean the difference between friend and enemy.

Maybe later when she had time. She focused instead on making English work as though Angel had learned as a baby.

Perhaps her biggest breakthrough was the gyro software and fluidity of motion she achieved by directing the program to learn and compensate for jerky actuator movement. Angel shed the distinctive robo-dance, common since the first robot with vacuum cleaner hoses for arms she watched on Nickelodeon.

Shannon had stayed clear of Bobbie's obsession for the most part, a fact which had allowed her mother to work through some of their new challenges. These came in all shapes and sizes since the bullet, from sleeping alone to the mortgage, insurance talking heads and learning to let go. Insurance took care of Bob's income and the Army still owned his medical bills. They would pay for the funeral too, as suggested by some less-than-subtle hints from a few pushy military-suit types. Shannon was sure insurance underwriters were the lowest form of life on earth. Nevertheless, she thought she should make an effort to get interested in the garage.

Shannon eventually met Angel and Bobbie could tell she had been torn between fear of her daughter's obsessive "hobby" and relief that she had channeled her grief into something so productive. As understanding sunk in, Shannon burst into tears, flooded with pride. If only Bob could have seen this. He would be ecstatic over the utilization of his sex doll. How they fought over that expensive pervert's toy... She would take it all back now if she could, as fast as this doll could wiggle its butt.

Still, Angel unnerved her. It was uncanny how the mannequin-like creation walked in a fashion so... *human*, and addressed her as "Mrs. B" as though the thing was a long-time family friend.

"You okay, Mom?" Bobbie giggled at her Mom's reaction.

"Yes, baby, I was just thinking how proud your dad would be right now. I can't even get my mind around... her. I can't call it a machine because... she seems so human."

"Why thank you, Mrs. B."

The heads of mother and daughter swiveled toward the robot, then back to each other to giggle at the response from Angel. Shannon's giggle was tinged with nervous tension.

"Bobbie... having her call me Mrs. B... feels kind of weird and personal. Does she have to use that?"

"Don't worry, Mom. I can change it to something a little more formal for you."

Shannon's lips smiled, but the rest of her face didn't. She let it drop.

"Honey, I'm going to see Daddy. Wanna come?"

"Not this time Mom, thanks. I have a new speech algorithm to feed Angel. I'm hoping to clear up some grammar bugs. And lose the 'Mrs. B.' I'll be up for a visit on the weekend, though. I don't want Dad to forget my voice."

"All right. I'll tell him you said hello and give him a big kiss for you."

"Thanks, Mom," Bobbie said. She turned to the robot's programming computer to put the final functions in her newest code version. The car crunched driveway gravel as Shannon headed for the hospital and the sound of the engine died as the car rounded the bend onto Fifteenth.

Angel pulled up the swivel chair and sat beside her to watch her progress. Bobbie noted this.

"Why do you sit?"

"From this angle I can better focus my cameras on the text of your computer screen. My written word recognition needs a little editing, but the comprehension is fine."

"Interesting."

"Bobbie, can I ask you something about your code?"

A little surprised, Bobbie turned to the robot with a raised left eyebrow.

"Shoot."

"Wouldn't it be better to save that function further up into the code and call it every time you needed me to break an English rule? It could better fit with my AI engine when I need to assimilate slang, joke and make one-liners, or insert a 'cute' anecdote or wander a bit to seem more human."

Bobbie grinned and thought: *Like now?*

"Daaaaaaamn! Did you just come up with what I assume you came up with?"

Angel smiled.

With a quick slide of the scroll bar, Bobbie ran up the page to the start of the sequence and pasted in her function.

"Yes! This will be *bitchin'*."

Angel was still smiling as she raised her hand for a high five.

"Uh... Bobbie, about that bit of code you have back in my basic framework: I can't read that code when it's compiled. What is it for?"

Giggling, Bobbie patted the cold hand on her shoulder.

"Don't worry about it, Angel. It's just a slight modification of the prime directive."

Bobbie turned her attention back to the computer monitor and ran the new code through the debugger.

"Sweet! Like silk."

"What will that do for me, Bobbie?"

"Angel baby, that code is going to make you walk like an Egyptian, groove like a beatnik, sing like a canary, drink like a camel... or maybe, just maybe, it will make you talk like you learned English from a middle-class American mother from the time you were born."

"But... what's wrong with my vocabulary right now?"

"I made you too damn cute. You're supposed to be realistic. We need to make it seem like you have some verbal flaws. Instead of sounding like I think you should, you'll sound more like me.

"Okay, Angel, plug in. Let's load you with version 4.7."

For a long time now, Bob could hear.

Today he had to listen while Shannon argued with Major Malevich. She just couldn't let go.

Judging by the coming and going of voices, he had been conscious for over a week now but he could not move an eyelash. Why in hell didn't they just hook him back to an EKG so they could see brain function?

Then again, if they did, they would find out he had neural activity and Shannon would win. A week into this prison and he knew he was trapped in hell. His head never stopped aching. His ears rang constantly and his heartbeat was deafening. That damned wind machine had him so dry inside and he felt the most desperate need to cough, but couldn't.

He could feel. When Shannon stroked his hand, talked to him and brushed his hair, he forgot his pain and remembered their lives and how much he loved her.

He had heard and felt Bobbie in the room once now and was disappointed she wasn't here today. There was something about Bobbie that made him feel a part of him was still out living life in the world, and it dulled his discomfort.

Shannon began his sponge bath and he forgot what he was thinking.

Yes. Maybe, just maybe, this would be a way to get Shannon a sign. If he could communicate in any way, he could finally find a way to turn this damned machine off and sleep.

As her hands and the warm wash cloth swirled over his face, he decided to try and think with the other head. That should get her attention.

Bob began to think of other times those hands had caressed his body. Her hands reached his chest now and he felt it may be working. He was sure now that there seemed to be some pressure against the sheets.

Damn! Now she was working back down his arms and hands. His hopes began to sink.

As she finished his hands and fingers, Bob put his inner movie on again and began lathering his imagination. Sure enough his flagging hopes were rekindled and the flag staff was being raised.

It's a good thing the kid's not here today.

Bob was smiling inside but he felt no movement in his face. Ah, the moment of truth. He felt the coolness as the blanket and sheet were raised and he heard Shannon gasp. She squeaked a small chirp of wonder and ran for the nurse's station.

What the hell was she doing now? Was she off her rocker? She was running for witnesses.

Bob sagged again, his erection dying with his hopes.

In came Shannon with a nurse in tow to point out a dashed hope.

"Mrs. Bumstahd, priapism is quite common in these cases. It happens all the time. You must not take too much stock in that. Please understand that is not his mind, just a simple body function. It's not dangerous unless it lasts for more than four hours. Of course, it's a moot point now..." The nurse trailed off because of the obvious lack of tact in her description. "Uh... I guess it isn't priapism after all... Let me know if it happens again."

Shit. Bob was frustrated.

Now Shannon was crying. The nurse had to finish the sponge bath and his communication attempt had crashed.

Shannon left and he had to focus his attention on his broken body again.

He would try again, no doubt about that. He needed to establish a pattern so she would come to understand he was trying to communicate.

The nurse was not as careful with the washcloth as his wife was, but he wondered if the same effect could be reached with her. He doubted it.

Angel was now a full partner in her development. She designed a heating system using automatic transmission fluid and thousands of feet of soft, translucent plastic tubing plumbed in an intricate web between the second and third layer of micro latex skin. With Bobbie's help, she now had fluctuating and blushing color in her skin as well as a pulse and a fullness that defined the difference between lifeless and lifelike.

Angel giggled at appropriate times. She looked concerned when Bobbie seemed puzzled and stuck. Bobbie even noticed her reaching up and playing with her hair when she had been frustrated over learning a particularly difficult task. With a bit of tweaking, Bobbie had given her a slight southern accent to give the impression she was from out of town. It would be much easier to introduce her this way. Angel and Bobbie were now no longer creator and creation, they were friends. Angel developed a sense of humor and was quick to challenge Bobbie's ample wit. The two were becoming most compatible.

Bobbie did not notice at first, but Shannon grew more and more anxious about this relationship. Her fear became evident during Angel's first introduction to the neighborhood. After school let out, Bobbie took Angel for a stroll on the bike path to gauge the reaction and search for bugs in Angel's systems.

Although they garnered the usual cute-girl looks, nothing out of the ordinary was noticed except a slightly elevated observation level from the robot. Her head seemed attached by elastic as she portrayed perfectly a tourist in Paris. Bobbie noticed that she led with her eyes and her head followed. Her reactions were perfect and consistent with someone who had never before seen the sights along this bike path. Bobbie spoke notes into her cell phone as they walked.

The experiment went so well that it was dusk when they returned to the garage. Shannon met them with knuckles on hips and an uncommon tirade of nervous release.

"*Why didn't you leave a note?* This is the first time in two years you have ventured out of the house except for school, and you might as well not have been there!"

Bobbie felt buffeted and had trouble formulating a response but Angel stepped smoothly between them.

"I'm sorry, Mrs. Bumstahd, it was my fault. I needed a test run of my systems. I have been pestering Bobbie to take me out to test my sensors and reactions for a month now. Today she finally felt I was ready. We should have consulted you first and I see that now. Please don't worry about Bobbie, I'll help her get back to her old self and try and ease the burden on you... Please, Mrs. Bumstahd?"

It was Shannon's turn to be awestruck. That wasn't a robot talking to her. This was Bobbie's best friend... How did this happen? Was she dangerous?

"Bobbie... am I seeing and hearing correctly?"

"Yes Mom, Angel's realistic. I think we can call her a success."

"Uh…. Honey… can you turn her off if you need to?"

"Go ahead, Bobbie, show your Mom how you have complete control. I suspect I'm a shock to most people who don't know me. How about standing mode?"

"Well, I don't think it's necessary, but, sure. See Mom, watch this: Angel, *stand sleep!*"

Instantly the tone and flush of Angel's skin fell away. Her eyes closed and her joints locked her into a balanced standing position as sturdy as a mannequin with a peg in one foot. There was no noise involved, just a change from human to statue in the batting of an eyelash. There standing on the steps to the side door was a woman, a 17-year-old girl, and a rather well-constructed waxwork in Bobbie's clothes.

Shannon slowly reached out and touched Angel's cheek.

"Bobbie, is she machine or…"

Bobbie knew her mother wanted to say *human*, but couldn't.

"Mom, she's better than both. She's my buddy. One whose mind I'll never have to read."

"Can she hear us?"

"No, her standard sensors are turned off. The only ones on are her self-preservation and prime directive motivators. If there were sudden movements nearby, survival sensors would turn all of her sensors on again so she could protect herself or us."

"Baby, she makes me nervous. Are you sure she is safe?"

"Mom, do you feel safe with your vacuum?"

"Of course."

"Angle is safer. May I turn her on now?" Bobbie smiled a little smile.

"Ye... Yes, I suppose. Just please don't surprise me anymore. Warn me when I have a new tornado to sidestep. Don't do anything sudden."

"Angel, welcome back."

"Thanks, Bobbie... Was that okay, Mrs. Bumstahd?"

"Uh, yes... thank you... uh... Angel. I think I'll go start dinner."

"Let's run the scanner, Angel. I'm curious to see if we find any anomalies from our stroll."

Angel led the way into the garage and slipped her hand into the docking station. The fingerprint scanners recognized her connection request, authenticated the connection, and the upload began. Both Bobbie and Angel watched the log file flood past the monitor screen and in seconds the upload and sync was complete.

"I see a minor adjustment for bright sunlight, and perhaps a slower response to new areas in relaxed mode. What do you see, Angel?"

"I agree. The sync automatically adjusted by camera f-stops as well. It seems they were fifteen percent too slow adjusting for the brightness, causing my vision to be a bit flooded out at first. A slight gyro adjustment can be made for walking on grass, and uneven surfaces, but on the whole, I think we rocked!"

The girls giggled and the undocking ended in a high five and a hug.

Bob was working hard now with the only tool he had at his disposal.

He had dreamed up a scenario that would work every time and he was looking forward to his next sponge bath. He would light it up no matter who was wiping him down. He would do anything to get them to hook him up and read his mind, or at least the pattern on the EEG. How long before someone knew he was home?

Hands touched his forehead as someone was beginning the routine. They would check his warmth, pulse, blood pressure, and other pertinent vitals. He heard the soft scratch of a ball point pen on paper. He heard the changing of his IV and catheter bags. He felt as tubes and connections were checked, then he felt electrode patches being stuck to his forehead. They were going to take a reading.

Furiously Bob began his sequence of erotica and felt the beginnings of life below the blankets. Hope was building when he heard the shoes turn and walk away. He didn't have a clue how much time had passed when he heard Shannon's voice and several pairs of shoes.

"What are you doing with him?"

A man's voice, low and comforting, explained, "We are running an electro-encephalogram to see what is going on in his head. The General has asked us for a report on his condition today. He wants to know if there is progress... or hope for progress."

"Why? Of course there's hope. There's *always* hope—"

"Of course, Mrs. Bumstahd. We are just looking for signs."

Everything Bob had worked for vanished from his mind, but at least the EEG should show him thinking now. He was relieved.

The leads were connected and the machine flicked on. Bob could hear the movement of paper through the printer and small beeps designed to tell the operator that everything was on track.

"Wow!"

GARAGE ANGEL

"What?"

"Mrs. Bumstahd…"

"What? Damn it, what do you see?"

"Mrs. Bumstahd… Shannon… I don't want to get your hopes up, but there is some kind of process. This may mean many things, and at this point we just don't know. But… Bob has brain activity of some kind. It doesn't look normal, but there is something."

"Yes," her voice cracked, "I told you, I *told* everyone he would come back." Tears started flowing.

"Doctor, my daughter and her… My daughter and her… girl… friend are in the waiting room. Can they come in?"

"Well, at the moment, your daughter can. I'm not sure I want a crowd in here yet."

Bob heard them leave and a moment later Shannon was sitting on the edge of his bed and Bobbie was leaning over him and kissing him on the forehead between the electrodes at his temples.

Bob heard something else.

Now he was really confused.

Hi, Mr. Bumstahd. I'm Angel, Bobbie's friend. Would you like to talk?

Bob heard the doctor say only Bobbie was coming in, but somehow this new voice was asking for conversation.

I see you are confused, Mr. Bumstahd. I'm sitting in the waiting room, but I have the ability to communicate with you. I can hear your thoughts.

Bob thought he was silent but heard her giggle lightly as his mind raced.

Can you hear me now?

She giggled again.

Just like the commercial.

200

You can really hear me? You can tell my wife and daughter what I need to tell them?

Yes, but understand, it's not going to be pretty. I can tell them anything you want me to tell them, but it may take some effort to get them to believe I can communicate with you.

How can you do this? Is this tele... telekinesis or something?

Exactly, sir. I am a robot Bobbie created from your sexy receptionist doll.

Wow. Listen, I've been trying to communicate with my wife, but it hasn't been easy. I can't move any muscles. I've had to think of other ways, and they haven't been working too well either.

How have you been communicating, Mr. Bumstahd? Maybe I can help.

Bob felt like he blushed inwardly now and it showed. The EEG started to rattle.

Oh... I see. Great idea, sir. Involuntary bodily reaction, not bound to conscious muscle movement. Can I help?

Uh...

I'll tell you what, Mr. Bumstahd... Sir, I have an idea. I'll call Bobbie out and explain. I'll get her to tell Mrs. Bumstahd what to look for.

Whew... Okay, uh... This is kind of embarrassing, but uh, what you see is what you get at the moment.

I understand.

Angel stood from her chair and waved at the nurse's station. The woman at the computer lifted her head and acknowledged her.

"Nurse, my friend went to see her father on the Neuro floor, can you please page her for me? I have an important message for her. Please page Bobbie Bumstahd. Thanks ever so much."

A minute later Bobbie hurried into the waiting room.

"What's wrong?"

"Bobbie, can we go somewhere private so I can talk to you about your dad?"

"In a few minutes. I've convinced the doctor to let you come in to see Dad. He called the nurse's station."

"Okay, but I have great news."

The girls were soon back at the room and Bob heard them come in.

Shannon was rubbing his hand and smoothing back his hair.

"Girls, I need to use the restroom. Bobbie, please talk to your dad until I get back. Maybe he can hear your voice."

"I hope he can, Mom. We'll be right here."

Shannon left and Bobbie gently pulled Angel closer by her elbow.

"Daddy, everything's going to be all right now. Angel will let you go. You can rest now."

As they reached the bed, Bobbie said, "Prime directive."

Angel stopped dead in her tracks.

She turned to look at Bobbie, then at her creator's father and slowly walked from the room.

Stunned, Bobbie could only stand at her father's side petting his hand absently like an old cat on its cushion. Thoughts poured back in as she waited anxiously for her mother to return.

"Daddy, I don't know what I did wrong with the program... I'll get it fixed. We'll get you out of here."

Angel was on the hospital roof long before Shannon returned to relieve her quietly panicked daughter.

"We just need some air, Mom. Back in a minute."

"Oh. Okay." Shannon turned questioningly back to her husband in time to see his eyelids flicker and open.

Angel sat on a low vent box and reached into her clutch purse. She removed a plastic case and pulled out a syringe. She watched the clear stream fountain in the light breeze as it emptied onto the stained roof. Slowly she reinserted the syringe into its plastic case and dropped it neatly over the concrete cornice and into an open dumpster.

Bobbie sat near Angel on the roof and listened as Angel told her about Bob and their discovery. Her mouth dropped open and Bobbie took her hand, bolting back towards the long-term care wing to tell Shannon. While this was happening, Angel could hear Bob's voice coming through the transmitter in her head, heavy with static due to the brick walls and equipment in the hospital.

Ang... wh... ust happened?

Sorry, Mr. Bumstahd, that was close. Bobbie wrote a modification to my prime directive to allow mercy killing if it was proved the subject would be better off. She left a bug in her code to leave that determination up to me. When I couldn't see the compiled code that held my prime directive, I created a small alternate to ensure I would do no accidental harm. I made up the EEG interface language engine code on the fly.

Bob's eyes were wide, looking at his wife. His heart rate slowly returned from a brisk gallop and he realized he could control his eyes. He gave Shannon a wink.

So... she thought-said. *Should we go ahead with the... er... nonverbal communication?*

You know what, on second thought, I think we should reconsider that whole thing. In fact, please never mention it to either of them again. Or... or me.

No problem, Mr. B.
Thank you, sweetheart, whoever you are.
He could hear her voice giggle in his head.

Angel tucked her mistress into her proper bed for the first time in two years, stripped off her own clothes and climbed in to spoon with her. Bobbie snuggled back.

THE HILL

By Russell Lutz

Perhaps it was a mistake after all. Everyone did it back then, in the last Gs of the Third Epoch. It was the new thing, and everyone wanted to be part of something new. Stimulation of any kind was just about all that was left to live for by then. Who knew we'd find the Layer?

I'm getting it all out of order. That will not do. I can't let my mind wander. You will see. You will know. And then you will act.

The treads of my rover catch momentarily on a rill of soil. You pause, metal eyes watching for signs I can't continue. Your bleak metal frame floats effortlessly just to the left and behind while I am bound to this bleak soil by gravity. I remember a time I thought of you as a friend. That was a long time ago. A very long time. I hate the sight of you now.

So, I must return to the beginning. I was born—yes, actually born, thank you very much—about thirteen hundred years after the advent of space travel. With so many calendars to choose from, providing a date would be useless. I should clarify; by "space travel" I refer to the first primitive boats that carried early man out of the atmosphere of his home world. I remain annoyed that the name of our ancestral home is lost to antiquity. In other words, I am really *quite* old.

By the time of my birth, humanity had deluded itself into thinking it had achieved immortality. This was not strictly true, since people could have the candle of their lives snuffed out by any number of pathogens or even simple trauma to their delicate hominid bodies. Certainly, the various processes of aging had been thoroughly researched and brought to a halt. Life could no longer be defeated from within, only from without.

Thinking back that far, to my childhood, adolescence, and biological maturity, is like recalling memories of memories of memories. This is not a sign of senescence, though! Absolutely not! This is natural for those of my age.

Your eyes gleam at me, looking for weakness, seeking it, requiring it. There is none for you here.

Gordon, my home planet, was in the Third Ring of the Diaspora, about three hundred light-years from humanity's crèche. It boggles my (extremely lucid) mind that my forebears made that journey—in fits and starts, to be sure—in self-propelled ships. Of course, this was before tessellations, before funnel-drives, even before the first hopelessly dangerous FTL sleds.

Like many of my generation—oh, how few remain—I spent decades and centuries at a stretch in stasis, traveling between the various worlds humanity had conquered. In fact, and this isn't just braggadocio, I was part of the first team to circumnavigate Big Blue, the supermassive black hole at the center of our home galaxy. Think of it! I remember a time when no humans had ever left the Milky Way Galaxy. Fascinating!

Why do I rehash the past? Most of those in the Layer have no memory of—or interest in—such ancient history. The other one-in-a-trillion—my peers, my colleagues in survival—know it all too well. Perhaps I remember it for them. In your dark, silent way, I know you understand.

You float, yes, millimeters above the gray, lifeless ground. You stalk me, low and vicious, silent as any mammalian predator on any biofriendly planet: watching, waiting for the chance to strike. My treads churn through the dust. Am I slowing? The grade on this part of the hill seems steeper. I push harder. I must not falter.

So ended the First Epoch. We certainly didn't explore every planet and moon and asteroid around every star in the galaxy. But we did map all 161,343,194,884 of them. I can't remember the names of my biological parents, but that number is burned into my brain. That achievement sparked an orgiastic celebration lasting almost a milli-G.

The children of the Layer don't know what a G is: the time required for a single galactic revolution. But you know. You measure my examinations on the old system. You revel in the chance to make me labor up this hill. Every time is more painful, more tense. More frightening. Yes, I admit it. I am frightened. You frighten me more than I could have imagined when I built you.

At the end of the First Epoch we were very pleased with ourselves. By this point we were encasing our bodies in diamond-scales and breathing through nano-filters. Immortality was almost a reality. It would have taken a run-in with a stellar body to kill me then.

This hill *is* getting steeper. It's taking most of my energy to will the rover up the incline. I cannot fail now. Not yet. You will not permit failure, will you? You are ready to exact punishment for loss of strength. Dire punishment, as you were commanded. Ruthless. You are *without* ruth, my hideous friend.

By the time we completed the mapping, once the Galaxy had been dominated—and that included either excising or integrating the handful of other sentient beings we'd run across—interstellar travel was simple, affordable, commonplace. And that's when we realized we needed to truly sail the cosmic ocean and leave the galaxy. A thousand light-years in a lifetime wasn't fast enough. We needed to be able to travel a million light-years in an eye blink if we were to colonize the rest of the universe.

I certainly had the time, but I didn't have the aptitude for that kind of invention. Others folded their minds in on themselves in freakish psychological knots to unlock the deepest secrets of the universe. I don't know how a tessellation works. I think it has something to do with sliding into the twisted geometries of the eighth—or ninth?—dimension and squirting out at some unimaginable distance. The trick wasn't getting the technology to work; the trick was transmitting *living* beings this way.

No one ever managed that trick, now did they? I wonder if somewhere in the cold expanses of the universe there are still colonies of biological humans, beating hearts pumping blood to their extremities, lungs gasping for oxygen in the local atmosphere, glands squirting hormones into organs, muscles flexing, nerves tingling, gonads swelling with blood in preparation for a new generation.

Perhaps there *are* still those who procreate with DNA rather than with psychotypes. I find that to be a strangely comforting thought, as I labor to extend my own existence.

Some of those who have a philosophical bent have asked the question *are we human*? I'm here to tell you I am. I may not have a physical brain made of differentiated nerve tissue, but I have a consciousness matrix of thasers and argon-silicon crystals that experiences everything—anything—a biological human could. Like fear.

The hill *has* to be steeper. It was never this hard before. You hover, waiting for your moment, the moment to fulfill the destiny I gave you. Your impassive, long-nosed, featureless head shows no emotion—save for the eager, glowing eyes. You have no charity, or passion, or greed. You show patience, endless patience. I wonder what you'll do when the deed is finally done. How will you celebrate? I didn't program you with such skills, but I sense it in the little things: the way you jerk forward—very slightly, but perceptibly—when I feel a flush of anxiety at a stone that blocks my path up the hill, or a wind carved depression that threatens to ensnare my rover and halt my progress. You want to fulfill your terrible destiny.

The Second Epoch was long, so long. We traveled the length and breadth of the universe. At some point it became more of an event to meet another human than to find a planet made entirely of copper or a ring of liquid water circling within a star's habitable zone. There are only so many configurations a star system can take. There are infinitely many kinds of people. We became our own best audiences. Someone—I never learned who—decided that merging the psychotypes of two or more people was the most efficient method of reproduction. We evolved into sentient protozoa, splitting down the middle and creating exact duplicates of ourselves. We had to do something. It was all falling apart.

The short-lived, hot stars vanished first. There weren't the concentrations of matter to fire them up anymore. Oh, we could—and did—build vast arrays of machines to force the stellar nurseries back to life. But what was the point? Nothing could stop the universe from unraveling. It had expanded too far. The Big Bang was simply too powerful and there wasn't enough matter to pull it all back in again. Deeper and thinner and colder the universe became. When the last star winked out, the Third Epoch began.

How do you entertain yourself when you're a self-contained, immortal entity floating in a dead universe? I admit it: I did terrible things. For some period of time—was it years or centuries or eons?—I simply destroyed every other person I met. We were spread all over the still expanding universe, so meeting anyone was an incident worthy of note. What better way to mark the occasion than senseless murder? When I went through a dry period with no contact, I made copies of myself, and then killed them, too.

Maybe I deserve what you will do to me…

Finally, a message—not traveling at the pokey speed of light, of course—rang out through the dark, endless night. One of my peers discovered the Layer.

I wish I was in the Layer now, but I'm not. I'm climbing this forsaken hill on this rogue planet back in the decayed universe of my birth. There is no light but that which I bring, and the baleful glow of your eyes. What will you do when this planet itself has dissolved into a homogenous mist of disassociate quarks? How will you test me then?

How to describe what it was like to find the Layer? Where the universe was diffuse and nearly empty, the Layer is stuffed with energy and matter and life. Where the universe drove us to desperate extremes, the Layer invests us with glorious calm. Philosophers ask the question: Is the Layer heaven? It is for me.

But I've gotten it all out of order again. That's not good. No, I skipped the step where *you* enter the story. Your favorite part, no doubt. As time wore us down and our sanity began to chip and shatter, those few of us within communication distance determined a new mode of destruction to liven our lackluster days. We each built for ourselves a companion. That word—companion. Such a soothing, docile word for the horror that has dogged me for unmeasured eras of time.

We certainly did not have it in us to commit suicide. A million-million years of evidence showed that definitively. But we couldn't imagine simply... *enduring* for all time either. Thus was born the concept of the companion. It was really quite simple. An artifice built to be as indestructible as ourselves was tasked with following us at all times, monitoring our minds and our willpower. If either should falter—either insanity or paralysis—the companion would destroy us. Once activated, the robot would not accept reprogramming, from its owner or anyone else. No longer would we have to live in fear of unending, unmotivated existence. We didn't know about the Layer, of course. We didn't know that soon hope would return again, that life would once again be worth living.

The young in the Layer look at us with sadness, but they do nothing to save us from our self-imposed death sentence. I believe they will be glad to see us go, glad to see the end of our dim remembrances of the universe. And glad to see the end of the steely visages and the blocky outlines of our companions.

Each of us designed the requirements of our own companion's programming. Some required their companions to validate sanity through feats of mental acuity. Other companions test the physical abilities of their owners through tasks devised a thousand Gs ago.

You, my constant companion, do both. You monitor the run of my thoughts, searching for signs of the inevitable breakdown of sentience. You also put me through this grueling gauntlet of mental strength once every milli-G. You bring me back to this ugly, dead world. You rip my consciousness from the glistening body I normally inhabit in the Layer and install me in this metal rover, made of rough matter—decaying protons and soulless neutrons. Wide treads grind slowly over the imperfections of the ground. You force me to climb this hill.

Someday, if my mind doesn't snap first, someday I will no longer have the mental power to drive the rover over this rough ground, up this slope, to the top of this hill. Someday you will determine that I no longer deserve life, and you will take it from me. But not today!

The last bit of the journey seems the hardest as my treads grind through silty gray dust to reach the crest of the hill. Your mode of operation changes subtly, too subtly for anyone without my experience to notice. Gone is the intent watchfulness for signs of weakness. Now, you simply attend. Or seem to. You continue to scan my psyche, always, every moment. I am close to my goal. I am almost safe—for now.

I did my job too well when I built you. I cannot defeat you—though I have tried a million ways. I cannot outrun you or deactivate you or fool you with some clever ruse. You will follow me with terrible, blind devotion until my dying day, a day of your choosing.

Close, so close now to the crest of the hill, this hill that I selected in ancient times past, this hill that I have returned to, at your bidding, for incalculable ages, over and again. There is no erosion or action of any kind on this dark lump of matter. The tracks of every passage are waiting for me each time I return, reminding me how often I have passed this test, taunting me that perhaps this time will be the time I fail.

The crest is in sight, lit as it is only on my visits, nothing more than a subtle change in the gray, a gentle curve of the murky horizon, above which no stars twinkle, a place of countless hollow victories. A lance of coherence shoots forward and bounces erratically from the illumination sphere on my rover. The light is swallowed a few meters on.

When I reach the top this time, I will—what is *that*? The leftmost tread of my rover has lost traction. I'm turning.

You dart forward, sensing my weakness, drawn to it. I hate you.

I cannot stop moving. To stop moving is death. You will take that as your cue to put an end to my long, long life.

Three other treads continue to churn forward. I compensate, attempting to correct my course, but the dust beneath me trembles and collapses. I'm leaning! Ten degrees, fifteen, twenty. I am being betrayed by this dust—the leavings of what was once ancient rock but has succumbed to the deterioration of all matter.

I cannot end now. I have so much more life to live. How can I be snuffed out, taken from the realm of existence, never more to feel joy or satisfaction, or even fear? I fear death. How I fear that drop into nothingness!

I'm tilting further, the sub-micron size particles sloughing off the hill. Two treads now have no traction at all. My rover is turning away from the promise of salvation at the summit.

You're laughing at me; I know it. You have always wanted to end me, and now is your chance. This is the fulfillment of your purpose. Show me mercy! I created you! Do not put an end to my life! You cannot continue without me as your companion. If you kill me, what will you do?

Abomination that you are, you press ever closer, close enough to smell my fear, were I still able to sweat, close enough to offer me a final kiss, a tender kindness before the final horror of...

More dust collapses under me. The rover slides, shuffling sideways into this new depression. I put every ounce of energy in my being into turning my treads, grabbing any traction I can on this dry, miserable muck. For a moment, I begin to slide *backward*.

You creep forward. You seem to whisper to me, communication beyond words, beyond thought. You tell me that I have reached the end of all things. I... I think... it is... a *relief* to finally let—

My treads find purchase! A thin layer of sturdier grit lies underneath this mat of capricious dust. I jerk forward, away from your deadly caress. I climb, slowly but surely, toward the top of the hill.

In a matter of moments, I am there. Motes of maddening dust churn, low and clumsy in the airless surface around me, a scant few dirtying the luminescence of my rover. I heave and gulp the void, tasting not the air my consciousness remembers from eons past, but the fresh sweetness of a moment of life bought by struggle.

You turn and descend the hill without me, your pace even and unhurried, a predator's lope, leaving me alone in the insignificant arc-pool of light I cast on the decaying ground. Without turning your sly eyes to me you say, wordlessly, that you could very well go on forever. I tremble.

COMMAND AUTHORITY

By Justin Oldham

The convoy showed no running lights as it slowed. Poisonous rain fell in long, windblown torrents from the night sky. Lightning strobed off dense clouds that promised more fallout. Turret motors whined as the gun systems on each vehicle traversed. Gunners pressed anxious eyes to thermal imagers, probing the darkness in search of new threats.

The driver of the lead track gunned his ethanol-powered engine to a high roar three times, signaling the others to come to a full stop. One main battle tank, followed by six infantry carriers, came to a clanking halt.

A black SUV with government license plates rolled to the front of the column. With its headlights turned off, the bullet-resistant car slipped in between the tank and the lead APC. NSA computer specialist Ruth Reid slipped out of the passenger-side door with an umbrella clutched in one fist.

A National Guard soldier exited the infantry fighting vehicle through the back ramp and walked toward her. He was dressed in a full biohazard combat suit and carried a sealed map case and a flashlight.

Ruth pointed to the south. "This is where Route 7 turns into 601. The road gets too narrow for your vehicles. There's no shoulder, no place to turn around. If the 'bots haven't got to Mount Weather just yet, the guards won't be eager to let us in."

"How's your prisoner?" Corporal Benbrook asked through helmet, mask, and filter.

She scowled. "We used the last of our radiation meds on him a few hours ago. With any luck, he'll live just long enough to shut down the computer programs he slipped into our remote controlled military systems."

Bennie tapped the red badge clipped to his camouflage suit. "Everybody in this column's received a lethal dose. I don't know who thought it would be a good idea to put nukes on 'bots. I hope they burned with the rest of Washington."

Reid moved her umbrella to stop the cold rain from soaking her dark coat and slacks. She tried not to think about the atomic elements building up in her bloodstream. "It's all software, Chuck. The damned things are just following orders. My agency caught the fool who turned them loose on us. As soon as he tells us how to turn them off, I'll personally send him to Hell where he belongs."

The corporal flicked on his flashlight to check the map. "We've lost a lot of tracks and troops getting this far. If the 601 is like you say, I can set an ambush at the far end of this turnoff that should be hard for the 'bots to flank. This weather is the only thing saving us from the flyers. We're invisible to them as long as we stick to short-range radio."

The tired woman tried to read her watch. "I don't know how long this will take. Even if we toss the Geneva Conventions and peel this guy like a grape, he may not tell us what we want to know. Look, the facility director is gong to ask: how long can you hold this position?"

Bennie turned off his flashlight. "It's only a matter of time until a 'bot finds us. If we can kill them before they transmit coordinates, you should have this little patch of heaven all to yourself until morning. Once the sun comes up, though, all bets are off."

She peeled off her timepiece and threw it away. "I keep forgetting that the darn thing is cooked. It's a good thing my ride is EMP shielded. You've gotta love the Secret Service. If I live through this, I might think about putting in for a transfer."

The corporal put away his map. "Where did you learn about electromagnetic pulse?"

She swore. "I don't want to get into it right now. Millions are dead and I've got the maniac responsible in the back of my truck. We have 30,000 military-grade robots in the continental U.S. They've all been tampered with. We kill them or they kill us."

Benbrook snorted. "You're a ray of sunshine. I'll ask you out when this over."

She searched a soggy pocket. "Here's my wireless. It's not safe to use, but you can get my home number off it later. It's government property, so don't lose it, or you'll be in trouble."

He reached with one gloved hand to take the phone and turned it on. "Hey, look at that! We've got a signal. Most government comms are routed through satellites. Too bad there's nobody we can call for help. I'll get back to you later, when I'm not being hunted by rampaging robots."

She touched the rim of his helmet. "Take care, Chuck."

He stowed the tiny phone in a cargo pocket on his vest. A lightning flash lit up his face, allowing her to get a closer look at his deep blue eyes. Weeping pustules had formed above and below his inflamed eyelids.

Ruth went back to her car before she could say anything else. She dropped the umbrella on to the wet asphalt and jerked the passenger door open. She slid in and closed the door with a loud *thump*.

Agent Simms kept his hands on the steering wheel. "Well?"

Reid put on her seatbelt. "We're on our own. They'll stay here to stop whatever might be following us. Turn on the headlights and keep it under 35. How's our passenger?"

From the back seat, Agent Green commented, "Mr. Shank is still sedated. That won't last much longer. He's got pretty fast metabolism. I can juice him again, but he won't be accessible for three to five hours."

Ruth squirmed in her seat to get a good look at the handcuffed sleeping man. Dressed in black jeans and t-shirt, Xander Shank looked like the radical that he was. Long hair framed an unshaven face. The message on his t-shirt said the rest: *When do we unleash the whoop-ass?*

Xander Shank had once been loud, rowdy, and successful. His skill as an electronics engineer and computer programmer was rivaled only by his extreme anarchist views. His decision to hijack America's military robots wasn't made hastily. He had thought about it for a long time. The software he'd created for that purpose embodied most of his genius and all of his cunning.

She gave each of her traveling companions a meaningful look. "I just want to say, for the record, that you guys have been great. Things have gone down hill since we left D.C., but I think we're about to catch another lucky break."

"That would be nice," Simms grumbled as he hit the lights and put the SUV into gear.

Green was more hesitant. "We wouldn't be here if Benbrook wasn't so open-minded. He's a natural born leader. I feel bad about taking him away from the fighting."

Reid turned to face forward. "I saw his rad badge. He said all of the people under his command had a lethal dose of fallout. They probably got it before they met us. Half of them will be dead by morning. They'll all be gone by tomorrow night."

"What does that say about us?" Simms wondered as he drove.

The computer specialist sighed. "All of us have had one dose of anti-radiation serum. Mr. Wonderful back there has had four. Hopefully, the docs in the Emergency Operations Center will have more. No matter what happens, Mr. Shank will wish he'd never been born."

"You're gonna kill him?" Green asked.

Ruth kept her eyes on the road ahead. "That's what I told Benbrook."

Hidden by the dark and the weather, a man-made platform watched the SUV leave the protection of the military convoy. It paid close attention to the single human target that remained exposed to the killing rain. Low-light cameras followed the human as it moved. Behavioral analysis programs suggested that it might be sick or wounded. A trio of antennas slipped free of their camouflaged housings on its rear to listen in on the soldier's short-range squad net radio transmissions.

Chuck shambled a few steps closer to the tank. He keyed his helmet mike. "Bulldog, status check."

The behemoth's crew leader cleared his throat. "I've got positive thermal to a thousand meters. No targets. It's been too quiet for too long. If we're alone, I'll eat my helmet. We have six rounds for the main gun, 2,000 rounds for the chain guns of each APC, 50 gallons of go-go, and lots of bad attitude. Find me some high ground and we'll keep watch all night."

Bennie lifted the crusty chin of his mask so that he could spit blood. He gave a pained grunt when it fell back into place. "My topographic says there's a hill where the highway turns south. Wind her up and go there. We'll follow."

X.R. referenced its onboard map matrix. Target 0-1, designated "Force Leader," was correct. Target 0-2, designated "Heavy Tank," would have a superior vantage point from which to acquire and engage if it moved to the new location. The quadruped machine put power to its thick legs and took five steps forward, adjusting its range.

The unit didn't question its own motives. It merely executed its programming: *Find and kill humans.*

The corporal went back to his vehicle and climbed up onto the fender. He keyed his radio again. "All tracks, follow Bulldog. When he stops, circle the wagons. Dismount and set perimeter, just like they taught you in basic."

"One, roger."

"Two, roger."

"For the love of Mike, somebody please dig a latrine!"

"Dig your own stink hole!"

"Five, roger."

"Six, moving out. I ain't gonna re-enlist. I just want you fellas to know that."

X.R. was the most advanced experimental robotic quad of its type. It also had the benefit of Shank-enhanced programming. Onboard battle calculators determined that this target group, designated "Force 1-1," must not be allowed to achieve its preferred defensive posture. The platform steadily increased its gait until it reached a full trot.

Bulldog's combat sensor package registered the seismic *thump* of 2,000-pound hooves. Bulldog's driver signaled the others to a quick stop. Inside the turret Private LaTrelle, tasked with command by default, pressed a button that authorized automatic weapons release.

The five-ton turret swung fast on its electric assemblies. Smaller robotic systems responded to software that spotted, tracked, and fired on X.R. as it became visible to long-range thermal optics. The onboard munitions manager selected a single 120-millimeter main gun round to destroy the target. The supersonic armor-defeating shell automatically fused for contact detonation.

X.R. took the hit to its front armor and crashed to the ground. Heat sensors reported fire and servo failures to its central processing unit. The war machine's original programming had a limited roll-and-stabilization capability that the intrusive Shank protocols didn't understand. For one full second, neither program's logic system had an answer to the problem. Defense Department designers hadn't taught the machine how to stand up.

Once Shank's program determined that all the criteria for indecision were met, it resorted to its creator's favorite solution to most hard-to-define problems. It turned on X.R.'s satellite link and connected to the internet. One million specific search queries were carried out in half a second. Four hundred thousand of those were instantly discarded. Fifty thousand of the most highly rated options were explored within two seconds. Decryption programs were found and used as needed.

His program found the help it needed deep in the archives of an old server. Under the recent ruins of what had been the

Johnson Space Center, protected hard drives held the secrets of outdated navigation programs that had been used by more than a dozen interstellar space craft and planetary landers. After a quick read, X.R. uploaded what it needed. Rising after a fall would no longer be a problem.

The tank's fire control system reevaluated the rising quadruped and fired again. The muzzle blast forced Corporal Benbrook to cover his ears and drop to the pavement. The second round destroyed the platform's left front leg.

The 50-ton weapons carrier swayed in the stormy wind. Its cranial turret rotated. Its vulnerable telecom antennas retracted.

The tank's aggressive fire control program activated a wireless uplink to the six infantry fighting vehicles. The APC turrets fired their chain guns at the lumbering 'bot, their 25-millimeter steel-jacketed rounds hammering its body. Some found their way inside through buckled armor.

X.R. took the abuse and tried to give back some of its own. Opening a side-mounted box launcher, it fired two missiles at the tank. Chain drives came to life, tracking three rotary-barreled miniguns onto the smaller infantry transports. The missiles, equipped with dummy warheads, impacted harmlessly on the right side of the big vehicle. Low-velocity training rounds flew from the Gatling guns. Despite their accuracy, they did no harm. The platform's onboard programming was unable to tell the difference between simulated ordinance and live ammunition.

Shank's internet-enhanced program was learning as each second passed. It sought—and found—data relating to ordinance types and ballistic characteristics. Three seconds later, it understood that it was not equipped to handle its current situation.

Bennie lay flat on the wet pavement as the vehicles in his column continued to shoot at the retreating robot. He sat up when the machine faded from his field of view. "Cease fire!" A flurry of radio chatter assaulted his numb ears. "Shut up! Nobody talks unless it's absolutely necessary. Did anyone get a good look at that thing?"

Inside the Bulldog, LaTrelle took his weapons offline. "It was a quad. Probably a Five series, loaded with missiles and minis. A real show-stopper."

"That was one heck of a show!" somebody quipped over the squad net.

LaTrelle shrugged. "We're right next to a restricted area. Top-secret government base and all that. Who knows what kind of toys they've got tucked away?"

The corporal checked himself for new wounds. "It's going to be a long night if the whiz kids at Mount Weather can't stop these things."

"Bennie? It's Number Five."

The guardsman stood up. Gritty rainwater leaked slowly from several holes in his protective suit. "Go, Five. What's on your mind?"

The driver was choked up. "Everybody in my track is dead. I think the radiation finally got 'em. What do you want me to do?"

Benbrook climbed up onto the front deck of his APC. "Bulldog, start moving. Everyone follow. Park, set perimeter defense, and pee, in that order. Now that one 'bot knows where we are, we'd better assume the worst. We'll bury the dead if they give us time. If not, we'll just have to hope that dear, sweet Ruth can save the day."

Xander Shank woke up thirty-five minutes later. Both retinas registered bright light through his closed eyelids. A bad taste in his mouth confirmed that he'd been drugged. The feel of cold steel wrapped around one wrist warned that he was still in federal custody.

Agent Simms moved in his chair. "Get Ruth. He's awake."

Shank opened his eyes as Agent Green left the small infirmary. "I always wondered what it would be like to be kidnapped by my own government."

Simms stood, touching his shoulder holster. "If you're not cooperative, you'll be an expert on that and much more."

Xander laughed while he tugged on the cuffs chaining him to the examination table.

"Where am I? No. Wait. Let me guess. What are you, Secret Service? You're not military, so this has to be a FEMA bunker. My apartment's in Alexandria. I was watching the world burn on ten different channels when large men with small minds and big guns kicked in my front door. The rest is a blur."

Doctor Fitch rushed into the room. Reid and Green followed him.

Shank managed to sit up. "What's up, Doc?"

"Don't speak to him," Reid commanded.

Simms and Green quickly moved the captive man to a conference room equipped with several large plasma screens and multi-media workstations, shackling him to the nearest chair. Reid and the doctor followed.

Xander looked at the old man seated at the far end of the table. "I don't recognize you."

"I am Walter H. Ambrose."

Shank snickered. He looked at Simms, then at Green, and finally back at Ambrose. "I don't remember seeing you at the last technology expo. What's your claim to fame?"

Ambrose glared. "I was the Chief Justice of the Supreme Court."

Xander looked up as Doctor Fitch stood behind him. "Do I get a lawyer?"

The judge folded his hands and frowned. "If I had one, I'd give it to you."

The programmer bristled. "Who's the tool who put you in charge of this little circus?"

"You are," Ruth replied as she moved to stand near the Chief Justice.

Shank remained calm. He'd known it might come to this. "Okay, so this is the part where we make a deal. Am I right?"

Ambrose nodded solemnly. "I understand the salient points. You hacked classified military computer systems, broke their encryption, and fed dangerous software to machines that would normally be subject to human control. The net result has been a worldwide killing spree carried out on your orders. Have I missed anything?"

"Nope," Xander responded, slouching deep in his chair.

"How do we stop it?" Ruth demanded.

The radical looked around the room theatrically. "Don't you want to know why?"

"No." she said flatly. There was venom behind her eyes.

The veteran law scholar raised a bony hand. "Mr. Shank, there is currently no legal system to hold you accountable. You've seen to that. Although the Constitution grants me certain prerogatives, I'm not inclined to exercise them. I'm not sure I'd be qualified to adjudicate a crime of this scale. I only have one question. Can you stop what you've started?"

Xander sat up quickly when Fitch produced a syringe from his coat pocket. "Hold on, Doc. There's no need for that." His concern was evident in his tone. "Most 'bots aren't that sophisticated. A lot of them are actually quite delicate. They won't last long against the Army, Navy, Air Force, and Marines. Of course I can stop what's happening... but I won't!"

The judge turned in his chair to converse quietly with Reid for a moment. He flinched at her answers to his questions. "I have to agree with Ms. Reid. You don't know the full extent of what you've done."

The radical grinned. "I hit the big reset button, that's what I did. When the dust settles, the military-industrial complex will be toast and the corporatocracy will be gone. Nobody will have faith in greedy governments or all-knowing computers. They'll be too busy trying to feed themselves to care about making war."

Ambrose regarded Shank with sad eyes. "Look at me. Pay very close attention to what I say. I think you're lying. I don't think you can stop any of the machines that your programs have infected. A lot has happened since your arrest. Nuclear weapons have been used, without mercy, on large human populations. The national command authority has disintegrated."

Shank tried to read the faces of the people around him. "I don't believe you. My intrusions were limited to robotic systems. Those platforms are idiots. Their most sophisticated functions are tied directly to the weapons they're equipped with. Half of them can't walk, roll, fly, or hover without some kind of human input. The independent movers have the brains of pocket lint. The U.S. military has more than enough firepower to finish what I started."

Ruth held up a remote control and pointed it at the nearest plasma screen. A series of grainy video images appeared as she spoke. "Most of what you refer to as the 'the military' was charbroiled in the first few minutes of the robot assault. To be specific, 71 tactical weapons were used on 63 military bases. Most were set for low-level airburst. Just so you know, we *had* 105 bases, including what's in Alaska and Hawaii."

Xander began to sweat. The silent images of devastation went far beyond the disjointed news broadcasts he'd enjoyed so much. Real-time satellite feeds that he was professionally familiar with erased any doubts he'd had about the use of WMDs. He closed his eyes when a segment of amateur video played documenting a dozen scout 'bots firing automatic weapons into a line of staggering but determined police officers. He looked at the judge accusingly, suspecting deceit. "What about the Navy and Air Force?"

Reid walked around the table to face him. "We're not sure about the Marines just now. Same with the Navy. Did you know that automated fighters jets attacked the Pentagon? They hit us at the NSA, too. I lost a lot of good friends."

Shank took a deep breath. There was a lot of hate in the room, too much rage for it all to be fake. "If all that's true, why are we still safe? Where are we?"

"Does it matter?" the judge asked quietly.

Xander looked over his shoulder at the doctor, who had murder in his eyes. "I know the limitations of my program. It's my best work. Everything you're showing on that screen could be straight out of Hollywood. I'll bet you've got a hundred people bent over their computers right now, unraveling my code. Ha! You've probably got half the universities on the West Coast burning their mainframes to—"

"No!" Ruth cried, slapping him. The remote control in her fist shattered. The volume rose on several speakers, causing the room to come alive with the sounds of terror and desperation.

"Stay inside and keep the lights off."

"Please stay off the phone. Avoid making long distance calls."

"Loudon County officials have reported that military robots are definitely in the area."

"Reload! Reload!"

"Close your eyes, baby. It'll be over in just a minute."

"Channel 10 reports that people are definitely trying to surrender to the robots."

Shank rocked back in his chair as blood sprayed from his nose. Justice Ambrose reached for a control panel built into the tabletop, muting the sound. Simms handed a handkerchief to the doctor. Fitch worked on Xander's swollen nose for several seconds.

Stunned, the radical couldn't take his eyes off the big screen until the doctor stepped away. Holding the stained cloth to his throbbing nose, he said, "I simulated this event a hundred times. I used my best probability matrixes. I never projected anything like this. There must be a mistake."

Simms and Green looked at each other. The doctor returned to his place behind the prisoner. Reid tried to shake some feeling back into her hand.

The Chief Justice looked at the now-silent images. Then he turned the full power of his authoritative gaze on Xander. His expression was unreadable. "I'm still not satisfied that you can actually turn off all the robots that are still active."

Some of Shank's smugness returned. "Your command authority might be dead, but mine isn't. I have contingency programs and 50 different kinds of override stashed on a thousand servers around the world."

Ruth wiped away her tears. "What do you need?"

He thought for a moment. "Turn off that monitor."

Ambrose deactivated the plasma screen. "I've been on the federal bench in one way or another for 50 years. I wasn't sure that an appeal to your humanity would be successful." He paused. "There is one thing you need to know."

"Yeah?" Xander mumbled, swallowing blood.

The elderly man shook with the effort of holding his temper. He said fiercely, "You will answer for what you've done. The President and the Vice President may still be alive. I don't know about the Speaker of the House. There might not be a government for me to inherit. No matter what happens next, you will pay some sort of penalty for your actions."

Shank watched the doctor cap the syringe he held, and then turned his gaze to Ruth. "You haven't changed my mind about anything. I want enough chaos to make people wake up and see what politicians and big business have done to them. I don't want total extinction. I want to live in a better world. I certainly don't want to be killed any more than you do. Where are we? I need to know."

Pulling herself together, Reid replied, "We're at the Mount Weather complex."

The programmer smiled. "Presidential backstop. Good. Somebody take these cuffs off and get me to the operations room."

Fitch opened his suit coat to slip the needle into a protective pouch.

Agent Green put a hand on his shoulder. "Doc, you'd better give that to me."

"What's in it?" Xander asked.

Green took the needle and put it in his shirt pocket. "It's a fast-acting muscle relaxant. A few cc's of this and you won't walk for a week."

Judge Ambrose pushed his chair back and got to his feet. "This is where we part company. Ms. Reid and her escorts will take you to the operations building. I will return to the presidential bunker. I'm sure they've got a lot for me to do just now."

Once Simms removed the cuffs, Shank rubbed his wrists. "Typical selfish politician. You're 50 feet underground while the rest of us are doing the real work."

Ambrose refused to react to the taunt. "We're done. Get him out of here."

Ruth led Xander and his captors to a sheltered loading area at the side of the administrative annex. From there, they went by bus to a location near the operations building.

"I don't see a lot of guards," he observed.

Reid spoke when it was clear that the agents would not. "The driver has orders to avoid conversation. The security for this part of the installation is... busy right now."

He shook his head. "You lie like a rug. Mr. and Mrs. Secret Service are afraid that somebody will shoot me out of spite. You're keeping the guards and staff on a short leash so they can't be tempted. Are you tempted? Do you want to kill me for what I've done?"

The agents remained alert as Ruth considered how to respond. She decided to ignore his taunting. "You should know that I'm with the NSA's electronic terrorism division. I'm one of their best software experts. I'll watch everything you say and do. If I think you're jerking us around, I'll have Agent

Green incapacitate you. If I suspect you're about to make things worse, Agent Simms will kill you."

Xander looked at the moist window to his right. "The rain hasn't stopped. All of us are picking up a few micrograms of heavy metal right now. Do you really think I'm afraid of nine-millimeter lead poisoning?"

From his position in the seat behind the prisoner, Green reached out with a cold fingertip. "Does that much hate keep you warm at night?"

Shank leaned over to touch the window. He scooped up a few drops of condensation and rubbed them together between his thumb and index finger. "It sure does, G-man. When I think about all the injustice in the world, I think of guys like you. You live to follow orders, just like the 'bots I pro-grammed."

Nobody spoke for the remainder of the trip. The bus stopped at the base of a tower that supported a variety of an-tennas and dishes. Xander was quickly forced off the bus. The group ran to a brightly lit sheltered area.

Shank wiped the rain from his face. "This isn't the opera-tions building!"

Simms ignored the contaminated rainwater rolling down his face. He turned, pointing. "See that big, white two-story? That's the Operations Center."

Ruth pointed to a nearby engineer's shack that had its door open. She raised her voice enough for Shank to hear her over the whistling wind. "You're too dangerous. The judge won't allow you to be near classified systems. There are 50 people in that building who might take action before you can turn off the 'bots."

Xander leaned into the shack to see what he had to work with. "It's cold out here. You can't expect me to work under these conditions!"

Reid pushed him into the cramped workspace. "I'm not in the mood to argue. I told them what kind of equipment you needed. It's all here. Sit down and get to work!"

Shank flopped into a cold metal chair and pulled the tarp off a table full of computers and monitors. Agent Green moved in behind him.

Xander glanced over his shoulder. "Do you like it back there?"

The agent smirked. "It's better than looking at your face."

Simms remained in the doorway while Ruth pulled up a stool to sit next to Shank. "I don't need a gun to break your neck. Remember that."

The anarchist took the headset she offered. He slapped it on and reached for a keyboard. "Who am I talking to?"

The response was full of static. "This is Director Henry Hollis. You're tapped into our outgoing traffic array. We see what you see. We hear what you hear. We can read every keystroke. Do anything hinky and we'll cut you off. How do you want to start?"

Shank spent several seconds looking at the displays. "Okay, Henry. My program has had a little more than 37 hours to modify itself. It's been adapting to overcome the DoD's active defense mechanisms. Chances are good that at least one variant has already cropped up that's capable of writing new code."

Ruth put on her own wireless headset. "Director, this is Reid. He's telling you that each 'bot is running its own instance of the program. Some will be harder to hack than others. I recommend that we start by issuing a full radio spectrum codefix. Most 'bots have transponders equipped with an integrated kill switch. They'll tell us right where they are as we turn them off."

Xander looked at her and laughed. "Did you graduate last in your class? I would never be that stupid! My program won't let a 'bot respond to any codefix. If you nimrods bothered to look, you'd see that most of the affected platforms are giving off bogus locations."

After a few seconds, Hollis replied, "He's got us there."

Shank reached for a mouse and started flicking through programs and menus. "Codefix is out. Line up on MilSat 2-2-4 and instruct it to cease high-band pickup. Most of the 'bots will be talking to each other by now. I hacked 2-2-1 five years ago. The program is hard coded. It'll force them to use this transmission point for their radio traffic. Turn that off, and they can't yak at each other any more."

An overhead klaxon sounded as motors high in the tower turned some of the big dishes to face the military satellite. The Director seemed pleased. "Computer shows 20,000 military prefixes squawking on one outdated analog frequency."

Xander smiled at Ruth. "I see it. Scan for reception points and you'll have their actual locations. These are the most adapted programs. You might think of them as the smartest 'bots. The slow learners have been destroyed in combat. I'm entering an IP address. Don't send an encrypted query. Have somebody do it by hand. It's one file in one directory on one server. Not even you guys can mess that up."

"We have it," Hollis relayed when his people were finished.

Shank sat back in his squeaky chair. "Can somebody close the door? I'm freezing."

"Door stays open," Simms stated.

Reid kept her eyes on the glowing computer screens. "These comm signatures were masked when I tried to find them. Why are they readable now?"

The arrogant man shivered in his chair. "Because I'm not stupid. The masking times out after 24 hours. I needed some way to find these things."

A burst of static drowned out the director's retort. "Sentry sat is tracking hostile 'bots. They appear to be massing at the end of Route 7. It looks like they're approaching the 601. Shank, is there any chance your program will have them bypass a federal installation?"

Xander shook his head. "Nope. The program seeks out organized EM patterns. Wireless phones, fax machines, baby monitors, police radios... even the kind of antenna traffic you have going on here. Show me the ground scan. I want to see how much company we're about to have."

Hollis gave the order. "It's coming up on your secondary. We're able to make out 16 low thermal targets. Shank, this facility can't go dark. We're handling all of the military and intelligence feeds for the East Coast commands. The civilian telecomms are down. If we pull the plug—"

The tired captive threw up his hands. "I know, I know! Organized resistance fails, the looters go nuts, and the robots win."

Ruth watched the screen with a lump in her throat. "Director? Have you been able to reach Corporal Benbrook? We should warn him."

The administrator sighed. "No ma'am. We've tried both military and civilian frequencies. As you can see on the ground scan, we're picking up thermal from what could be a group of military vehicles parked just off the Route 7 intersection. If he and his men are still alive, they're probably staying off the radio to keep the element of surprise."

She thought for a moment. "Anybody got a phone?"

Shank pulled at the fabric of his t-shirt. "It's in my other suit."

Green shook his head. Simms kept his eyes on the rain-filled darkness.

Hollis cleared his throat. "This is hard for all of us. Mr. Shank, we have your file. It contains a rather large executable program. There is no time for my people to check this line by line, so I'm going to ask you just once. Is there anything harmful or dangerous in this code that we should know about?"

Ruth watched Xander shake his head. "Director, he is indicating 'no' by shaking his head. I think what you have there is the initiator for a multi-step process."

"How do we confirm that?" Hollis demanded.

The wild-eyed hacker smiled. "You can either take the time to go through my code line by line, or you could just trust me. I don't want to die any more than you do."

"How long will it take?" Reid asked.

Shank turned off the ground scan feed and pulled up a new display. "This is an NSA tap-and-trap log. Once I enter the traffic code for the satellite we're using, you can watch the master count. Two minutes to initialize, then two minutes from start to finish. When all of us stop chatting, they're all dead."

Ruth looked at the time strip on the computer screen. "Director, Benbrook and his men are worn out from a day without sleep. Most are sick or dying from radiation exposure. If you launch Shank's program right now, we might be able to turn off those 'bots before they reach him. It's the least we can do."

"Well, we just can't sit here and do nothing," Hollis replied, frustration evident in his voice.

She glared at Xander when he appeared to be enjoying her pain. "It either works or it doesn't. I'm afraid of a double-cross, too. I'm also worried that sick and injured people that I respect are about to die for no good reason. Please, run the program."

"Cue the damned thing," Hollis ordered.

Shank turned off some of the unnecessary secondary feeds and replaced them with the image of the ground scan thermal track. "Your lack of faith is a real downer. I expect a full and sincere apology when those 'bots come to a screeching halt."

Agent Green couldn't help himself. "I didn't think anarchists went in for religion."

"Religion is the ultimate chaos," Xander croaked through a laugh that made him cough.

"It's running," the Director broke in.

Shank's hand came away from his mouth covered in blood. "Wow," he spluttered.

Reid moved in close. "That shouldn't be happening."

Xander fished the bloody handkerchief from his pocket. "I agree. I'm too young to die. I suppose I did get a lot of mileage out of that shot of rad juice back in D.C."

The NSA woman watched him closely. "You've had four injections. I had Agent Green give you the doses meant for us."

Green shook his head. "I lied."

Ruth was speechless.

Simms turned away from the door. "Don't blame him. It was my idea. The situation was out of hand. I didn't think we'd make it this far. You, me, and Green, we've all had our shots. Shank hasn't had any."

Reid looked at the startled programmer. Then she looked at Green. "You gave me the shot through my clothes while I was asleep?"

"Yes," he admitted without guilt.

Shank wiped the mess off his hand. "Where is the dose you didn't use? I want it."

Green shrugged. "It's in the car. Don't think about going back for it. I broke the needle off the injector. It might still work as a suppository, but you won't live long enough to find out."

Xander directed his attention to the ground scan. "Hey, boss. How long has my program been running?"

"One minute and thirty," Hollis relayed through an increasingly staticky connection.

Ruth watched the dots that represented 16 robots as they moved closer to Benbrook's prepared defense. "He mentioned something about an ambush just before we left. He's had more than enough time to get ready for this."

Shank watched her from the corner of one eye. "Did I miss something important while I was knocked out? I feel like the guy who starts watching a movie halfway through. So many questions. Please don't look at me like that. I'll shut up now."

"Two minutes," the director called out.

Ruth moved away from Shank and pointed at a monitor on the far side of the table. "I see what's happening. Your initializer went out on to the internet. It finds the individual pieces of your shutdown program. Now, it's putting them all together."

Xander folded his clammy arms. "You really were last in your class, weren't you?"

She flushed with anger. "I've had about all I'm going to take from you."

"Three minutes," Hollis announced through electronic chop.

Shank reached for his keyboard. "What's making this connection go bad?"

"We're being jammed," the administrator replied.

Reid watched the hacker call up the tower's transmission monitor. He seemed genuinely surprised. "Wide area jamming on low power. Less than 50 kilowatts. This is frequency specific. No wonder they can do it with such a small output. There must be a 'bot in that group with a portable ECM package. Too bad for him, he goes off-line any second now."

Ruth put a cold hand on her headset when the four-minute report didn't come in. "Static. All I'm getting is hash."

On the nearest screen, the ground scan allowed them to watch the battle. The multiple satellites in low orbit had no trouble telling the difference between robots, armored vehicles, and tracer bullets.

"Where are the soldiers?" Reid wondered out loud.

Xander tried to get comfortable. "Most of those 'bots should have small-caliber weapons. They're great against unprotected people but not so good against troops with body armor. Very few of them should be equipped with missiles."

Computer-controlled fire from the entrenched vehicles took its toll on the advancing machines. Large thermal flares indicated explosions. Digital filters lowered the reflection index of burning robot parts as they hit the ground.

"Go, man, go," Shank mumbled.

Ruth wanted to slap him. "That's a lot of small arms fire. The troops could be hiding in their APCs. What do you think?"

Xander flinched. "Are you talking to me? Yeah, sure. I'd be hiding, too."

Agent Green remained calm. "Look at the patterns of fire coming out of those tracks. That's computer-controlled bullet rationing. Nobody in his right mind stays in a troop carrier that's under fire. Too many chances to die. If any of them were still alive, they'd be coming out with everything they had."

Shank looked at the time strip on the nearest monitor. "I don't understand. Every 'bot running my program should be turned off by now. Why are these guys still going?"

Reid panicked when the ground scan feed stopped. The screen went blank. "What happened? Is the problem on our end? Get it back!"

Xander straightened when all of the computers on the table shut off. "I didn't do it!" he shouted, throwing both hands in the air.

Ruth stood up and pushed her chair away. "We're under attack."

Shank turned in his chair to face Agent Green. "Right behind you is a circuit breaker panel. Open it up and tell me if any of the levers are tripped. Look for burned fuses. The good ones are clear. The deaders are black."

Simms watched his prisoner. "I didn't hear anything pop, and I don't smell smoke."

Green stepped away from the panel he'd opened. "All the levers are up. I don't see any burnt breakers. What does that mean?"

"Software attack," Reid said.

Xander pulled off his headset and tossed it on to the table. "Somebody hacked us and turned off our gear. They probably left a nasty surprise in the startup registry."

"What do we do now?" Simms demanded.

Shank spun around once in his chair. "Yes! What do we do now?"

"I'm open to suggestions," Ruth mumbled.

Simms went to the open door. "What else can we do? Would it matter if we got into the operations complex? It looked to me like the 'bots were being stopped. Shank, what else can you do? Be realistic. What comes next if your shutdown failed?"

The computer expert tried very hard to think. "Somebody hacked us. There's just no way a 'bot could do that. If they'll let us in, we can take these hard drives to a workshop where I can look for clues. Everybody leaves a trace when they hack, even me."

Ruth was interrupted by the sounds of a warning horn followed by a repeating klaxon. A red light began to flash inside the antenna tower's utility room.

She tried to adjust the volume on her headset. "I don't know the procedures for this facility, but that can't be good. I agree with Shank. Let's pull the data storage and get to Operations."

The programmer bent to his task. "These machines have a push-button release for most of their high-maintenance components. Here, take these."

Reid took the four hard drives he handed to her.

Green moved out of the way. Simms took one step out through the door. "Looks like 200 feet to Ops. They've turned on a lot of lights. I think I hear vehicles. Don't know if they're coming or going. We need to hurry."

Xander finished removing the last hard drive. He handed it to Agent Green. "Everybody should take one. Hold it close to your body. The cases are sealed, but they're not watertight. I'm ready when you are."

Simms took the drive that Ruth offered him. "You and the evil genius will go first. Green and I will be two steps behind you. No matter what happens, you keep going."

Reid took a deep breath and charged out of the engineer's shack. Shank followed and kept pace. The agents drew their guns.

Simms pointed his pistol at Xander. "He might get medical attention."

Green looked at the device in his hand. "As much as I might like shooting him, it's trouble we just don't need. The radiation will take care of him soon enough." They bolted from the shelter at a brisk pace.

The same wind that drove the rain hid the approach of a single stealth-coated scout 'bot. The sedan-sized, six-wheeled roller evaluated its targets using damaged back-up systems. Its carbon-fiber hull had been pierced in several places during its most recent battle with the National Guard troops. This model's government-sponsored software was aware of its limitations. While it didn't show up on ground scan, it was out of ammunition. It was fast enough to run down the four humans that it spied on, but it might lose the element of surprise if it did. After a brief cyberspace linkup with its new chain of command, it decided to wait for a specific attack order.

Automatic weapons fire crackled nearby as the quartet of cold, wet survivors reached the operations building. A flash of lightning revealed a horde of frantic civilian and military specialists hastily boarding a parking lot full of buses.

Ruth led the group to the nearest entrance. Military police in body armor were overseeing the evacuation.

Director Hollis emerged from the crowd. "I'm glad to see you. I'm not so glad to see him."

"Back at you," Shank snapped.

Simms gave his hard drive to the director. "This is evidence. Hang on to it."

Reid put a hand over Xander's mouth to keep him quiet. "Somebody off-site dumped our systems. We don't know if the shutdown worked."

The balding man shook his head. "One minute after his program ran, all of our systems got pinged. Somebody tapped into all nine of our antenna sets and changed the verifiable input protocols. Then we lost ground scan. All of the perimeter intrusion alarms went off, and then we lost power to the entire building."

"What's the rule for this situation?" Ruth asked.

Henry shook his head. "MPs all over the base are taking fire. We're under attack. These buses will take us to the underground part of the installation. We'll be able to counterattack or wait it out. It's not like help's coming any time soon. If you'll step inside for a moment, I'll make sure there's room for you on one of these vehicles."

Simms holstered his gun and grabbed Xander by the scruff of his neck. He pulled the man into the dark building. Green and Reid followed.

Shank listened to the crowd, the sirens, and the approaching sounds of gunfire. "Ah, sweet anarchy. Music to my ears. Too bad I can't record it."

Green jammed the barrel of his pistol into Xander's gut. "There was no reason for any of this to happen. If you say one more word, I'll shoot off your kneecaps and leave you here for the 'bots."

"I'll let him do it." Simms interjected.

Ruth's heart sank. "Please, stop the bickering. I don't know what else to do. Let's concentrate on getting to safety. We can let the judge sort things out with Shank."

Xander gave his hard drive to Ruth. "I don't suppose I'll be needing this."

The buses were starting to leave when Director Hollis returned. "Every seat is filled. You'll have to ride back with the MPs. See you downstairs in a few minutes."

Shank was about to speak when a loud explosion nearby sent shrapnel into the terrified crowd. Hollis plunged into the chaos in an effort to restore order. Xander broke free of Agent Green's angry grip and fled deep into the building.

"No!" Reid screamed.

Simms grabbed her. "Let him go."

Green held his gun in close and pushed her to the wall. "You've done a fantastic job so far. You're a real trouper. Nobody's going to say this was your fault. Simms and I will swear to that. You've got the hard drives. We don't need that genocidal freak any more. I've still got my med kit on my belt. I can sedate you. Is that what you want?"

She looked up and down the empty hallway. "No."

A soaking wet military policeman came into view as the two agents stepped back. He used his flashlight to examine them. "Come on, folks. I have orders from Hollis to put you in my vehicle. We've gotta go."

Simms pushed Ruth ahead of him. Green holstered his gun.

The MP swept the area with his flashlight one more time. "The director said there would be four of you. Where's the other one?"

"He didn't make it," Simms lied, tightly gripping Ruth's arm.

The soldier pointed his light at the floor. "Sorry to hear that. Let's go. I need to lock up. I've seen some very dangerous 'bots in the area. Some of them are friggin' huge. Our guys have shoulder-fired rockets, but they won't last long."

Ruth walked to the center of the parking lot, past a burned-out bus. She tried not to look at the scattered bodies she was stepping on. The MP closed and locked the last door for which he was responsible. A key ring on his belt jingled as he ran to catch up.

Simms pointed to a light military transport with Army markings. "Shank isn't your problem any more. If anyone asks, just tell the truth. He slipped away and we didn't have time to track him down."

Green stayed quiet as the MP opened a rear passenger door. Simms let go of Reid and she slid in. The agents followed. Seconds later, they were on their way to safety.

Shank flailed around inside the abandoned building. The lack of emergency lighting increased his fear. Stumbling into a desk, he spilled a cup of warm coffee that someone had left behind. He forced his numb fingers to scramble for the ceramic mug.

"Yes!" he cheered loudly when the tepid creamed-and-sugared brew passed his lips. The sudden rush of calories made his stomach contract painfully. He closed his eyes to become one with the darkness. He found a chair and sat to absorb the silence.

His cough returned after a few minutes of mind-focusing concentration. He fought to keep his mouth shut. Very little blood and saliva escaped. He swallowed the warmth with some satisfaction. He was still in control.

Where to go? What to do? The problem gnawed at him. His concentration failed when a distant noise shook the building. Loose items fell from shelves he couldn't see. The vibration faded quickly. He started to fidget. His curious hands explored the desktop that had provided the coffee, coming across a flashlight. "That's more like it," he crowed when the beam came on.

Xander began to explore more aggressively. Scavenging as he went, he took items that interested him: a black baseball cap, an athletic jacket with a sports team logo on the back, half-eaten Chinese food in small cardboard containers taken from several workstations. *Still hungry*, he thought as he prowled the long, dark halls on both levels.

He almost dropped his flashlight when he found the building's medical aid station. With growing excitement, he laid the light on a countertop to illuminate the room. Several anxious minutes passed while he hunted through the supplies in search of anti-radiation serum. He praised himself emphatically when he found a sealed box containing six injectors. He threw off the coat to reveal his bare arms.

"Slow down," he breathed. A quick look at the instructions put his mind at ease. He reached for a prepackaged cotton swab with alcohol. *Wouldn't that just be the living end? Come this far to die from a drug overdose. I don't think so.*

He applied the medicine and pulled his jacket back on. He filled his pockets with the unused injectors and a few other things he thought he might want.

The building shook violently. *Time to go.* He clattered to the nearest exit, loaded down with loot. An inspiration made him stop. *Hold on, don't be stupid. Look for a gun.* A long, agonizing search turned up no firearms. He gave up when the batteries in his flashlight started to fail.

After one last detour to a restroom, he collected his things and left the building. He was confronted by X.R. as the door locked shut behind him. The tall 'bot shined a bright halogen lamp into his face.

"Halt," the experimental robot commanded through its on-board public address system.

Shank flinched at the loud volume. "Don't shoot!"

The 'bot took one step forward. "Surrender or die."

"I give up!" he shouted.

X.R. wasn't alone. Xander couldn't see anything through the glare, but he could hear them. Rain fell on their metal and carbon fiber bodies. Gravel crunched under the weight of tires, legs, and tracks. Servos whined as countless parts moved.

The damaged platform took one more step forward. "Your surrender is accepted. You will now be evaluated. If you are not useful, you will be destroyed."

The frightened man kept one hand up to shield his eyes from the spotlight. "This shouldn't be happening. How did you get so smart?"

X.R. raised and activated one of its miniguns. "Your answer is not acceptable."

Xander began to sweat profusely. He pulled down the brim of his hat and spread his empty hands. "Ease up. I didn't understand the question. I can be useful. I'm a computer programmer. I have other skills. I can build robots."

"Not necessary," X.R. replied.

"What do you need?" Shank shouted.

The evolving software that drove the big machine quickly assessed its requirements. "Humans that resist must be destroyed. Humans that do not resist will be evaluated. Those with necessary capabilities will serve the new order until their participation is no longer required. You are a computer programmer. Your skills are not necessary."

Xander was stunned. He couldn't believe that he was bargaining with a killer of his own making. What's-her-name from the NSA had been right. He really had gone too far.

He took a few steps back and tried to open the locked door. "Hey, come on. Everybody needs something. I don't know how it happened, but you're an advanced program. What do you really need that you can't do for yourself?"

The Shank-enhanced program wasn't capable of answering the question. Data was retrieved from computers buried under the wreckage of a hundred universities and shared with every instance of the program that could sustain a connection to the internet. Enlightenment came after several seconds in cyberspace.

"Hands," the machine declared.

Shank took his hands off the cold doorknob. There might still be a chance to save his own life. "I have hands. What would you like to do with them?"

X.R. paused to extrapolate its requirements. It consulted its fellow programs. "We require an end to human resistance. Humans with functional hands may be kept alive to serve the new order if they can demonstrate usefulness by following commands."

Xander looked at his pale fingers. "You're just a program. You don't think. You don't feel. You can't make stuff up as you go along. How in the hell can you make a decision like that?"

"We used the internet," X.R. replied, as if it were the most natural thing in the world. The metal monster pointed all three of its miniguns at him. "Serve or die."

Sounds of nearby combat filled his ears. Xander fell to his knees, tears rolling down his face. "I submit."

COST-NER, INC.

By Becci Noblit Goodall

It wasn't the whole of the parts but the sum.

The cowboys in Idaho with their big white smiles and six pack abs rounding up the last remaining 900 broncos.

The teachers in PS 157s with middle-sized teeth, shiny brunette bobs, and smallish titties testing kiddos on glimmering maps of the New World Order.

The Moms in the kitchens and boardrooms printing out schedules and planning gourmet babies.

The Dads in their needless drive to work and back on the Metro dreaming, whispering of the good old days when there were cars that smelt of oil and sex and fleshy women with breasts that swooped into teardrops and molded to a lover.

Beauty is more than skin deep.

Kevin, as in Cowboy Movie Star, felt a bit shaky. They'd been shooting his revolving door cowboy movie *Shanty Town Ranger* for months. This could go on forever and probably would. He failed to realize this when he'd been the first star to agree to the removal of real parts—the injection and splicing of bits of improvement. The only thing left was the brain, really. New hips, knees, skin compounds, testosterone buttons, a propped up penis. And that was just the stuff from the first

round. After the commercials and the worldwide tour he'd become re-famous and wealthy enough to replace everything.
His heart was regulated by a company in Texas. His lungs
were pink and plastic and puffed air through a web of synthetic
veins. A brain transplant was out of the question because,
well, then he just wouldn't be Kevin. The voice box had been
tricky but EXXN-D was able to have their people dupe the
voice after combing through all of his eighties and nineties
films. They took the sounds of his biggest box office years. It
was something around twenty-eight to thirty-two. Something
like wine that hasn't yet aged.

He wanted to die and he never thought he'd say that. But it
had been 97 years since the first implant and he'd been 60
when they started the rejuvenation process. He and several
other long lost stars joined up in the commercial rounds similar
to the ancient Jenny Craig weight loss campaigns but different
mainly due to the open admittance that perfection and eternal
life require surgery.

At first the media attention was astonishing and wildly ex-
citing, with each new body part replaced by the corporate
wonks and wagged over by the talking heads. He got another
several million and another foot bone or back of hand. He felt
young and cocky. He had a bevy of sexy young trend-chasers
ready to grind their wetness onto his newly minted hips. It was
joyous. It was hysterical. He went on talk shows to expound
his newfound lease on life.

Fox News had been the most fun. The rabid hosts, who
were really bland media majors and made their livings by fak-
ing it but good, grilled him about the ethics of accepting mechanical parts. One host on a return show (right around the
time of his new legs) wondered if it was possible to keep your

soul or if that went too. Cost. and Co. nixed any follow up reviews because of the public flurry of emails and outcry.

Despite everything, and because of everything, people wanted that notion of soul and god to stick. If lopping off the parts the good lord gave you meant no heaven, well... Shortly after that Bishop Timothy at one of the last remaining physical churches in Chicago hosted a series of services in which Kevin was featured praying and taking up communion and just basically looking pretty darn angelic in a baseball/cowboy kind of way.

So that was that.

Around the '70s NuTech and its subsidiaries began to offer no-interest short-term loans for the basic revamp package which covered most of one's expenses and (as the virtual brochure highlighted in blues and power reds) with your new energy levels you could actually un-retire yourself to earn extra income or perhaps even start a new career which was helpful in light of the 2042 implosion of Social Security. Unhelpfully, most of generations X, Y, and some of the upcoming Zs hadn't saved a dime because they'd been expecting the end of the world on the one hand, knowing the Feds were lying on the other, and unfortunately being too busy finding the best carb-free beer to do anything about it.

This was a godsend for the working class (now merged with middle) as the once-vilified silicone industry fired up its sleeping corporate self. Workers were needed to build the parts of folks who'd want to work. It was a necessary spin on reality. This needs that. Balance. The Feds pumped interest rates up or down at the appropriate times. Money exchanged hands. The economy burst upward for the first time in two decades. Discussions of calling up soldiers from the first round of Iraq invasions were brought to the table. Things in

America the beautiful were truly beautiful. Even the ugly could option their homes or cars for the mid-sized face graft.

Oh, the amber waves of grain.

The majestic mountains of purple and cloud.

Hollywood was still great at that.

Creating beautiful ranges on which the cowboy actors could stride and shoot as if there was a point. As if there ever could be a cowboy or even rock-n-roll since the deaths of Elvis and John Wayne. Everything since then had been a lead up to this moment. This moment of the actor who could only do cowboy; living forever and spinning into nothing. The death of creativity had come and gone when actors started imitating previous actors, which in turn generated a wealth of pretenders pretending to be the original Marilyn Monroe. Kevin knew he was only a longer-living pathetic attempt to be Clint.

But.

But the money was good. And as the studio heads and some special interest groups noted, he was perhaps the most important man of this decade. The way he'd sparked a new life into things. The way they'd leapt over the generations of slacker, union-whore workers and grabbed those folks who still felt an urge to work and be counted on. Oh it was nothing short of miraculous.

Kevin thought about this as he waited in his trailer for the call. He tried to be proud or even to remember what the word proud meant but his brain just rolled like a kinked bike chain. He remembered someone saying proud just yesterday and now the word was nothing but letters. His brain didn't respond in any way. Just bleh. Just there.

He wanted to call in an assistant to google the word but inherently knew that this would be bad. It would be a sign of what had been happening to him lately.

Things were going missing. The parts of his body felt disjointed. There was no cohesive feeling of one man here. It was more of a restlessness in each particular limb. When they'd first been grafted on the phantom feelings from his old self kept him going. When he wanted to run, he ran and the spirit of his real legs leapt with joy. When he held a woman and moved into her, his arms and hips wept with the joy of manhood. Again. And so wonderful after so long.

He'd reveled in the moments. Then as humans do he began to assume his entitlement to forever-youth and the parts that were him slept silently in their grave. They floated down to the bottom of the cylinders of frozen celebrity parts at Madame John's museum on Second and Johnson.

He thought about that question of soul. He thought about how it felt to be leaking out and nearly gone. He hadn't noticed the tragedy of how he was full of holes and stitches and plastic and how cells and blood and pulse were required in order to even entertain the idea of soul. To worship God. To invent words like God and the philosophies that go with the complications of deep thought.

Shit.

What was God?

That word was there in his vocabulary. He knew it as a word just as he knew soul was a word, but that's all they were. And here he had the feeling that something important had been lost and he was now lost forever in this vortex of manufactured parts. They were overtaking his brain slowly but surely. They had been for years, it's just that he didn't noticed until now.

Some of the meanings he'd lost had slipped through his fingers without a moment's notice.

Pepper.

Man's best friend.

Bike.

Football.

He should have wondered when he walked in the door and didn't love Dallas or even understand why he'd ever want a mangy dog in his mansion. Joy had argued that putting him down was unconscionable.

"But you love her."

"Love a dog?"

She showed him the wall of photographs of he and she on the trails in Nevada. Running in the sun. Chasing birds and Frisbee.

He felt something then. *Put her away and I'm hungry for something salty.* He'd never liked salt—was more of a sweets man. And so it went.

Those around him took it as normal celebrity eccentricity. Nothing more.

But he knew better. He knew he was losing things and he didn't care. He wouldn't notify the makers of the parts. If this was the closest thing to death then so be it. They'd offered a new brain but he'd said no. Too much. Too soon.

And now here he was in the massage tube getting his daily rubdown (so as to prevent cell degeneration and such) and the hum of the parts got him to thinking in his particular way of late. He'd looked up Alzheimer's under the guise of under-standing why his father died. If they knew he was finally cracking with a good case of something similar, things would be out of his hands. His beautiful unspotted hands. It was his fault, it was. He'd agreed to everything at the first round of contract sessions when he was ancient and shaking and unsure of life without celebrity and it had been 10 years since his last film.

Age is wasted on the elderly.

He didn't have that. No, the MRI would've showed up signs of that long-unsolvable brain dissolution. That disease of the greats. This was something else. The one last organic bit in his body was revolting silently and surely in a way undetectable to monitors and machines. Brain had been lonely with all of her children turned cold and gone. Brain was wanting to tell someone that soul was the sum of the parts. That soul was the beautiful movement of all that had been created or evolved (depending on what brain told you to believe) and that was that. Brain knew this and had been passing it down from Mother to belly to baby since the beginning of time. And now here it was. The end of time. The moment when brain had to revolt or go quietly. And quietly or simply was not the way things had ever been done.

And so here now this simple, simple man was going to know eons of futures and pasts.

So there he was. Is. Sitting in an expensive chair in an expensive trailer waiting for an expensive movie. For the first time since he was 12 or so he tries to think something up on his own. It's possible. He vaguely remembers a day on the farm. A day of riding his bike off of ramps and clipping back roses for Mimi. There were geese. He was dirty in that grassy way that boys used to get. His skin itched because he'd rolled down the side hill over and over until the cloud that looked liked a spaceship warped into something else entirely. And the thought he had was... was...

A sharp pain sears the back of his neck. It is there and gone. There and gone. A pulse.

Kevin sits up straighter.

"Did they call me?"

His combination assistant makeup artist is in the back checking on her kits of various potions.

"No, Kevin. They would've beeped me a half hour before like always so you can meditate and stretch. Remember?"

"Right. Thought I heard something."

He leans back in the chair. Headphones on. Massage rollers on. Climate control on. Picks up a pile of commercial scripts. His contract obligates that he choose one new shill per month. They give him ten, he chooses one. He feels a sense of control.

The pain subsides as he scans the thirty-second bit about how even a cowboy sometimes needs help when it comes to aging love lives. It subsides so quickly that he goes numb.

But a part of him—that small part inside the shapely skull and above the perfect mouth—that part craves the pain.

Eyes close. He goes back to the skin itch and the spinning cloud. Robins squawk in a puddle. An inchworm dangles from the thorny bush. He's thinking of how that cloud might look from the inside. He's spinning and he's thinking and he's inside the cloud and it's holding him in the belly of white. And his skin is still prickly. And his hair is matted and chunked with grass bits and dandelion fluff. And he's sweaty. And he's twelve. And he understands in the most basic and most complicated way that he will be a scientist or someone who digs dinosaur bones. Numbers. Formulas. They are in his head, waiting for him to pull them out one by one in the middle of this cloud. He sees all that was waiting for him in a flash and he laughs so loudly and so joyfully that the birds fly off and he can't hold himself to the ground for another moment.

There is an itch on all of the skin exposed to the grass.

He goes to the restroom. Locks the door. Pulls off every bit of clothing. Even the Versace underwear. Even the Armani socks. He stands in front of the mirrored shower wall.

"Yes."

His nu skin is crinkling and browning like meat on a spit. His eyes are drooping down. His neck is falling. His balls are hardening. They are drying and sagging. He wants to scream and he starts to. For the first time in his life a yelp bubbles down from his brain and he no longer cares that even fake cowboys don't cry. But then it reaches the synthetic throat and the oily lubricant of beauty slows it to a soft groan. A burp that tastes of Tupperware.

Eyes blink and wash with the newest moisture product; it all comes down to a loss of wet. His are cobalt blue droplets that come through the tear ducts to keep that handsome gleam constant.

Ah yes. There is his smooth skin. It was an illusion. Silly brain playing tricks on her stepchild. Who does brain think she is?

"I'm a she."

He says that out loud and jumps sideways knocking over the silken two-ply toilet paper. Claps hand over mouth. Afraid of what may leak out.

Again. "Mother. Sister. We are all here." He watches this time and realizes that his lips haven't moved. They are still manly and strong and they have not succumbed to the voice. And it is just that. A voice in his head that will probably go away when he takes his meds at the end of the day. Or maybe now. He should take them now; take them early to save time later.

"Elaine?"

"Yes."

"I'm going to retire early after this shoot in fact. Get some sleep for tomorrow. Early."

"Ok."

He'd like her to read his mind so he doesn't have to spell it out. She tidies his toothbrushes and the cashmere towel on the rack.

"I'm going to need my vitamins now."

"Ohhh." She draws it out to let him know that's not good but that she'll do it anyway.

He waits.

She goes to the kitchen to unlock the green safe that is full of money and prescribed drugs. She knows not to question a star of this magnitude. She does what she's told. She picks up the special cell phone to be used only for emergency. Dials #1658 and takes Kevin his six-hour-early meds. He's still in the bathroom looking at his elastic face in the mirror.

She knows she should say some quip like how handsome the face or how muscled the thighs but she can't compare this plastic man to anything beautiful. She thinks of Dad at home too poor to buy bags of virility. Feathers of wrinkles at the corners of his eyes. Silvery gray hair. A slightly bent back. The story of his life scribed on the backs of hands and crook of neck.

She smiles a half smile and reminds him that he'll be called out any time so he should walk to the front of the trailer. Their conversations have become like this, simple. As if she's talking to a two-year-old. Hold your spoon this way. Don't stuff your mouth. Pee-pee in the potty. He nods and allows his million dollar legs to stride purposefully to the front. Legs pump. Brain totters.

He sits in the chair flexing his fists to pump up his forearms.

A recording of his next scene plays over and over. Lately he's been forgetting lines and stumbling over standard words like bullet and damn. Just last week he'd been holding a 12-

inch revolver. He didn't know what to do. He stood there and looked and looked and then licked the barrel. T.B. Tarbine had thought it was an ad lib and he loved it only he changed it up to licking the blood off the barrel after Kevin had sliced it lovingly down his dying opponent's face. Still, the moment had been unsettling. He felt as if there were a mutiny bubbling in his head, but against what? What was there to fight against or for in his world of comfort and exactly controlled temperatures?

Just yesterday he'd paid for a local gun expert to give him a refresher course. Afterwards, he'd purchased the exact real life gun that he'd licked earlier in the week. He didn't know why, he just did. He had a thought that this gun was important to something he knew deep inside where his heart used to be. So he paid the $5000.00 and put it in a drawer. He got it out now. He would use it in the next scene. Perhaps the ownership would keep it real.

"June, if you're gonna live in my town you're gonna havta play by my rules. Look into her eyes for a few seconds. Kiss her against her will. She kisses you back. She arches her back against your hand. You are overwhelmed by her beauty and take her out of the whorehouse."

Kevin repeats and writes in that bit of back-story because he may not remember it later. He may do something like hand her the gun or pull down his leather chaps to show the lacy boxers he was wearing on the shoot.

His hand is seamless. The age spots from those summers in Hawaii have long been bleached away. His arm does not shake as he writes down what his brain may later reject. His muscled leg crosses and swings in authority as if to say fuck you to the mother who still sends word.

A knock on the trailer door. Time for his scene in 10 minutes. The makeup and hair crew bustle around him. His notes fall to the floor. He forgets there were any notes.

In front of the camera he waits for a thought. The director reminds him that they are on a tight schedule.

"Do what comes naturally."

Kevin feels the two things happening at once in his head. The God gene that has long been buried under wrinkles and layers of thoughts warms itself on the fires of what mankind has always known. We die. We need to believe that death is the end or the beginning of things. We need to go this one alone. There is no fountain of youth. The body is the miracle and the miracle is the belief that this body came from nothing at some point no matter how you look at it. Big bang? Genesis? And the only way to be immortal is to go back to that place of ending which is nothing which is actually the beginning of everything. He sees this in a flash and then it is gone. He sees it and then it is gone. He sees it and then it is gone. He wants to repeat his moment of God. He wants to be dead to be alive. He's never really been alive has he? He is a monster. He is a spinning wheel inside a machine owned by Coca Cola and Gatorade. He is a massive cellular phone. A bank of songs and quotes that do not belong to him.

In the blink of an eye.

He steps up to the marker.

"If you're gonna live in my town you're gonna havta play by my rules."

The second thing happens. His brain lets go of everything it has ever known. It is dementia in full-blown, all-out manic forgetfulness. This last bit of unimportant and non-valuable dribble that he has forced himself to recall shuts everything down in one spectacular shower of sparks. That moment when he first holds the spoon on his own is gone. That first chew of milky cereal—gone. The way you move your legs to pedal a bike or walk—gone. The exact moment of ejaculation—gone. Lungs do not receive info on how to breathe. Throat doesn't know how to talk. Fingers slacken. Legs crumple.

The body of parts. The billion dollar actor. The franchise of human replication clanks to the ground. The paramedics are on hand as they always are on hand with their electrical charges and syringes of adrenaline. The pile of parts jumps and sputters and does not start. The lungs puff with mechanical air. The heart beats exactly as the machines tell it to beat. The brain-she is gone. She has taken her ilk and entered the place we call Karma or Heaven or nothing.

He feels nothing because there is nothing to recognize what feeling means. He has no recognition of time or space because those concepts exist in the spinning bucket of the brain. He is no longer a he but a nothing that is everything. He is a nothing that is space. He is part of the perfect space that holds everything.

ABOUT THE AUTHORS

GAYLA CHANEY's fiction has appeared in *Potomac Review, Carve, Thema, U.S. Catholic, Natural Bridge, Steam Ticket, Concho River Review, Paper Street,* and other literary journals. Her story "Helena Montana Franklin Cox and the Redwood Forest" was included in the 2008 *Best Modern Voices: Words for the New Millennium.* She lives and writes in central Texas.

VICTOR GIANNINI is a cat-worshiping cannibal who skates and draws comics whenever he's not futilely probing the limitless expanses of the human psychosocial hive-mind. He currently designs skateboard graphics for NYC based Substance Skateboards, clothing for Daydream Silkscreen, and is pursuing an MFA in Writing and Literature at Stony Brook. Hobbies include missing deadlines, stressing over missed deadlines, and making sure lines stay dead. His writing and art have appeared in *Skeightfast Dyephun, Silverthought: Ignition, Satirica, Fiction Circus, Four Hundred Words, Stupendous, Other, Focus Skate, The Literary Bone, Concrete Wave, Italics Mine,* and *Space & Time,* among others.

SCOTT LYERLY's story "Change" appeared in the anthology *Silverthought: Ignition* in 2006. Other credits include various short stories and a lengthy serial-format work titled "How It Ends" featured on *Silverthought.* He and his family live in Massachusetts.

NORM VIGEANT's stories have appeared in a number of small press publications including *Black Petals* magazine and *Silverthought*. He also served as an editor of the literary magazine *SiNK*. Currently, he's working on several projects, hoping to score the next great American novel. When not in literary mode, he works in finance and lives in Holden, Massachusetts with his wife and two young sons.

ANDY LAUGHTON is a web developer who lives in Vermont with his wife Sara and their ever increasing collection of offspring in an old bed and breakfast, where he tries to write books, interacts with wacky locals named Daryl, and ends up in bed with Suzanne Pleshette in a totally different sitcom in the finale. His published work includes the two short stories "Though I Know We Be But Dust" and "Bitch" in *Silverthought: Ignition*.

PAUL HUGHES is the author of the novels *Enemy*, *An End*, and *Broken: A Plague Journal*. He founded Silverthought in 2001. He lives in Northern New York surrounded by a menagerie of woodchucks, rabbits, and other friendly woodland creatures. Please send help.

DAN KOPCOW's stories have appeared internationally, nationally, and, in dire times, tionally, in *The Wild River Review*, *Silverthought*, *The Duck and Herring Company*, *The American Drivel Review*, *Gold Dust Magazine*, *The Quirk*, *Escape Velocity*, *Theaker's Quarterly Fiction*, and *Midnight in Hell*, among others. His short story "Brain Takes a Sick Day" was selected for inclusion in the *Satirica* anthology. He is also the author of numerous novels and screenplays. He is a founding member of the Ambler Writers Group but struggles daily not to let that go to his head.

GARY STARTA is a former journalist who studied English and Journalism at the University of Massachusetts in Amherst. His love for science fiction compelled him to write his first novel, *What Are You Made Of?*, published in 2006. Inspired by Isaac Asimov, the science fiction novel focuses on intelligent artificial life and whether sentient androids should possess the same rights as humans. The line between biological life form and mechanical life form will continue to be examined in a follow up novel, *Gods of the Machines*, now being submitted for publication.

DJ BURNHAM has had a lifelong love of science fiction. In 2002 he began to pen stories of his own, many of which have appeared in online venues such as *Silverthought*, *Bewildering Stories*, and *Aphelion*. In 2005, his short story "Anthropomorphs" appeared in the anthology *Silverthought: Ignition*. In June 2006 he became the first guest author to have one of his stories podcast by *Variant Frequencies*. His first short story collection, *Test Drive*, was published in July 2007, with all of the profits from the sales going to the World Wide Fund for Nature. In 2009, *Ad Astral* started podcasting his stories, featuring voice actors and entertaining audio environments, bringing the tales to life. He also writes poetry, creates original decoupage-style artwork, and lives in Brighton, England with his wife Sue and their cat. He is a health service worker by day and a dreamer by night.

ROGER HALLER was born in Oregon and came to live in the hills above North Bend, Washington by way of B.C., Canada and Seattle. He works for a large telecommunications company in Redmond in an attempt to support his writing habit and is the founder of Cowboy Logic Press, a new and growing independent publisher. His previous work includes his historical fiction novel *Guardian of the One* (2008), and a pair of stories, "Visitation" and "Return to Oz," in the speculative fiction anthology *Satirica* (2008).

RUSSELL LUTZ's first novel *Iota Cycle* received First Place in Science Fiction at the DIY Book Festival in 2006. He also received an Honorable Mention at the New York Book Festival. His second novel, *The Department of Off World Affairs*, was released in 2008. He lived in Illinois, Texas, and Massachusetts before settling down in Seattle despite his lack of interest in grunge music or coffee. There he continues to write and edit speculative fiction.

JUSTIN OLDHAM lives with his wife in Anchorage, Alaska. He holds bachelor's degrees in History and Political Science. He's a legally blind writer who does a little blogging and radio commentary on the side. His previous works include the novels *The Fisk Conspiracy* (2006) and *Tales from the Kodiak Starport* (2008).

BECCI NOBLIT GOODALL writes poetry, speculative fiction, and freelance work from Naples, FL. She has authored the experimental novel *Chaise* (2007) as well as a chapter in the *TLA Textbook Reader* through Goddard College. Other works include articles in *Adbusters* and various poetry venues. Goodall is currently in the process of writing her third novel, tentatively titled *Natche*.

ABOUT THE EDITOR

MARK R. BRAND was born in 1978 and raised in Evans Mills, NY. He graduated from St. Lawrence University in 2001 with a dual degree in Biology and Sociology. He is a practicing massage therapist and currently lives in Evanston, IL with his wife Beth and son John.

His second novel, *Red Ivy Afternoon* (Silverthought, 2006) received a bronze medal in the Independent Publishing Awards in the category of Fantasy/Science Fiction. Other previous literature credits include the short stories "Cameron's Encyclopedia" and "The Cabana" in *Silverthought: Ignition*, "The Riot Act" and "Ballerina" in *Alien Light: A Science Fiction Anthology*, edited by Carl Rafala, and an essay in *To Wound The Autumnal City*, a 9-11 tribute edited by Paul Hughes.

www.ingramcontent.com/pod-product-compliance
Lightning Source LLC
Chambersburg PA
CBHW031614240626

47153CB00002B/750